THE SHEPHERD

D. L. Beaumont

DEDICATION

For my husband, a man who said two little words
When I told him my darkest secret.

When you whispered, "It's okay," I knew you loved me.

PROLOGUE

Evie

Numb. That's the only word that could be used to describe me. I feel nothing but hollow—gutted.

I absentmindedly run my fingers over the wrinkles in the nicest black dress I own. The sequins on my shoes make me ill. These shoes are for parties. But, they were the only ones that match this dress. His favorite dress.

My long, red hair is draped over my shoulder. I cannot pin it up. Today, I need it to hide me from the world.

I sit under the small tent erected for loved ones who mourn the loss of those that lie in front of me. They are asleep. They are together. The tiny white coffin will rest beside the large black one in the cold, wet ground.

I am surrounded by my friends and my family, but I have never felt so alone. My mother sits to my left, while my father, who is always so strong and put together, sits to my right, slumped forward with his head in his palms. My mother, my comforter, squeezes my hand and whispers softly, "It's okay to cry, Evie."

I cannot cry. I have no tears left. I can only sit and stare blankly ahead and listen to the roar of the summer wind that encompasses me. I have thought about my life and pored over the decisions I have made, things I have done, and I cannot pinpoint one thing that I did to deserve this. I have lived my life determined to hurt no one.

Just last week, I gave my lunch to the homeless man that sleeps on the bench two blocks from where I work. I volunteer at a family service agency as a guidance counselor for single mothers. I go to church, faithfully. I pray for and love people I do not know. My job is a public service.

I will never survive this small vial of wrath that has been poured over me—a wrath I will never understand.

Just last week, I was a wife…to a man who loved so fiercely and tenderly at the same time. He was the second man I ever kissed, the only man I made love to. He was the one who made everything better. He always told me everything would be okay. And, he was always right.

I will never be okay again, because he is not here to tell me so.

Just last week, I rocked my precious baby boy to sleep. I sang to him while he watched me intently, studying every feature on my face while he laid back and stared up at me. His little eyebrows rose up every time I hit a high note, and he smiled when the crescendo played out softly. He was captivated by my voice.

I will never sing again, because my baby boy will not hear my songs.

We worked hard and prayed harder for the blessing that was given to us. Five years of trying finally paid off. He was handed to me as a screaming little bundle and taken from me in the silence that has roared in my head for days.

Our little blessing lies lifeless in a box. No heartbeat. No sweet baby breath. No twinkling blue eyes blinking up at me. No smiles. No giggles. No precious squeals that I relished in. No grunting that I will lie in bed and listen to as the night settles around me.

I did love the man that will rest beside my son. But now, I hate him. I hate him because he left me here. Alone.

The same baby boy that I thought of every single second of the day, he had forgotten on a Tuesday morning in late July.

CHAPTER ONE
Two Years Later

RHETT

I sat back in my chair and pinched the bridge of my nose. As the judge called for a recess, I wanted nothing more than to follow the defendant to the restroom and do what I do best. I'd only need a few minutes to clean up the mess.

Drug dealers make me sick. If I have to hear one more sob story about how they need to sell drugs because their families will starve to death if they don't, I might yak right in front of the judge's bench. I've even told them, on record, that every place in this city that flips burgers is hiring.

The man, or boy rather, that stands on trial today is a nineteen-year-old Latino, Antonio Sanchez, who has been charged with manufacturing, possession, and distribution of methamphetamines. Lots of them. I've worked on this case for months and am determined to put this fucker away.

I have been a deputy prosecuting attorney in St. Louis for four years now. I enlisted in the military when I was eighteen, served for six years, deployed twice and finally, after being wounded, was discharged. It is no secret to anyone who knows me that I do not, will not, and cannot tolerate bullshit.

While I served my beloved country, I earned my bachelor's degree in English. After being discharged, I went to law school and graduated at the top of my class, despite the tragedy that almost destroyed me. I used my own destruction as my fuel to build myself up again. I turned thirty last month (*bummer*), and I happen to be the youngest deputy prosecuting attorney who has practiced here.

I love this job. I'd say it's what I live for, but that would be laughable. Putting criminals away feels good. But, I have to admit, putting them in the ground feels better.

I loosened my tie a little to relieve the pressure on my neck. Sanchez's boohooing was wearing thin on my nerves. Save the tears for your mama. She's the only one who gives a damn about them.

As I ate my sandwich at the restaurant within walking distance of the courthouse, I felt a heavy hand on my shoulder. I looked up to see my boss, Winford Turner, sitting down beside me.

"He's working them today, huh?" he smirked.

"Yeah. I hope the judge doesn't buy into that bullshit," I said around my mouthful of food. "There's a reason I don't make deals often. This bastard is making me regret that. I could've offered him three years, instead of the full sentence these charges carry, and he would've taken it. If the judge is sympathetic, that fucker is going to be able to skip to rehab like a happy little girl."

"You're in a pleasant mood today, I see," Winford laughed. He always gives me grief about my *terrible attitude*. Hey, my terrible disposition is who I am. Circumstances and criminals turned me into this asshole. I've earned this attitude, fair and square.

I huffed, "I have no room, time, or give-a-damn for pleasantries. Don't act surprised."

He smiled. "I'm not surprised. I just like hearing you defend yourself. You're the last person I would come to for a good joke, but you always make me laugh." He leaned back in his chair and said, "Maggie thinks you're too pretty to act this way."

"Don't call me pretty," I growled. "That's probably the worst compliment a guy can get. You might as well tell me that I have a vagina."

He laughed. "I didn't even know you knew what a vagina was."

"Screw you," I bit and continued to chow down.

That was another thing.

Women.

I have not touched a woman since I lost my wife over five years

8

ago. Looked at them? Yes, but with little interest. I don't date and if any woman propositions you within the first ten minutes of meeting her, trust me, she's not worth the time. Hell, if she can't hold on to one man for longer than one night, she can't even be a good time, in my opinion.

I never kicked up many skirts, only a couple, and it wasn't because I didn't have the opportunity. I was focused and driven. I wanted a career, so that when I did settle down, I could take care of the one woman I wanted to play out the days of my life with. But, one night, I gave in. I messed up, then I manned up. It wasn't what I wanted. *She* wasn't what I wanted, but she grew on me. Then, she was taken from me.

I had no interest in losing anything or anyone else. So, I drove women out of my mind and replaced all of my vices with my ache for revenge.

After lunch, and when court was back in session, I sat and watched Sanchez enter the courtroom with tears streaming down his face. *Give me a break.* I'd love to mop his tears off of the floor with his face. I could...if I wanted to.

The verdict was read two hours later, and not to my surprise, the judge took pity on the poor little drug dealer. Two years, counting time served. He'd be out in twelve months for good behavior. But, the kicker? Overcrowding. His crimes are nonviolent. He walks until a bed opens up. I should've offered a deal.

Ladies and gentlemen, there you have it: our justice system. As a man who serves the public, I want to apologize for the shortcomings of this flawed system. I tried. I attempted to get a drug dealer off of the streets. This one kid has dabbled in the lives of hundreds of people and ruined those lives in his wake. On a national and global scale, the lives ruined by drug dealers surpass millions, and our officials have sympathized with these scumbags. I do have your best interests at heart, but I am one man trying to row up shit creek, without a paddle.

As I packed up my briefcase, I quickly glanced at Sanchez. He sported a little smirk that I have every intention of wiping off of his face in a moment in which he will never see me coming.

I smiled my brightest smile and gave him a little wink. He had no idea that he was a dead man walking.

***

I work my hardest to hand out little nibbles of justice while the sun shines, but when night falls, I serve it in abundance--on silver platters, if you will.

Stripped, scrubbed, then dressed by the time darkness comes, I try and prepare myself and my arsenal of weaponry for my next assignment. I never know any details about my subject until it's given to me.

Every Friday night I am handed a manila envelope. Enclosed are pictures of the subject, along with pictures of their next of kin, and a list of their favorite hangouts, the names, addresses and pictures of their closest confidants. The general whereabouts of the subject are always given, so it does not take long to find them. I don't even know their crimes. I trust they are guilty. I can know if I ask, and on occasion, I have.

In the daylight, I prosecute criminals. Under the cover of moonlight, I execute them.

I am a member of a small circle of justifiers. Our victims are not innocent or undeserving. We never kill without a purpose, one that is proven. From pedophiles to rapists and drug dealers to murderers, we are called upon to eliminate them.

There are five of us who carry out justice on those who are not worthy of life, and there is one who assigns our mark. I only know parts of her story, parts that she has disclosed. I cannot even research her, because I do not know her name. To us, she is simply *The Queen.*

We are all pieces in an elite group called *The Guardians.* All of our backgrounds are littered with military or law enforcement service. We all help each other, guiding and training each other, to make our group quick, precise, and untraceable. Through our experiences, we have learned the tricks of the trade—be on target and be invisible.

I was warned by *The Queen* the week prior that this night would be a big night—a dangerous mission. High profile.

I drove forty miles to an abandoned warehouse along railroad tracks where trains no longer travel. I pulled up in my BMW—the car I use for special occasions, secured with fictitious tags. I looked around the small parking lot and got out, retrieved my rifle and duffle bag of various weapons from the trunk. I could hear chattering and laughing coming from the loading dock. Everyone was here.

As I approached them, their attention turned to me. They are truly the nicest people I have ever met. All of them share compassion for the feeble and all of them have been touched by heinous crimes. We were all recruited, brought together by common ground, and coddled by the woman we fear most.

They all greeted me with smiles, handshakes, or slaps on the back, but I reserved a hug for *The Queen*. She's a foot shorter than my six foot, four inch frame, and thirty-five years older.

"You look ravishing in red tonight," I said as I kiss her on the cheek.

She smiled, sweetly. She reminds me of my grandma, if my grandma were bad-ass. "I told you tonight was a big night."

"You did. I just didn't know we needed to dress up," I said, smiling down at her.

She reached up and pushed my black hair from my forehead. "You look smashing, as always, my sweet boy. You don't need to dress up."

I pulled away and pulled a beanie over my head to hide my hair and break the wind.

We all take our seats at our respective places while *The Queen* stood at the head of the table with her hands locked in front of her. Her long gray hair was pulled up in a loose bun and her dark brown eyes scanned the room. She smiled at us all lovingly, the same way a mother would smile at her children in their finest moments.

I sit on her right hand, with good reason. *Pops* sat across from me, smiling from ear-to-ear.

He is the youngest here, but he has an old soul. However, his big green eyes, baby face and shaggy blonde hair reveal his youth. He is a new daddy to a three week old baby girl. Who wouldn't be smiling? However, he was named long before he became a father. He has been with us for over a year now, and from day one, he has been the go-to guy for advice or moral support.

His brother was abducted from their front yard when he was six. *Pops* was ten. He was found two days later in a drainage ditch less than two miles from their home. He lived with the guilt for most of his life. He told us that God had forgiven him for letting it happen and not saving his brother, so he would devote his life to teaching forgiveness. Explaining to him that what happened was not his fault would've fallen on deaf ears, so we listened in silence and tried to understand his logic. As a chaplain in the U.S. Army, he has earned our respect. He's prayed over more dying men than anyone I have ever met. He is our comforter.

Tinker sat beside him, resting his forehead on his fist. He was scanning over a newspaper article from his assignment from last week. The story made it to the very last page of the news section, in the left-hand corner, right below an article about an elementary school age kid and his love for turtles. No one really cares about a prostitute found dead in an alley. The only reason the article was printed was to notify those who ever came in contact with her that she was knowingly spreading HIV like a wildfire through the projects.

Tinker was an interesting person. His mother and father came to the states from Bosnia in the early eighties. They wanted him to have a better life that the western world could give him. Essentially, he had learned not to take things for granted. *Tinker* was a former cop from Kansas City who lost his badge for driving while intoxicated. He was highly decorated. A captain. A beloved member of the community. *Tinker* had endured a son's worst heartache. About a year before joining the group, an intruder broke in to his parents' house and stole his father's keys to the jewelry store he owned. The intruder never found the keys, stole six bucks from the coffee table, and killed *Tinker's* parents. Alcohol numbed *Tink's* pain, but cost him his career and the life he had known.

We all have something that soothes our heartaches. Liquor soothed his. Can't really blame him. He is a short fellow, but agile and fast. In his off time, he tinkers. It's his thing. Whether he's fixing up motorcycles or hot rods, he's always using his hands. He is an expert in hand-to-hand combat—a master of martial arts. He teaches us the truth and power of relaxation, and teaches us to calm the demons inside of us. He is our solace.

Whist is a mysterious fellow, but a true brute of a man, who always sits across from *The Queen*. His name is a synonym for quiet (so I read). *The Queen* gave him that name. He is quiet—there's no arguing that. I argued that when we said his name it sounded like we had a speech impediment, so we needed to call him something else. She told me to shut the hell up and we moved on. I was trying to be funny. She didn't laugh.

Whist arrived six months after I did. He was given away as a child. Yeah, I said, *given* away—to random strangers. Those strangers made him a drug dealer at the age of eight. By twelve, he was smoking his profits. At seventeen, he ran away, lied about his age, and joined the Marines. He lost his legs in a roadside bomb blast in Afghanistan. He almost died for his country, and now he kills for it.

The Queen found him lying in a parking lot, nearly beaten to death, two months after he received an honorable discharge. Racial slurs were spray painted on the pavement where he was unconscious. *Whist* was a black man in a predominately white neighborhood—a white neighborhood crawling with racist drug addicts. When a crackhead wants your car, he will beat the shit out of you and steal your prosthetic legs to get it. *Whist* was on life support for two months.

After learning of his kill shots and military accomplishments, she had to have him. *The Queen* and I would go visit him every day and she would make me read aloud to him. He pulled through and he was recruited. I had never seen gray eyes before—not until I looked into his. I am confident enough in my sexuality to say that they are nothing short of amazingly beautiful. But, the color is not what truly captivated me. His eyes see the mark and hit it. Every. Single. Time. He never misses. He is an expert marksman. His breathing is strong and steady. His hands never shake. He is our rock.

Blue is the only female on our team. She is tall and absolutely gorgeous…and I think she bats for my team (if you catch my drift). She uses her beauty to reel in most of her marks. She doesn't like the bloodiness of our dude tactics, so she is more covert with her deliverance. She is a sad thing, hence the name *Blue*. The only time I've seen her smile, it was sinister and the only promise it held was certain demise.

She worked for the CIA for six years before she lost her job due to extensive medical leave. A late night drink with her male partner stole her career. His romantic feelings for her and her sweet decline to his advances caused her partner to go ape shit, and he nearly turned her into a vegetable. After walking her to her door that night, he pushed her inside and raped her on her living room floor. Then, he tried to bludgeon her to death with things in her own house. To his dissatisfaction, she lived. She was told she would never walk again, but look at her…walking a bad man to his grave every Friday night. She is an expert in any type of intelligence, a hacker, a spy. She is our true guide.

We all work together, gathering intel, handing out tips and tricks, but we carry out our assignments alone.

Everyone here has tasted revenge…everyone except me. I still await the moment *The Queen* finds the men responsible for taking away my reason for living. So, I wait to be handed the envelope with my name written across the center in *The Queen's* whimsical cursive.

The Guardians are a special covert group that I am proud to call myself a part of, a major part.

Tonight, I will be the biggest part. I serve up the ultimate punishment for those who commit the worst crimes. Those are saved for me.

There are no real names here. Only identities. Names we give to each other.

I am a watchman, a protector, a keeper of sheep who cannot protect themselves.

Here, I am not Rhett Trimble.

I am simply *The Shepherd*.

CHAPTER TWO

Evie

"How's the Martin case coming?"

I jumped when my boss's voice boomed over me. "Good morning, Frankie. How are you?" I said, smiling up at my favorite old man. He'll be seventy this month, but still as spry as a twenty year old--claims he has the sexual appetite of one too. Kind of makes bile rise up in my throat a bit. I just can't picture Mrs. Charlotte in compromising positions, osteoporosis and all.

He entered my office and took a seat in front of me, propping his feet up on my desk. "Are you seriously doing that right now?"

He smiled and his bushy eyebrows went up. "My division. My desk. That's how I see it."

"Sure..."

His smile faded a bit. "The Martin case?"

Tippy Martin went missing from outside of Kansas City ten years ago. She was a bright and beautiful girl with a promising future...or so everyone thought. Her parents were the picture perfect family, if such a thing existed. Her father owned a successful oil company and her mother stayed at home with all three of their children. They were raised to be respectful and strong Christian pillars of the community, just like their folks. Tippy was the eldest. The only pictures I have seen of her show her to be young. She looks naive and a bit sheltered, wearing clothes that literally look like potato sacks. However, the stories that litter her case file tell stories of the girl's troubled life. Unbeknownst to her parents, Tippy dabbled in witchcraft and started using cocaine when she was fifteen.

With no money to her name, she exchanged sex regularly for drugs. No surprise really. Addicts will do anything to get their fix, including selling their firstborn. I know. I've seen it happen.

Tippy was murdered when she was nineteen. Her body was found four years later in a shallow grave in Senator Bill Craven's back yard. Construction workers installing his in-ground pool found her remains. The house had only been built for a year, and with his prestige and reputation, he was quickly ruled out as a suspect. Since discovering her remains, there have been no leads.

"I think I'm making some headway, but it's still too soon to be sure about that."

He smiled at me and stood. "You'll figure it out."

"Oh, my friend. You have so much faith in me," I said coyly.

He shook his head. "Why wouldn't I? You're the best."

I just smiled and shook my head, "Whatever. Get out of here. I think I hear the donuts crying out to you."

He laughed while leaving my office. "Yeah, yeah! Can't let diabetes slow me down!"

I looked back down at the file in front of me. I took all of the pictures out and laid them out across my desk. The pictures of her smiling and laughing create a war inside of me while I compare them to the pictures of her remains. I pick up her graduation picture. She was wearing the same pink shirt when she died. The crisp, light pink button up became nothing but a shredded, dirty mess that cocooned her small frame.

Pink is a happy color. A happy color for a sad girl.

I leaned back in my chair and rubbed my eyes. This occupation should bother me. Death should trouble me. But, it's funny. I feel closer to the family I lost when I do this. I feel like for an instant, when I finally solve the crime that wiped these victims from the Earth, that those who are gone are alive again—just for a moment.

I don't understand my logic or my heartache sometimes. I can sit and study gruesome photos all day long, but pictures of my own child, I can't bear to look at—especially the ones in which he smiles.

As I try to push their memory to the farthest recesses of my mind, I glance at the calendar. In two days, it will mark two years since they left me. The huge hole in my heart that they left, I have tried to fill with the satisfaction of giving others peace.

I've worked for the Federal Bureau of Investigation for eight years, starting two days after I turned twenty-one. I always wanted a badass job, and I finally got it...I thought. I started out filing papers, which was less than glorious, but quickly worked my way up the ranks. Within six months, I was placed in the evidence division. That is where I first laid eyes on Dash--and I instantly loved him. There was no question.

I was turned around, rebuttoning my uniform shirt that I had misaligned when he walked into the evidence room. "Are you going to eat that?" he asked smoothly, scaring the daylights out of me.

"Holy shit!" I screamed and flung my whole body around, with my shirt halfway unbuttoned, my ginormous breasts flashed him, barely covered by red lace. My face heated with embarrassment and it didn't help that he was the most handsome man I had laid eyes on since I started my job.

I turned around quickly and tried to tell my heart to pipe down on the palpitations. "I'm so sorry," I said, panting unattractively, fumbling with my shirt.

I could hear the laughter in his voice when he spoke. "It's all right. Trust me. After the night I've had, I could definitely use a striptease this morning."

I turned around slowly, after taking several deep breaths, and pasted on my best smile. "How can I help you?"

He handed over a bag with a small pistol inside. "I just need to drop this off. And this," he said, handing me a file.

"Okay, thanks. I'll take care of it."

"You're welcome," he said softly.

I expected him to leave...like everyone else always did. Usually, most people dropped off their stuff without even saying anything to me. Instead of leaving, he leaned over, resting his elbows on the counter. I looked at him for as long as I could stand. He possessed the bluest eyes I had ever seen and his crooked smile made my heart skip a beat.

While I fantasized about running my hands through his short, blonde hair, he smiled and tilted his chin up, "What's your name?"

"Why?" I asked shyly.

He cocked his head to the side, "Ma'am, it's my job to ask the questions. What's your name?"

"Evangeline. But, please, call me Evie."

His smile grew, "Evie. Just Evie?"

I turned my head, unable to stare into the blue depths any longer. "Evie Miller." I smiled. "And you are?"

He nodded and stuck his hand out for a friendly shake, "Dash Harrington. Nice to meet you Evie Miller." We shook hands and didn't let go for too many seconds.

"Dash?" I asked.

He grinned and nodded once. "That's right. Dash."

"Are you new here, Evie Miller?"

I finally shook my hand free. "I've been here for a few months, but I guess, technically, yeah. I'm new. *You* new here?"

He chuckled, "I've been here a few years."

I nodded. "Which division?"

He grinned and looked down at my half-eaten breakfast burrito. "Are you going to eat that?"

It was two hours old and cold as all get out. I shook my head. "No."

"Can I have it? I'm starving."

I chuckled. "It's cold. But, yeah. If you really want it. Sure."

"Thanks," he said as he picked it up and took a huge bite out of it. "Good burrito, Evie," he said, turning to leave the room.

"So," I said, stopping him at the door, "which division?"

He grinned. "Fraud."

I studied him for a moment. "Why do you have a firearm?"

He winked and turned the knob, pulling the door open to leave.

"You missed two buttons, Evie. Thanks for the burrito."

I looked down and nearly died. The only buttons I had missed created a gaping hole where my boobs were squished together, meeting in the middle.

In this building is where our love began--the same place it fell apart.

I sat back up in my chair and pushed the reverie away. It was too painful to think about.

Frankie poked his head around my door, "Ready to turn in the Gillespie case?"

"Yes, sir," I said. I pointed to a stack of boxes piled on top of one another in the corner of my office. "There it is."

"That's all of it?"

"Yes, sir," I responded.

"I'll get some guys in here to move it," he said with a smile.

"Thanks," I said, before he stepped away.

The Gillespie case was cold for thirteen years. I've had it on my desk for a year and a half. It is one of three cold cases that I had resolved in the last two years. It was a satisfying feeling to solve the unsolvable.

Two and a half years ago, I was an investigator in the Homicide Division, working my way up to a big promotion. I loved my job. While I was pregnant, I was moved to a desk. But, after my son was born, I was back in the field.

After the accident, I withdrew from everyone and everything that I loved. I didn't want to come to work, but I had to. So, my boss gave me a position where results really weren't expected. He figured I would work until I imploded, leaving this job behind. But, the opposite happened. I became more focused and more dedicated. I earned even greater respect from my peers. I needed something to take my mind off my own life, and I had the perfect job to do so.

The Gillespie case was solved and put to rest. Mark Gillespie was a respected member of the community in Kansas City--a model citizen. He was a city leader who was murdered in cold blood.

Because of my investigations, Mr. Gillespie's family could now rest because his killer had been caught. His murderer was a thirty-five year old gang leader that our city was glad to see off of our streets. Vincent Trellis pled guilty to the crime he committed when he was in his early twenties. He told of things that were undiscovered by investigators then and details that I had missed completely. Trellis was killed his first night in prison by a rival gang member.

Justice served. Kind of.

I don't just do my job. I am the job.

Eight hours later, I was no closer to finding Tippy Martin's killer than I was when I arrived. I was just cleaning off my desk when Frankie entered my office with a concerned look on his face, carrying a file.

"What's wrong?" I asked, taking in his expression.

He threw the file on top of Tippy's Martin's pictures and said, "Pack your things. You're going to St. Louis."

I looked at him, questionably then asked, "Why?"

"I know it's been a while since you performed in the field, but I was ordered to send the best investigators I have," he answered.

My heart dropped to my stomach. "What happened?"

"Senator Craven's son was murdered."

CHAPTER THREE

Evie

I wiped away my tears when I sat down on my couch. I really didn't want to do this. Going back out in the field was going to decimate my heart. I was quietly reminded by the stillness inside my house that I couldn't come home from a long day of fieldwork and be greeted by my boys. And...I couldn't walk away from this house.

Not this soon. I'd be back, sure. But, I could still smell his sweetness every day when I walked in the door, although he was long gone. I didn't want to leave, because I knew when I came home, the mustiness would replace the powdery smell I loved and couldn't let go of.

My sweet baby, Noah. Noah Allen Harrington. He was the spitting image of Dash. Especially with his blue eyes, he looked exactly like him to me. Everyone said they saw me in there too, but truth be told, I only wanted to see Dash in him. I loved him that much.

How could the most beautiful baby boy be taken from a mother who loved him so much?

I see on the news and read in reports how mothers discard their children every day. They don't want them and they choose to give them away or lose them on purpose or take their tiny lives. I wanted my baby—with everything inside of me. All I wanted out of life was to be a mother. Asking God for that over and over was the most selfish thing I had ever done. Maybe that's why he took him—*because* I was selfish.

I got up and walked down the hall to my bedroom. I walked past the open door to the nursery, but I didn't look inside. I can't just yet.

I stripped down to my panties and bra and walked into the closet. I ran my fingers over Dash's shirts that hung there, mocking me. I pulled his favorite blue shirt off the hanger and slipped it on, bringing the sleeves up to my nose and inhaling. He shucked it off and left it in the floor the night he died. I haven't washed it. If I close my eyes and breathe it in, I can still smell his cologne on the fabric. Maybe it's my imagination, but…maybe not.

I closed the closet door behind me, shutting myself inside and slumped to the floor against it. I pulled my knees to my chest and rested my forehead on them. I couldn't hold it in any longer.

For the first time in months, I gave in to my grief. I sobbed like I had never grieved them. I felt like I was losing them all over again. I felt like he could walk into the room at any minute, carrying our son, and tell me that he's hungry. I feel like he could lie down beside me and hold me close, and tell me to wake up—that all of this is just a bad dream.

I wailed until I couldn't catch my breath.

As my cries calmed, I whispered the only thing I would ask him if he could hear me, "Why did you leave me, you bastard?"

I made my way to my hands and knees and breathed in and out, slowly. I pulled myself up using the door handle because my knees ached. I stood and buttoned the shirt, closing my eyes and pictured his fingers doing the work. On nights I feel I can't go on, I do this. He never really leaves me if I keep his things ready for him to return.

I made my way to Noah's room gingerly. I must do this tonight, for tomorrow I leave little remnants of him behind. And, I know that when I return, his smell will have disappeared.

I stood in the doorway and looked around. I could barely see through the tears that clouded my eyes, and I could barely make my feet move forward. Finally, they moved on their own accord and carried me until I stood beside his crib. The blanket he slept under the night before he died was still bunched up in the left-hand corner. I loved how I would lay him down in the center and by morning he was curled up in that corner, with his little foot hanging between the spindles.

I picked the blanket up with tentative fingers, hating that I was destroying the makeup of my last memories of him. But, I needed to smell him. I pressed the blanket against my face and it so lovingly absorbed my tears.

I abandoned the crib and made my way to the glider where I nursed him. I lowered myself to my knees and rested my head on the seat, rocking myself back and forth, back and forth, while wrenching the blanket in my hands.

Before I fell asleep where I knelt, I prayed for God to make my heart stop beating. As long as it beats, it will ache. Before closing my supplication, I whispered the same words that I whispered every night, "Please tell my sweet baby boy that I love him and that I'll see him soon."

Wishing I could wake up in his presence, I fell asleep.

***

When I woke up, it was daylight. The sun beamed through the windows and the dusty furniture that surrounded me reminded me that I was still alive. Another prayer—unanswered.

I stood up slowly because my knees and back ached so much from sleeping sitting up.

The hot water of my shower washed away the tears that dried on my face and soothed my achy muscles and joints. It washed away yesterday.

I only had a few hours to pack the things I needed. I had no idea how long I would be gone, but it wouldn't take me long to find out.

A few hours later, as I'm zipping up my fourth and final suitcase for my trip, my phone rang. I considered not answering it, but if I didn't, my mother would come find me. So, I tried to compose myself and answer.

"Hey, mom."

"Hey, sweetie. What are you doing today? I was hoping to do a little bit of shopping, but your dad is being a grump today. I really don't want to take him. I thought maybe we could go together," she said sweetly.

My mother, God love her, is the kindest and gentlest person I've ever known. That would be a subjective opinion, if everyone who has ever met her didn't think the same thing.

I sighed, "Actually, I can't. I have to go to St. Louis."

"St. Louis?" she asked. There was no denying the apprehension in her voice.

"Yeah. For work."

"Another cold case?"

I paused and pulled my lips between my teeth and took a deep breath before answering. "A homicide." She sucked in a breath and there was a long silence. I thought she fainted. "Mom? You there?"

"I'm here," she whispered. "Why are they sending you? Aren't there enough investigators to choose from in that office? They can't just leave you alone? Let you sit this one out?"

I blew out a long breath, "It is a high profile murder case. Kansas City has been ordered to send its top investigators to St. Louis. Per Frankie, those orders include me."

My mom sighed loudly. "High profile? Who?"

I sighed. "Do you and dad *ever* watch the news?"

"Well, yes, sweetie. But, lately, almost every night, your dad has been pretty frisky and—"

"Mom!" I screamed, then smiled. "Nobody says *frisky* anymore! And, I don't want to hear that, so please, don't talk about that."

"Okay! High profile. You were saying?"

I walked over to the bookshelf where I kept my photo albums and pulled them all down. There were worse things than taking a fifth suitcase.

"Senator Craven's son was murdered this past Friday night."

She gasped, "Are you serious? Oh, that is terrible. Who would want him dead? He's done nothing but wonderful things!" She took a deep breath. "I'm going to cry, Evie."

I smiled. "Mom. It's not like you knew him personally. Quit being dramatic."

"But, Evie! It's so sad!"

"I know it's sad. It is horrible. So, I'm going to go. I'm going to work the case," I said softly.

She sighed, "Can you handle it, Evie? Is it going to be too much?"

I answered her quickly—a little too quickly. "I can handle it, mom. This could be a good thing. I loved my job then and I think I can still love it. I may not be able to just jump right in, but I…I think I need to do this." I didn't mean to, but I sobbed…just once, quickly.

My mother caught it. "Evie," she whispered, her voice etched with agony.

I couldn't help it. I started to cry. I hadn't talked about Dash and Noah for so long—almost like I was waiting to forget they were ever a part of my life. Their deaths were the reason that I couldn't hang on to happiness. Every time I smiled, it reminded me that I would never hear them laugh or ever see them smile.

"Mom," I cried. "I miss them…so much." I sobbed uncontrollably while I pressed the phone to my ear. I could feel my knuckles turning white from my crushing grip.

She whispered the only words she knew would comfort me, "I know you do, sweetie. I know."

I have always asked my mother the toughest questions, because I knew she had all of the answers. "Mama," I whispered, "Will it ever stop hurting?"

"No, baby. It won't." Her honesty was almost a sore comfort. In truth, I didn't want the pain to stop. The day it stopped would be the day that I let them go. They would disappear from my memory the day it stopped hurting.

I nodded, even knowing she couldn't see me, and pinched my eyes closed, squeezing my tears out, sending them racing down my face.

I said nothing for twenty minutes, while she sat on the other end of the line and listened to my breakdown. Through her own tears, she sang to me. She sang every slow hymnal that she could remember the words to. When she finished the final verse of *Sweet Hour of Prayer*, I felt like I could breathe again.

When I spoke again, my voice was a little steadier, "Mom?"

"Yes, baby?"

"Do you think God hates me?" I asked on a whisper.

My mother answered quickly, "Absolutely not. Baby, don't ever think that."

My voice became wobbly again as I spoke, "Then why did He do this to me?"

I closed my eyes and let her answer wash over me. "Because you're a special kind of strong, sweetheart. You're a rock. You were strong before…but I think He has great plans for you. Plans that require you to be indestructible. He allows people to be torn down, so He can build them up again. You are His proof to the entire world that even the greatest heartaches can be survived."

I took in several breaths before asking her my last question. "Do you think He knows I'm angry? With Him?"

My mom chuckled before she whispered, "He certainly does. You're angry with Him, yet you still crawl up to Him for warmth and comfort and for answers." She laughed, "He couldn't get rid of you if He tried, could He?"

"No," I whispered.

"I don't believe you'll ever stop hurting, but He loves you enough to send something…or someone…to dull the ache, my sweet girl."

I said the only other thing I knew to say. "I love you, mom."

"I love you, too, Evangeline. Go to St. Louis. Do what is required of you. Keep your mind open and your heart cracked. You never know what could happen."

"Thanks, mama."

"Goodbye, baby."

"Bye," I said softly before hanging up.

I loaded up all five suitcases and stood in the foyer. I closed my eyes, inhaling the scents of it, one last time. Before I stepped out on the porch and closed the door, I whispered, "I'll miss you, boys." I pulled it shut and locked it behind me.

I pulled away, looked in the rearview mirror and pictured my blonde-haired, blue eyed husband bidding me farewell, bouncing our baby in his arms, with that crooked grin plastered across his face.

I wiped away the last of my tears and promised myself that I wouldn't cry anymore today.

CHAPTER FOUR

RHETT

I expected outrage. I really did.

No human being with a heart could stand to see the face of America's Golden Boy plastered all over the news for days. If they only knew...

To see his smiling face on my television every time I turned it on was really bugging the shit out of me.

It was rare for me to ask to see the crimes of my marks, but I had to with Bradley Cravens. He seemed so...nice.

I don't really cry anymore, haven't in years—but the pictures *The Queen* showed me made my eyes well up. As I stared at the photographs, I placed my fingers over my lips and took deep breaths in and out. I had to look away from them.

Bradley Cravens was no golden boy. He was a sick and twisted motherfucker. Without a doubt, he deserved that bullet through his head—the bullet I put there from the back seat of his beloved Mercedes.

Before I pulled the trigger, I confronted him about what I had seen. He didn't defend himself. He simply told me to go to hell.

I informed him that hell was reserved for sick bastards like him. I looked in his eyes from the rear view mirror the moment the life disappeared from them.

The plan carried out flawlessly. I could not be traced. I had slipped out as invisibly as I had slipped in. As soon as the job was done, I left. I felt confident, when I stepped away, that because his life was over, thousands of people could get their lives back. That was where *The Queen's* true work began.

The Guardians take care of the criminals and *The Queen* takes care of the victims, if they are still alive. She works to rehabilitate them and introduce them back into society. She is not always successful. Many times the victims are just too broken.

However, some are able to pick up the remnants of their lives and move on. When it comes to Bradley Cravens's victims, the innumerable amount that were still alive, she truly had her work cut out for her. She needed a small army to not only find all of Cravens's victims, but to fix them too.

After a typical day at the office, I was looking forward to relaxing on the couch and enjoying a beer or three. I was just sitting down with my dinner for one when there was a knock at the door. Naturally, I grabbed my pistol. After seeing it was *The Queen*, I put it away and opened the door for her.

Her showing up at my apartment was extremely unusual, so I was surprised, needless to say.

I moved to the side to let her in. She smiled sweetly before greeting me, "How are you tonight, Shepherd?"

"I'm fine." I looked around my apartment like I was looking for something. I wasn't sure what. "A little nervous because you're here." I held her gaze stoically, not exactly sure what to say or think. "Not that I don't love your company." I didn't miss the envelope she was holding in her hand.

She grinned. "That's sweet. No need to worry, really. Not right now. So, how did it go Friday night?"

I nodded. "Good."

"Good."

I pointed to the envelope in her hand, "What's that? It can't be what I think it is. It's Tuesday."

She studied me before she spoke, "You probably already know the FBI is in town."

I nodded. "Yes ma'am. I heard that at the office today. A few of the agents came by and asked around the office for details and such."

"Did they say they found any evidence?" she asked.

"No ma'am. And they won't," I said with certainty.

"Good. We saved a lot of lives on Friday. You know this, right?" she asked softly.

"Yes ma'am. I know."

Her eyes, normally so confident, dropped to the ground. "I received word that the Senator is digging around where he shouldn't be. I'm not saying that he or anyone else has found us out, but something about him makes me uneasy." She looked back up at me. "This is the first time in years that I have felt this nervous about a mark."

She handed me the envelope. "What's this?" I asked looking on the outside. No name. Not my revenge.

She began, "Before you open it, I want to explain the assignment to you." I nodded. "You can refuse, but please understand that you're my only hope on this one."

"Okay."

"This is not a mark, in the traditional sense." She locked her eyes on mine and proceeded, almost in a rushed breath, while I listened. "I had some information sent to me about the agents who are working this case. I need you to get in that circle. They'll be leery about you because of your day job. So, being buddies with them is not going to work. They'll know you're up to something." She paused. "We must make absolutely sure they do not find out about us."

"I understand," I said a little too roughly. "What's the assignment?"

She let out a deep breath. "There is a certain agent, Evie Harrington, who will be working the case. She is damn good at her job. She worked Homicide for a while, but recently she has been working cold cases. She's solving the damn things left and right, it seems."

31

"Okay? What do I have to do with this?" I asked.

"The FBI headquarters, our source from that office reports, has ordered her to work this case. That's where you come in. That envelope contains every detail of her life, starting with her birth certificate. She's coming here from Kansas City. She should be here tonight."

"Here? Where's here?" I questioned, still a little confused.

She inhaled slowly and breathed out, making me wait. "Next door."

I felt my eyebrows pull together, "Next door where?"

"Next door to you," she said quietly.

I chuckled. "That's not possible. Mr. and Mrs. Castro live there. They've lived there for years."

Her shoulders slumped, "I had them evicted yesterday. They had until noon today to get out."

"What?" I asked loudly. I threw the envelope on the table and stalked to the refrigerator, pulling a beer out. "What are you doing? Why next door? What do you intend I do? What are you suggesting?"

I turned to her and her shoulders lifted back up, almost like she was regaining her bearings. "I want you to start a relationship with her. Get to know her. Find out what she knows. The closer you get, the more she'll open up."

I chuckled, "I'm sorry. You know I'd do almost anything for the greater good of mankind and for you, but I can't do this."

"Yes, you can, Shepherd. You can. And, you will."

"I won't," I said adamantly.

For the first time ever, *The Queen* showed weakness and fear. Her eyes welled up. "Please, Shepherd," she whispered. "You have to. No one can know about this. Everything we've worked for will be gone. More people will die and our cause will be lost."

I shook my head, "I can't." I cast my eyes to the floor. "She..." I trailed off. "Acquaint me with someone else. A guy. I can't...a woman? I...I can't."

Unexpectedly, I felt her arms around me. I automatically closed the embrace. "I know you think you let her down. Let them both down. But, none of it was your fault."

"Wasn't it?" I countered.

"No," she whispered.

"I did let her down," I whispered. "I didn't mean to, but I did." I paused.

"I'm not asking you to marry Agent Harrington," she said.

I laughed. "I know. Just being close to a woman reminds me of her. Of both of them." I shook my head. "It's just tough."

She pulled away slowly. "We both know that I've neglected and almost abandoned my search for those who took them from you." I nodded. "If you do this, I will start today and exhaust every resource finding those bastards, so you can have your vengeance. I promise you."

The temptation was too great. I needed blood. I needed retribution.

"Okay," I said. "I'll do it."

"Inside the envelope—"

I cut her off. "I don't want to read what's in there."

"But there are things that I think you should know about her," she said quickly.

I interrupted her again. "I think it's best that I go into this blindly. I don't want to know things she might not want me to know. I don't want something I know to slip that she hasn't told me."

"Do you want to see a picture of her? So you know who you're looking for?" she asked.

"No," I said, flatly.

The Queen frowned. "Can I tell you one thing about her? It's important."

I gave in. "All right. What is it?"

"She's kind of broken. In the worst way. You're kindred spirits. That's why I chose you."

She turned and made her way to the door. "Take the envelope," I insisted. "I don't want it here—haunting me."

She picked it up off of the table and turned around when she turned the knob. "Shepherd?"

"Yes."

Her lip turned up on one corner. "She's beautiful."

I smiled. "Pulling out the big guns, huh?"

"Most certainly," she said, softly, and left quietly.

After she left, I sat down on the couch and rested my forehead on my palms and studied the carpet.

A woman. Nostalgia slammed into me like a freight train.

I looked to my right, on the end table, and there they rested. Their faces smiled at me. My wife, Arianna and my baby girl, Haven. I would do this for them. They deserved justice.

It never hurt me to look at their pictures. I never tucked them away. I wanted to remember that they were in my life. I wanted to be reminded why I do what I do. Everything I do is for them. I was not the husband or the father that I should've been. If I had been, I would still have them. That's what I told myself.

My love for them pushed me as much as my hatred for myself. I didn't deserve the love of another woman. I was doted on by the sweetest girl I had ever met. She loved me. And, all the while, I treated her like an obligation. I did love her, tremendously. I was just too scared to show it. I wasn't *in love* with her in the beginning, but she...she was incredible. It was impossible not to fall for her. She was a tiny thing, with warm brown eyes and golden hair. Our daughter was a perfect combination of the both of us. She was barely a year old when her tiny life was taken.

I had been in battle overseas. I had seen death on a daily basis. I had seen starving children. I had seen dead children. But, even that couldn't prepare me for losing my own, especially in the savage manner she was taken.

So, I kept their pictures out where I could see them—where I could remember what their smiles looked like. I liked to remember the way Arianna looked at me—like I was the epitome of all of her dreams.

Even in death, they deserved all of me.

CHAPTER FIVE

Evie

I received a call before I arrived in St. Louis that an apartment was being arranged for me. For that, I was extremely grateful. However, an apartment meant long term, which was what I was afraid of.

After a terrible night's stay in a dirty hotel and after the extremely long day I had, I was thankful to have somewhere semi-permanent to rest my bones.

I had arrived at the St. Louis office about midday, and was briefed on what I would expect and given a file compiled with details already gathered.

After all that I already knew about Bradley Cravens and what I had read, I could not understand why anyone would want him dead. It was very clear that what happened was not an accident. However, it didn't look like a crime of passion or even vengeful kill. It was simple. Clean cut.

It was obvious, as stated in reports that the shot was taken from the back seat of Mr. Cravens's car. Someone had waited on him. Not only that, but there was not one fingerprint, fiber, or hair anywhere in the car that did not belong to the victim. The killer was certain to be groomed and squeaky clean. Thus, premeditation. A planned kill. An assassination.

Bradley was on his way home from a friend's house when he was shot. The car was found, still running, in the middle of the street, which gave me reason to believe that Mr. Cravens had seen the perp in his back seat and stopped the car. He either knew his murderer and didn't try and flee the vehicle, or he wasn't given a chance to escape.

The angle of the gunshot wound was evidence enough that the back seat was occupied. Although the suspect had not left any trace evidence of his or her being there, there was one piece of possible evidence, if it did not belong to the victim.

The piece of thin metal, found shoved in the back seat, appeared to be some type of broken dog tag of sorts. It resembled military tags to an extent, but it wasn't from any type of United States military branch.

It was our only clue—a broken piece of metal with the letters *"herd"* on it, with the number *"9"* directly under it.

We find the other piece of that tag, and we would find our killer. I was certain. But that was a tiny tag to be found in a city this big—if the killer was even from this area. Abandoning the only clue we had, I went back to trying to figure out a motive.

The life, credentials, and successes of Cravens spoke for themselves. He was certainly high society. He was gorgeous, and he appeared to have a huge heart. He was a volunteer as well as a philanthropist. He gave away millions of dollars each year to various charities. He was always having auctions and benefits to raise money for organizations built around helping those in need. He had not one mark on his record.

It made me sad that the life of such a good person was snuffed out.

His father, the Senator, was equally impressive. They both had lived their lives on old money from stocks and bonds bought by their ancestors in the eighteen hundreds. Instead of squandering their fortunes, they used them for good. They changed hundreds of lives.

There were parks, buildings, and even bridges dedicated to them—erected in their names.

I picked up a picture of him and studied it. His light brown hair, cropped perfectly, his chocolate brown eyes and warm smile made him look…perfect. I shook my head trying to understand the waste.

There was a knock at the door, startling me. "Agent Harrington," the secretary said, "Boss says to head on out. You've got a long day ahead of you tomorrow. Better get out of here and get some rest." She walked to me and handed me a sheet of paper. "Here are the directions to your apartment. It's in a good neighborhood and just a few miles from here. It's an extremely nice complex. I think you'll like it. It will be comfortable." I nodded. "It's fully furnished. The sheets are clean, so you should be able to climb right in."

I smiled. "Thank you. That's great."

"See you tomorrow, Agent Harrington," she said, walking away.

"See you tomorrow," I answered in kind.

I rubbed my eyes and sat at the desk for a few minutes, collecting my thoughts and trying to steer them away from the life I had when I worked these cases. At least this would keep me busy.

I cringed when I heard her say my name. After the accident, my coworkers just called me by my first name. *Harrington.* Dash. I thought back when he was alive and with me. We would often be at the office, in the same room and someone would call out, "Agent Harrington!" and we would both say "What?" at the same time. I smiled remembering how I laughed every single time. He would always look down at me and grin.

I wiped away a few errant tears, but couldn't stop myself from whispering, "I miss you." I felt like tonight was going to be a *blue shirt* kind of night.

It was almost eleven thirty when I finally found the apartment. If I had any life in my spirit or heart, I probably would have cussed the secretary out the next morning. Her directions were terrible, and I got lost in the most dangerous part of St. Louis. But, I would ignore her shortcomings, just like I ignored pretty much everyone else in my life.

I had withdrawn from the world and only spoke to people at work, and only about cases. I hadn't spoken to any of my friends since the funeral. I hadn't seen them either. I didn't believe that I resented them, but my heart could not take the beating that would come with seeing them with their families. I spoke to my mother almost every day, but that was it. In the beginning, our friends would constantly stop by, but I refused to answer the door. I wanted them to feel like I was dead too, because that's what I feel like inside.

I didn't want their sympathy.

I didn't want their smiles.

I didn't want their tears.

I didn't want them telling me that everything would be okay.

I didn't want them telling me that it was *their time to go.*

I didn't want to hear that they were at peace—while I was falling apart.

I wanted to hear that they were still alive—that they were coming back to me. I wanted to hear my son's needy cries—crying out to me. I wanted to hear my husband's voice in my ear while he made love to me, telling me that he'd love me forever.

Pulling my suitcases from the car, I had one thing on my mind. *Blue shirt. Blue shirt. Blue shirt.* I was about to crumble. I could feel it coming. I needed him. Like an addict that needs a fix—I needed to be as close to Dash as I could get.

When I saw the elevator was out of service, I hurried up the stairs, attempting to toll two of my large suitcases at once. I was almost to the door of my new apartment, when in my rush, one of the suitcases caught on the back of my shoe and I tripped.

I stumbled a few paces, but didn't catch myself in time. I fell to the floor with a painful thump, but not before banging loudly into the door in front of me.

Not only did it sound like a train wreck, it looked like one too. I held the retractable handle in my hand, while the suitcase it was attached to sat six feet away. Not only was it without a handle, but the back had busted along the edges and my DD bras were sprinkled along the floor of the hallway. Tears immediately began to stream down my face. I didn't need this. Not tonight.

I was just pulling myself straight, still in tears, when the door flew open.

"The hell?" I heard.

I stiffened. It was nearing midnight and it sounded like I was singlehandedly tearing the place down.

I turned around, and staring at me, were the most crystal blue eyes I had ever seen in my life.

CHAPTER SIX

RHETT

I was already on edge all night long. After *The Queen* stopped by, I couldn't get this assignment out of my head. Not only that, but as much as I was confident about the execution of my last assignment, this was the first time that the FBI was crawling all over the place, digging up what they could find. I convinced myself that they would find nothing, and tried to relax. But, I was finding that to be impossible.

I couldn't sleep. So, I decided to clean my gun. What do guys do when they can't sleep and don't have a woman to wake up to wear them out? We find our dirtiest gun and clean it.

That's exactly what I was doing when I heard something crash into my door. It startled the shit out me, and I grabbed my loaded pistol, keeping it to my side and without checking the peephole, swung the door open quickly, in the glory of my boxer briefs.

"The hell?" flew out of my mouth before I had the door completely open.

A woman stood, hunched in front of me with her back to me. I glanced down the hallway and her luggage was scattered from the stairwell to my door.

She slowly turned and her long, red hair veiled her face until she was facing me completely.

When she looked at me, my breath was literally stolen from me. She was absolutely the most gorgeous woman I had ever seen in my entire life. Although her cheeks were wet and ruddy, her hazel eyes showed the unbound depths into her soul. She was panting slightly.

Her full and pouty lips were parted slightly blowing out her frustrated breaths while sucking in calming ones.

Before I had a chance to speak, her captivating eyes landed on my gun. I saw her quickly reach for her holstered pistol.

In a rush, I held my pistol out to the side, holding it by the trigger guard with one finger, away from me, letting it dangle.

"Hey, hey, hey," I said softly. "I'm putting it down, okay?" I couldn't help it. I smirked. I bent over slightly and set it on the floor in front of my feet.

As I stood back up, I straightened my expression. She was a job. I had to remind myself of that. At the most, I would pretend to befriend her and only do so in order to find out what I needed to know.

I had already made up my mind. I was not going to get close. I was not going to get wrapped up in her charms, no matter how beautiful I was told she was. I was not going to get personal. And, I, sure as hell, was not going to touch her.

So, I tried to tap down the asshole I knew I was, but keep my guard up. You catch more flies with honey…and all that.

I was standing there staring at her, scanning her from her face to her feet. She. Was. Luscious. Curvy in all the right places. Her thick red tinted hair hung in beautiful waves down her back. Her simple gray cotton dress hugged every inch of her that it covered. Her breasts were more than a handful and her hips gave her that delicious hourglass shape. Her legs were tight and toned and her red heels nearly set me on fire.

I like red.

I smiled. "Rough day?"

She hiccupped a small chuckle and shook her head, bringing her hands to her face and burying her sorrow.

She was beautiful, but her sad eyes convinced me that *The Queen* was right. She was broken.

She wiped her face and tried to force a smile. "I'm sorry for all of the clamor. I apologize if I woke you up." She turned and started gathering her things that littered the hallway.

"Need some help?" I asked.

She shook her head. "I've got it. Thank you."

I knew she was embarrassed and I didn't want to make it worse, but she looked like she was going to fall apart at any second. I abandoned my doorway and helped her gather her belongings, while watching her tight derrière as she was bent over in front of me.

Kneeling beside me, she spoke, trying to stop me. "No, please. You don't have to do that," she said in a rush.

I looked down and realized what I was picking up. I held three of her bras in my hand and was reaching for her thong. I don't know who was more mortified..her—because they were her underwear. Or me—because I hadn't touched a woman's undergarments in so long, I felt like a prepubescent boy.

Instead of ignoring the warmth in my cheeks and putting them back in her suitcase, I dropped them like hot potatoes. "Sorry," I said quickly and stood as fast as I could.

She looked up at me, as if she were about to speak, and we both realized, at the same time, that my junk was inches from her face.

"Holy shit!" I yelled, jumping back away from her, and taking my hands and covering myself. Why in the *hell* didn't I put on pants? "I am so sorry. Holy shit."

Then, the unexpected happened.

She started laughing. And, it was the most beautiful sound in the world. I stared at her and smiled when I saw her eyes liven up for just a moment before it flickered away.

Chuckling, I said, "I'll be right back."

I ran into my apartment, after picking my gun up and carrying it inside. I quickly slipped on a pair of worn out jeans and a t-shirt and joined her again in the hallway. She was still sitting where I had left her, but her things were secured in her suitcase.

I smiled when I knelt down beside her. "That was probably the most embarrassing thing that's ever happened to me."

She smiled, "Don't worry about it. I needed a little laugh after the day I've had."

"You too, huh?" I asked.

"Yeah."

I held my hand out to her. "Now that we've seen each other's underwear, I guess we should introduce ourselves." I smiled. "Rhett Trimble."

She took my hand and shook it lightly. Girly grip. "Evie Harrington."

I remember when I was a kid, I was going to cross a fence that I wasn't aware had an electric charge pulsing through it. I grabbed onto the wire, attempting to push it down for me to cross over, and it zapped the shit out of me. Even though it hurt like hell, I couldn't let go of it.

Evie Harrington's hand was the wire. After holding on to her hand for longer than I should have, she whispered, "You can let go now."

"Sorry," I said quickly, letting go of her hand. I blew out a rush of air. "So," I started, "Moving in?"

"Yes."

"Which apartment?"

"Two-oh-two," she said slowly.

I smiled. "Ah. Welcome home, neighbor."

I couldn't believe what a goober I was being. I needed to get my shit together. And fast.

"Why don't you go unlock the door, and I'll carry this one, since the handle is broken," I suggested.

"I can get it," she argued.

I gave her a sideways glance. "I can help. It's what neighbors do."

"Okay," she relented.

After she opened the door and pulled one of her suitcases inside, I followed her, carrying the other.

"Holy crap," I said as I sat it down on her couch. "That thing weighs a ton."

She smiled. "Yeah."

I looked at her. "Have any more?"

She nodded. "I do—in my car. But, I can get those."

I shook my head. "I can help you. It's late and no one should be down by the street this late at night by themselves. This is one of the most dangerous cities in America. You know that, right?"

She chuckled. "Yeah."

I gestured to the door. "Lead the way."

Without argument, we managed to get everything inside of her apartment in only a few minutes. I almost found myself wanting to stick around and talk to her. I felt drawn to her. *Kindred spirits.* I couldn't help but wonder in what sense *The Queen* spoke of.

After I put her last suitcase down, I headed for the door. I was turning the knob when she said from behind me, "Thank you so much. I'm sorry if I disturbed you."

I smiled at her. "It's not a problem. Anytime. And, you didn't disturb me. I was awake." I chuckled. "You did scare the shit out of me though."

She chuckled in kind. "I'm sorry."

I winked at her and pulled the door open and stepped outside, and slowly started to close it. "Stop apologizing," I said softly.

The door latched behind me and I went back to my apartment. I dropped down on the couch and let out a deep breath. I expected beauty and brokenness. But, I didn't expect the impact that those things would have on me. Maybe if she was just beautiful, I could've handled it. Or, maybe if she was just broken, I could've ignored it.

She was so stunning and she was so sad. Her blues went beyond having a tough day. It takes something tragic to steal the life from someone's eyes. Despite the entrancing hazel, her spirit was lost…somewhere deep down inside.

There was one thing that bothered me about her more than it should have. Other than the moment I first saw her, she never met my eyes. It was almost like she was hiding from something or someone—or like she didn't want others to see into her soul.

She was on the verge of crumbling when I found her. She was in tears. And, I made her smile.

I made her laugh.

What's worse than that?

I wanted to do it again.

CHAPTER SEVEN

Evie

Holy. Tattoos.

Instead of scoping out my new residence, I immediately pulled off my shoes and crawled onto the bed, pulling my knees to my chest. The fiasco in the hallway turned into the brightest part of my day.

Blue eyes. Every time I saw a pair of blue eyes, I thought of Dash. But not this time.

Dash's eyes were deep blue and beautiful.

These blue eyes were so light, like the blue of the sky on a summer day. The light blue was a sharp contrast to his olive skin.

I hadn't seen that much of a man in two years. Was he ever…all man.

His corded arms and legs showed every bend, flex, and haunch. His chest and stomach were rippled with definition. He was definitely taller than my five foot seven inch frame, and his presence seemed to tower over me.

He was absolutely, underwear model gorgeous. I can attest. I saw him in only his underwear.

Rhett.

I closed my eyes and could see his face. His dark wispy hair fell just above his ears, partly hanging, splayed across his forehead. His lips were full and were gorgeously showcased by the trimmed facial hair, a tad thicker than a five o'clock shadow, which covered his jaw and traveled up to meet his hairline.

I only looked at his face once, but I could remember it well. He was too handsome to stare at. His eyes were too mesmerizing. As much as I might have been tempted to look into his eyes again, I didn't want him to see me. And, I didn't want him to see through me.

When I first saw him, I should have been scared. I really should have been. If I would not have seen his face first, I would have been. Usually when someone has that many tattoos, they are in a gang or simply up to no good.

Both of his arms were sleeved in tattoos. Not just symbols or tribal markings—but an artist's graphic work. His chest was completely bare of tattoos, and his back almost was. Words covered the top of it and I read them when he walked away from me. If I wasn't familiar with them, or had never heard them, I wouldn't have been able to read them so quickly.

In the most elegant cursive I had ever seen, it read: *Vengeance is mine, I will repay, saith the Lord. Romans 12:19.*

I was raised to learn that verse and believe it. And, this gorgeous man believed it enough to have those words inked on his body. It was strange, but in that moment, I felt trusting of him.

He had a professional composure and gait. And, he was friendly.

The pistol took me by surprise. Even in my profession, I've not seen many people answer the door with a weapon drawn. As he was putting it down on the ground, I saw within the ink the letters U.S.M.C. Marine Corps. I relaxed…somewhat.

He neither limped nor stumbled, but as he headed to his apartment, I almost missed the indentation on the inner thigh of his right leg. The flesh on a large part of his upper leg was obviously missing. His steps never revealed the damage most likely caused by war.

Wounded.

That's what he was. Beautifully wounded.

Forget wounds. Forget blue eyes.

I tried to clear my mind so I could wind down after the long day. I pulled myself up off of the bed and went in search of my fifth suitcase—the one full of pictures of my husband and my son. I picked it up and carried it to my temporary bedroom. I sat it down on the bed and ran my fingers over it and finally built up the courage to unzip it. I closed my eyes and blew out unsteady breaths as I listened to it open. I pulled the top open slowly and peered down. And, when I did, my breath caught. During the drive, my albums had shifted and two of the pictures had come out of their respective sleeves.

I reached down and picked them up and stared into those blue eyes that captured my heart. He faced the camera, peering up at me with those piercing blue eyes and with that lop-sided grin plastered on his face. He held a white stick that sported a plus sign in his hand. I had peed on it and he didn't care. I flipped it over and on the back were words I wasn't aware that he had written. In total guy-penmanship, he wrote: *Finally, baby. I've waited for this moment since the day I met you. I can't wait to be your 'baby daddy.' I love you, sugar…more than I love myself.*

Reading those words made me angry. Enraged, I threw the picture down on the floor and my tears came in waves. I stomped out to the balcony and screamed into the night, "You did not love me! You did not! You fucking liar!" I whimpered and my rage broke me. "If you did…you would've stayed," I whispered. "You would've stayed with me."

I gripped on to the railing and inhaled the night air. It was hot and muggy and made my face stickier with my tears. I panted and tried to catch my breath. Before I abandoned my perch, I closed my eyes and let the tears roll down my face, letting them fall to my chest. I whispered, "I loved you, and you left me on purpose. I hate you. I hate you."

In the shower, I wailed. I missed him. I needed him. I loved him and I hated him.

After I dried off, I walked naked to my suitcases in the living room. I dug until I found it. I pulled the wrinkled blue shirt from its resting place and pushed my arms inside. I could smell him in that shirt and my heart seemed to calm instantly.

I looked at the clock and it revealed that I was already into my D-day by eight minutes.

Two years ago, I kissed them both goodbye with every intention of seeing them again.

Two years ago, my husband wore this shirt to work for the very last time.

Two years ago, I had a son who had just turned ten months old.

Two years ago, everything was perfect in the morning and destroyed by the afternoon.

Now, I am dead inside, and all I have are pictures and this stupid fucking shirt.

When I finally laid down to sleep, I had no more tears. I had no energy, except to whisper my anthem to a God I could not see. "Tell Dash I don't know if I can forgive him yet. And, tell my precious baby boy that I love him, and that I'll see him soon."

And, I fell asleep.

***

I woke to knocking on my door. After pulling a pair of shorts on and glancing at my phone to see I had nine missed calls, I raced to the door. My hair was a rat's nest and my face felt tight and puffy, and my eyes felt swollen.

I pulled the door open to see my "assistant," Rhonda, smiling at me. She was taller and slimmer than me with shoulder-length brown hair and coffee brown eyes. The secretary slash intern would be my shadow and helper on this assignment. I wasn't too sure how I felt about the company, but I didn't have a choice. Rhonda, my new best friend, held a cup of coffee in front of my face.

"I've been trying to reach you," she said in a sing-song voice.

Lord, she was going to annoy me, I could already tell.

"I called you nine times. Do you have any idea what time it is?"

I shook my head while trying to sip my coffee.

She smiled. "It's past noon."

I felt my eyes go wide. "Are you kidding me?" I shouted.

She laughed. "Nope."

"Holy crap. I'm so sorry. Give me ten minutes. I'll be ready."

She shrugged. "Please, take your time. I already covered for you. I kind of took the blame. I got to thinking about those directions and I…I think they were probably really shitty."

I nodded. "They were."

After showering and dressing quickly, Rhonda and I were walking out the door. As I had my back to her, locking the door, I heard the deep, smooth rumble from the night before right behind me.

"Hey, Rhonda," I heard him say.

I turned around in time to see her stick her hand out to him. "Hey, Rhett. How's it hangin', pal?"

He chuckled. "That's a tad personal, even for you, perv."

She laughed. "Well, you know me!"

His eyes cut to mine as I stood there gaping at him. He was dressed in gray slacks that hung low on his lean hips, tidied with a belt, and a crisp light purple shirt sealed at the top with a fashionable tie. The tattoos I saw the night before were completely concealed. His dress shoes completed his professional look. Still gorgeous, with his wispy hair in disarray. The sky blue of his eyes caused my heart to drop to my feet. He smiled. "Hey, Evie. How are you?"

I looked to Rhonda. Then, back to Rhett. Then, back to Rhonda before speaking. "You know him?"

Rhonda looked at me, smiled, and nodded. "Yeah. He's the deputy prosecuting attorney, so I deal with him often."

He smiled like he was satisfied with himself and laughed. "Deal with me? You make me sound like a tyrannical child. Work together. Say we *work together* often."

"Okay. We *work together* often," she said sarcastically. "Coming home for lunch?" she asked.

His eyes left me for a moment, a moment that felt entirely too long. "Yeah. I left a file here, so I had to come and get it before my hearing this afternoon."

Rhonda smiled. "Distracted much?"

Once again, his eyes landed on me and he smirked. "A little."

I looked down at the ground and busied myself, putting my keys in my purse. "You ready?" I asked her.

"Yep."

I started walking away as quickly as I could, and I heard her following me a few steps in. "See you later, Rhett."

"K," he announced at our backs. "See you tonight, Evie." I could hear the smile in his voice.

I didn't turn around. "All right."

As soon as we hit the stairs, Rhonda let out a dramatic sigh, tossing her head back, resting the back of her hand on her forehead. "Be still my heart. Rhett Trimble touched this hand." I smiled and shook my head. "Good Lord, if I weren't happily married, I'd climb that like a damn tree! He's a fine specimen of the male species, isn't he?"

I attempted to be passive. "I didn't notice."

"What?" she screeched, stopping on the stairs as I continued downward. "Hold up!" She rushed to catch up. "He was eye-," she paused, "...f-ing you in the hallway and you didn't notice?"

I kept walking, exiting the building. "No, I didn't. And, could you keep your voice down? You're yelling! I'm sure everyone in the stairwell heard you."

"There wasn't anyone in there, and who gives a rat's ass? I don't know of anyone who would disagree with me."

We climbed in her car (I hate being a passenger, by the way) and headed to the office. My curiosity got the best of me and I started asking questions. "So, prosecuting attorney, huh?"

Her eyes flashed to me and she grinned. "Deputy prosecuting attorney, yes."

"Why did he call you a perv?"

She smiled. "Because I am."

I turned to stare out the window. "He good at his job?"

"Yeah. He's kind of an asshole. Although I squeeze in every sexual innuendo I can during our conversations, that little thing you saw in the hallway—that's the nicest he's ever been to me."

I faced her. "You're kidding."

She shook her head. "Nope. Everyone says he has a burr up his ass, but he has his reasons for acting that way. My cousin went to law school with him and he said he was always a really nice guy."

"Why do I feel like I don't want to hear this?"

She spoke softly, "Because you probably don't. He was mar—"

I cut her off. "Don't tell me. Please. I don't need any sad stories today." The purse in my lap gave me something to do with my hands, so I started playing with the metal latches, flipping the front pocket open, then closed. Since Rhonda was kind and I had an aching feeling that she would become a friend, I whispered, "Today is my D-Day."

There was no laughter in her voice, only curiosity. "What's that?"

My eyes welled up and I whispered, "My Death Day. Two years ago, today, I lost my family." I looked at her and tried to fake a smile. Surprisingly, only one tear fell.

She let out a heavy sigh and reached over and stilled my hands. Her watery eyes caught mine for a moment. "I'm sorry," she whispered.

She squeezed my hand and her comfort had me squeezing back. "I heard about what happened. You'll be my strong girl today, okay?" She looked at me and nodded. "You can do this and if you can't, I'll take you home and we will start again tomorrow, nice and fresh. Okay?"

My face drew up for a moment before I willed my tears away. "Thank you," I whispered.

She didn't let go of my hand until we reached the office.

CHAPTER EIGHT

RHETT

I almost lost my case at the hearing that afternoon. I just couldn't think, and every time I closed my eyes to gather my thoughts, all I could see were Evie's hazel eyes. She was too damn beautiful for her own good. Her hair appeared a deeper shade of red today and my fingers tingled to touch it.

I don't remember ever feeling this way about a woman or being so distracted by one. Every time she looked at me, I felt like I was being sucker-punched in the gut. I had the urge to pull her close and tenderly kiss all of her tears away. Like a lovesick woman, I rubbed my fingertips over my lips as the defense attorney gave his argument. If the defendant wouldn't have broken down on the stand and admitted to his terrible deeds, I wouldn't have won. My argument was lacking, and my arguments never lack. The judge, when I saw him in the restroom, asked me if I was okay. I lied and told him yes.

The truth was that I was most certainly not okay. A storm was brewing inside of me, and I had no control over it. I needed to get close to her, and not even for my assignment. I needed to be near her for my own satisfaction, for my own longings. I had to know what had broken her, and I needed to hear it from her plump lips.

The day seemed to drag on and I checked the clock a hundred times, counting down to five o'clock. I was looking forward to her being on the other side of my bedroom wall.

When I arrived home, I saw a newspaper outside of her door, which I understood to mean she wasn't home yet. I immediately was bummed and felt my shoulders slouch, like a six-year-old boy whose mother just told him he couldn't have any ice cream after dinner. I was pissed when I realized that I was pouting. I don't pout.

It was almost nine when I heard a knock on my door. Like every other time, I was ready for any surprises. When I checked the peephole and saw my brother-in-law, Adam, smiling at me, I opened the door. Adam and Ariana were twins and looking into his eyes nearly killed me every time he was around. Adam supported us from the very beginning. I was close to him then, and I still am.

He walked in, still in his scrubs, and greeted me with a full-fledged bear hug. He was only a few inches shorter than me, but about fifty pounds lighter.

"Hey, brother," he said, mid-squeeze.

"Hey, buddy. How's it going? I haven't seen you in a couple weeks."

He pulled away, "Yeah. There have been some schedule changes down at the hospital, and I've been working more hours. It's fucked me up a little."

I chuckled. "Nurse Adam to the rescue."

He laughed in kind. "Nurse Adam is right." His eyes went wide. "Holy hell. I just met the hottest redhead ever, walking up the stairs just now."

My heart fell to my stomach. "She's home?" I asked curiously.

He cocked his head and grinned. "Waiting on her?"

I shook my head—a little too quickly before answering. "Nope."

He laughed. "Yeah. Doesn't sound like it. Who is she?"

I shrugged. "No idea."

"Bullshit!" he yelled. "What's her name?"

I relented. "Evie. Just moved in next door."

"Hmmm. Evie. Beautiful name for a beautiful lady. She single?"

I glared at him. "Why do you care?"

He smiled and lifted his eyebrows. "Pretty sure it's obvious. I'm single and…handsome." Within the bounds of my sexual confidence, I would have to agree—he's handsome. "And, she is…" he paused and shivered, "gorgeous."

I blew out a loud breath and said softly, "She is gorgeous." I turned to him before he could respond. "Want something to drink?"

He nodded. "Sure. Do you have any tea?"

That's one thing I always have. "Yep."

After retrieving us a couple glasses, and filling them up, I strolled back into the living room. Adam was not going to let this one die. "So…is she single?"

I shook my head. "I think so. Why? Are you going to walk over there and knock on her door and ask her out?"

He chuckled and leaned back in my recliner. "Nah. I'll leave that for you."

I scoffed. "What makes you think I'm interested?"

"Are you kidding me? You should've seen your face when I asked her relationship status. You were pissed a little."

I negated, "No I wasn't."

"Bro, you were. I've known you forever. And, I think this would be good for you. It's been five years. Ariana wouldn't want you to stop living."

My good mood turned bleak. "Don't, Adam."

His smile fell from his face and he continued, despite my plea. "I'm just saying. She would want you to move on. You've got to stop punishing yourself. We both loved them, and I can tell you right now, they'd both want you to be happy."

My hands started to shake. "Adam, I…" I was cut off by a loud bang from next door and a loud scream.

I jumped up and raced out my door with Adam hot on my heels. I pounded on her door like a crazed lunatic. "Evie!" I yelled as I pounded. "Evie!" There was no answer. I pounded harder. "Evie!" I turned to Adam. "Grab my keys from the coffee table. I guarantee that the landlord didn't change the locks." When Mr. and Mrs.

Castro went out of town, I kindly watered their plants. Chores equal spare keys around here.

I continued to call out to her as I banged on her door. As soon as Adam returned, I unlocked the door and went inside. "Evie," I called out again. Her apartment was silent as a tomb. I checked every room with no luck, until I entered the master bedroom.

There she lay on the floor, passed out cold, wearing nothing but a blue long-sleeved shirt and her underwear. If she were conscious, I would've ogled. But, ogling her in her current state would have made me an asshole. I was making my way to her quickly before Adam cut me off. I could see the stool she was obviously standing on overturned and one of the suitcases I carried in the night before was on top of her legs with the contents spilled at her feet.

"Don't touch her," Adam warned. "Let me." I bit back my jealousy, knowing his expertise would be of some use. He checked her over and tried to wake her up. After a couple of seconds, she came to and looked at us like we were from another planet. Adam smiled at her, the bastard, and she immediately smiled back. "You okay, baby?" *Baby?* What the...

She rubbed her head and blinked rapidly while trying to sit up. "Take it easy," Adam cooed as he helped her into a sitting position. He checked the dilation of her eyes and took all necessary precautions as I sat there and looked on at the beautiful mess.

She looked between the both of us half a dozen times before she spoke. "What happened? How did you get in here?"

Adam chuckled. "You fell off of that." He pointed to the stool. "You bumped your head and have a nice knot on the back of it." She rubbed it with her fingers and winced. "And, old Trusty Neighborhood Watch over there," pointing at me, "let us in."

He helped her to her feet and walked her to her couch and they both sat down. I handed her a blanket from the back of her recliner. I didn't care if she was cold. I needed her to cover up for *my* own good, sanity, and wood. She took it and covered up without any objection. She looked at Adam. "Who are you? Are you a doctor?"

she asked quietly.

He smiled. *This prick and his smiles.* "I'm Rhett's brother-in-law and an R.N," he answered and she nodded. "You may have a concussion and you probably need to go the doctor in the morning if you experience any nausea, vomiting, etc."

"I'll be fine," she answered.

"That may be so," he answered, "but you can never be too careful. It could turn into something serious. Do you have any family or anyone who could stay with you tonight? You can go to bed, but you need to be woken up every hour."

She shook her head to answer his question before speaking, "I'm just here for work. I don't know anyone, really. I have a co-worker that might come. If you think it's absolutely necessary, I can call her."

Adam agreed that was the best thing for her to do. I listened carefully to her side of the conversation. "Yeah. Okay. No. I understand. He just said it was best. I'm sure I'll be fine. Okay. Thanks. See you tomorrow." She hung up and shook her head. "She can't stay. She has a sick little girl." She peered at me for a moment before her eyes flickered to Adam. "Look, guys. Thank you, but I really think I'll be fine. And, to be honest, I'd rather just be alone tonight."

"You really shouldn't be," he argued.

The corner of her mouth tilted up. "Seriously. What's the worst that could happen?"

Without missing a beat, Adam answered, "You could die. Seriously."

Her smile fell from her face and she let out a heavy breath. I stood in silence, watching the scene unfold. When Adam turned around and winked, I knew exactly what was about to fall out of that asshole's mouth.

"*Neighbor* can stay." He turned around and grinned. "Can't you, buddy?"

I felt my nostrils flare and I shook my head. "I can't."

Adam turned and narrowed his eyes. "Why not?"

I didn't answer. My heart pounded out of my chest. I stared down at her and she looked up and caught my eyes. I couldn't look away, and it felt like she didn't want me to.

I was pissed for two reasons. One: he volunteered my ass and put me between a rock and a hard place. I shouldn't be near her, but I couldn't let her die in her sleep. Two: I *wanted* to stay. I was like a moth to a flame when she was around. For some reason unknown to me, a completely unexplainable feeling raged inside of me. I *wanted* to be near her.

I had only known her for two days. I'd only talked to her three times. She didn't know me. I was certain I scared the shit out of her the night before. There was no way in hell she would even let me stay with her.

As I sat there staring into the hazel eyes that held my gaze, and to my utter fucking surprise, she asked me, "Do you mind staying with me?"

Holy. Shit. This couldn't be happening. I broke our gazes and looked behind me like she was talking to someone who stood at my back. I faced her once more and pointed at my chest. "Me?"

She nodded, but didn't smile.

I spoke before she could. "But, you don't know anything about me." I shook my head. "I could be a serial killer for all you know."

Adam turned around and laughed. "You're a fucking prosecutor. Not a killer."

I stilled at his words. He had no idea how wrong he was. I couldn't stay with her. Despite what they believed, I *was* a killer. I could tell by looking at her that she deserved someone better than me. I would only hurt her, and I knew it.

Her eyes teared and I sighed and smiled. "Sure." She nodded and a tear ran down her cheek. "And, just so you know—I'm not...a serial killer."

She wiped her face and smiled. "I didn't think you were."

Adam stood up from where he was squatting in front of her. He slapped me on the back and winked. "Go get your sleeping bag, Trimble."

He started walking to the door before he stopped to wait for me. I asked her, "Are you absolutely sure?"

She nodded. "Yes. I don't really have a choice. If you give me about ten minutes, I'll change clothes and get ready for bed." I nodded and when I reached Adam at the door, I glared at him. Her sweet voice stopped me. "When you come back, just use your key to get in."

"Okay," I said and followed Adam out. As soon as I closed her door, I frogged him as hard as I could in his arm.

He yelped. "What the hell? That hurt, you asshole!"

"I know." I passed him and walked into my apartment. "What the fuck are you doing, Adam? What the hell was that?"

Adam answered, "She honest to goodness needs someone to stay with her tonight. You can't just leave her alone."

"This is not your place, Adam. You can't push me into something I'm not ready for."

"I know you. You're ready," he argued.

"You don't know shit about me!"

Adam's coolness fled. "I know I watched a woman love you with everything inside of her without that love being returned." His eyes teared and it caught me off guard. "She loved you anyway. And, just so you know *asshole*, she would want you to move on and find someone you *can* love. Find someone to love like she loved you."

I felt like he had punched me in the heart. "I *loved* her, you motherfucker. I still do," I seethed.

He nodded. "Maybe so. But, it was just a little too late." He picked up his keys from the kitchen table and pointed to the wall that Evie and I shared. "You're welcome for that." And he left without another word.

As soon as he shut the door, I felt my bottom lip tremble. I knew I was an asshole, but having my dead wife thrown in my face stung like hell. I felt like he had pushed his hand into my chest and squeezed the little bit of heart I had left.

I dropped down to the couch and picked up the picture from the end table and ran my fingers over her face a dozen times. I missed them. I had finally loved them and appreciated them the day before they were taken from me. A tear fell before I realized it. As I continued to stroke her face, I whispered to her as if she could hear me. "I'm so sorry, Ari."

I set the picture down and took a long, hot shower. I needed it. I gathered a few things I would need for my overnight stay and let myself into Evie's apartment.

When I walked in the door, she was sitting on the couch in pajama pants and an oversized shirt. No matter how big the shirt was on her, I could immediately tell that she was not wearing a bra. My eyes clung to her chest for a second too long.

When I looked her in the eyes, she didn't seem to be aware that I was staring at her goods. Before I could step out of her foyer, her words stopped me in my tracks. "Are you married?"

I blinked. I couldn't understand how she would've gained that assumption.

She spoke again. "Are you?"

"Am I what?"

"Married," she answered impatiently.

I shook my head. "No. Why would you think that?"

"That nurse guy. He said he was your brother-in-law."

Ah. It clicked. "He *was* my brother-in-law. I guess that's how you would say it."

"Was?" she asked.

"Yes. My wife…uh…passed away several years ago," I answered slowly. In a town this big with this much crime, I'm not surprised to know people don't know my story. I smiled. This smiling shit made my face tired, but I couldn't help it in her presence. "Are they still considered in-laws in that case?"

She sat there and stared at me, without answering my question. She slowly closed her eyes and took several deep breaths in and out.

I gave her a minute before speaking. I just stood at the door like an idiot for a moment before I moved toward her couch and set my things on the coffee table. "Are you…married, that is?" I already knew the answer because of *The Queen's* hasty visit, but I couldn't let her know that. And, I still didn't really know anything about her and I craved to.

She shook her head. With her eyes still closed, she answered my question. I knew what she was doing, because I had done it thousands of times. She was willing away her tears. "My husband passed away a couple of years ago," she whispered.

Kindred spirits. Kind of broken. The Queen's words came back to me in a rush. She had lost as I had lost.

"I'm sorry," I said immediately. That was all I could say. She looked up at me and her eyes welled up. I knew then that she was more shattered than I had ever been. Her undying love for who she had lost was evident and it made me unreasonably jealous. I was jealous of anyone who could love that deeply. I was jealous of the receiver of her love. I was jealous of a dead man.

She tried to clear her face of any emotion before speaking. She was so beautiful with her strawberry hair piled on top of her head and her face completely bare of any makeup. "So, how does this work?" she smiled. "How many concussed people have you taken care of?"

I laughed and the tension in the room relaxed. "Quite a few actually. I was in the military for several years and deployed a couple times. Sometimes there is nothing to do in the desert besides beat the crap out of each other." She smiled. "Needless to say, concussions were a common occurrence." She kept her eyes on me. *Finally*, I thought. I couldn't stand for her to continuously look away from me. "So, you'll go to sleep, and I'll wake you up every hour and make sure you're not vomiting and whatever. And, I'll get you anything you need. This is going to suck; I'm not going to lie about that. You'll hate me by the time dawn comes, trust me." She nodded. "I suggest no reading, no TV, nothing strenuous for certain.

And, you will most definitely need to see a doctor tomorrow."

She agreed without any argument. She and I stood at the same time, and I noticed the blanket and pillow on her couch. She looked at me sheepishly. "Is this okay? I'm sorry. I have another room, but there's no bed in there."

I smiled. "It's perfectly fine." I would have much rather slept in my own bed. But, sacrificing my comfort was worth her close proximity.

As promised, I woke her up every hour. I don't want to sound like a creeper, but I knelt beside her and watched her sleep before I attempted to stir her awake. She was so gorgeous, I ached. She smelled divine and I knew I would smell her scent for days.

She woke up every time without incident. Although I didn't sleep at all, it was so worth it. While she slept, I sat in the chaise lounge in her room. I couldn't sleep. I didn't want to sleep. So, I laid there and watched her closed eyes dance around in her dream world.

After she fell asleep during the fourth hour, I looked over by her closet to see her suitcase still open with its contents spilled out. I walked over and crouched to pick them up.

Photo albums.

I opened the suitcase and it was packed full of them, at least ten of them. The cover of the first album displayed a picture of a young Evie on the right and an attractive blonde-haired guy to her left. They were beaming at the camera, standing in front of an old wooden barn. The man's right hand was in front of his chest, with his thumb in the air and his pointer finger aimed at Evie. They were holding chalkboards, each of them with a different phrase scrolled across it. His read, *She Stole My Heart*. And, hers read, *Now, I'm Stealing His Last Name!*

Happy. She looked so incredibly happy and so incredibly in love.

Against my better judgment, I opened the album to the first page and stared at the image of Evie, with her red hair twisted up on her head looking away from the camera; her husband held his eyes closed while kissing her on the cheek. In the corner was written a message in black marker. It read: *If this is a dream, please don't wake me up. —Dash.*

I put the album back in the suitcase and zipped it up. When I picked it up to put it away, one picture was face down on the floor. Naturally, I bent over, picked it up…and flipped it over.

My heart sank.

Evie was a mother. She smiled up at me from the picture, obviously in a hospital bed, holding a brand new baby boy. The blue cap gave it away. Her eyes were teary and she looked exhausted, but her smile radiated.

She was beautiful now, but she looked like a totally different person in the picture I held. Her eyes were bright and red-rimmed with joy. They were colder and darker now. She almost looked lost now. I couldn't help but wonder what happened to her and her family. I was aware that her husband had passed away, and I was almost certain that her son was gone as well. No one who had something to live for looked as lost as she did now. If her husband and her son were gone, she must feel like she had nothing to live for.

Just like me.

I carefully put the picture in the suitcase with the others, zipped it up again, and put it on the top shelf of her closet where I believed she wanted it. I got a few hours asleep, but losing sleep over her was worth it.

For the rest of the night, I watched her—watched her battle her pain in her sleepy state. It was beautifully sad.

When she woke up, I was getting my things around to go back to my apartment. She walked into the living room, rumpled and beautiful from sleep.

"Good morning," she said. Her voice was quiet and scratchy and sexy as hell.

"Good morning," I said in return. I picked my phone up off the table and walked to the door. "I have to run. I have a hearing this morning, first thing. I hope you don't mind, but I called Rhonda and told her you need to see the doctor. She's on her way."

She looked dumbfounded. "You didn't have to do that," she answered softly. "You've done enough. Thank you so much for staying."

I smiled before opening the door and stepping out, "You bet. Anytime." I paused. "Do you want your key back?"

"Keep it. You never know when I'll bust my skull open and need you again."

I nodded and pulled the door closed. I felt like I was running away like a whipped puppy.

As I got ready for work, I straightened my tie and stared at myself in the mirror. I had to finally admit what I had been trying to deny since the moment I saw her:

She would become more than an assignment to me. I had to know her.

All of her.

CHAPTER NINE

Evie

By some small miracle, I did not have to spend the night of my D-day alone. I had my very own watchman. Although he woke me up half a dozen times throughout the night, I slept like I hadn't slept in ages.

Every time I opened my eyes and saw him standing over me, my heart constricted. It felt good…having him there with me.

I did have a mild concussion. Doctor's orders: No work for a week. I hoped that the case would be solved within the week I was gone and I didn't have to do anything. My supervisor was very understanding, stating that there were too many hands in the pot already.

However, not working got the wheels in my head turning and every so often, my eyes would flicker to the top of my closet where my suitcase was—the suitcase Rhett obviously had put up for me. I really hoped that he didn't see the evidence of my life that I wanted to hide from both of us.

I wiped away a single tear as I released a long breath. Two years ago today, I woke up alone for the first time in years. But, not today. I felt like my demons were kept at bay as I rested while being protected by one of the most gorgeous men I had ever laid eyes on. He hardly knew me. Didn't know me, really. Yet, he had stayed. For me.

For the first time in two years, I wanted someone near me. I spent the day putting my things away and trying to do everything possible to keep my mind off of everything. I couldn't handle it. I took it easy, but could not stay idle.

At a quarter 'til six, there was a light knock at my door. My heart thumped wildly in my chest for one reason. I knew who stood on the other side rapping on it with such tenderness. Glancing through the peephole only confirmed what I already knew.

There he stood, looking tired and rugged, rubbing his eyes with his fingers. I opened the door, not really caring what I looked like. Right when he saw me, his wide grin sent my heart straight to my throat.

"Hey there," he said, softly. "I brought vittles," he said, holding up a bag from a local burger restaurant.

Like an idiot, I gaped. And, stood there. He looked around my shoulder and kind of waved the bag back and forth, almost in front of my face. "Can I come in or…"

Without taking my eyes off of him, I said softly, "Yes." However, I continued standing in the doorway, staring.

His mouth turned up in a gorgeous smile before speaking. "Are you uh…going to let me in?"

I jumped slightly and shook my head to clear it, dropping my gaze from his mesmerizing blues. "Yes. Sorry. Come on in."

I cleared the doorway. While he walked in, he called over his shoulder, "I thought you blacked out on me for a second." He turned, grinning. "Thought I was going to have to give you mouth-to-mouth or something."

My gaze snapped to his and his eyes dropped to the floor as he looked around for somewhere to put the bag of food. He almost looked embarrassed or like he didn't mean to say that out loud. He shook his head and cleared his throat—loudly.

His blushing face looked up at mine and he chuckled. "I don't know where the hell that came from."

I smiled and let out a short, breathy laugh. And, much to my surprise, a joke rushed from my lips. "I may need chest compressions, too."

The air filled with his rich laughter. I stood with a smile on my face, not sure of what to do or say next. I fought the urge to be embarrassed.

I had not cracked a real joke in two years. Just being in this man's presence for no more than three days had me tearing down my barriers and revisiting little pieces of my old self. The smiles. The laughs. The jokes.

His voice interrupted my thoughts. "I'm glad you finished that. I thought I would have to file sexual harassment charges against myself."

As I laughed out loud, tears pricked the backs of my eyes. The sound of my laughter was so foreign, it startled me. I laughed for the first time in a long time two nights prior to this one. The last time I had laughed before that night was the morning of the day I lost my family. Dash, who was preoccupied buttoning his shirtsleeves, not watching where he was going, ran right into the doorjamb in the kitchen and busted his nose. I laughed so hard that corn flakes and bananas went tumbling out of my mouth.

Most men would be pissed if their wives gloried in their clumsiness. But as Dash reached for the paper towels to clean the blood racing for his lips, he looked at me with teary eyes and purple nose and smiled and said, "I love your laugh."

My smile fell and I sucked in an unsteady breath at my reverie. Rhett's smile fell as well. I was so tired of bringing those around me down. I just wanted to crawl in a hole and die in unholy peace.

"You okay?" he asked, stepping up to me.

"Yes," I answered, looking up at him.

"Feeling any better today?" he asked, genuinely concerned.

It took me a couple seconds to compose an answer, having to tear away from his crystal blue gaze. I smiled and looked in his general direction. "Yes. Thank you so much for staying last night. I probably would have been perfectly fine without you babysitting me, but I am grateful." I shrugged. "And, thanks for not killing me."

The slight smile that was dancing across his lips dropped immediately and he visibly stiffened. I instantly took it back, putting my hands in front of me, in a surrendering gesture. "I'm kidding. Totally kidding." I turned my back, scurrying away embarrassed and recovering from my obvious joke fail. "Want something to drink?"

I heard him rub his hands together. "Sure. Tea? Sweet?"

I turned and shot him a narrowing look. "Why is that a question?"

He shrugged and answered seriously, "Depending on where some people are from, they don't believe in sweet tea." I smiled and he nodded and furthered his point. "Where I was raised, sweet tea is the only beverage for people of all ages. It comes in bottles…for infants. We start 'em early."

I chuckled. "Where did you grow up?"

"A, uh… little town in Arkansas. A spot in the road really. Griffithville, to be more specific. My grandma still lives there. Back roads for miles and miles. Strangely, they all lead to grandma's house. Farm country. My roots are those of a pure homespun country boy. Can't tell it much now, though," he said, smiling.

With teas in hand, I entered the living room and he was taking a seat while pulling burgers and fries from the crinkly paper bag.

Without looking up, he started to speak, "I didn't know what you like, so I just went pretty standard here. Tomato, lettuce. I think there's mustard on it, too." He opened up the wrapper and pulled the bun off the top, and handed it to me after setting the bun back on the burger. "Yuck. There's mustard. That's yours."

I slowly took the handled burger. I couldn't help but smile a little. "Are your hands clean, because you just totally had your hands all over my sandwich?"

He stopped what he was doing, holding a carton of fries suspended in the air and faced me. "You did not just call that a sandwich." I nodded, not comprehending what his point was—until he finished. "My grandma calls burgers sandwiches." A smile pulled at the corner of his mouth. "You're such a grandma," he teased, his voice heightening slightly soprano at the end.

I chuckled and attempted to correct him, "I am *not* a grandma."

He set the fries down on the table and turned to face me, his blue eyes boring into mine. "Do you know what you have on the back of your toilet?"

Of course I did. "It's an air freshener." He chuckled. "What?"

His shoulders shook with laughter. "That's a granny air freshener; it's nothing more than a silly looking cone with gross hard gel, or whatever, in the middle that collects dust quicker than an old granny vajayjay." He stared at me with a huge grin on his face. Then, he finished by yelping, "Granny!"

To my own astonishment, I bowled over with laughter. Cackling burst from my lungs and tears moistened the corners of my eyes. I looked over at him and he just sat, staring and grinning at me. As I wiped the tears from my eyes, I fought the urge to allow my constant sadness to overtake this moment. The heaviness that I constantly felt in my chest let up, if only for a moment. His eyes continued to dance over my face, almost like he couldn't look away, because if he did, this moment would be lost to eternity.

I had not eaten dinner with anyone in two years. I always found some excuse to avoid it with my parents. I didn't want company. I wanted to be alone. But, with this man, whom I had one major loss in common, would I share this meal. We danced to the same sad tune. We had both buried the half of our pair. We both went to bed alone on a day we woke up with our better halves.

My mother encouraged me to attend grief counseling, even suggested that I talk to my pastor. But, I didn't want to talk. Talking about them was their device to convince me to move on and leave them in July. I didn't want to leave them. I only wanted to hold on to them.

Before I realized I was speaking, I whispered to him, "I haven't laughed in two years." To my horror, my eyes watered and my lips quivered.

Rhett smiled sweetly at me and nodded. "You should do it more often. It's a lovely sound. Most days, I don't laugh, myself." He shook his head. "It's hard to smile when your heart hurts. Kinda makes your face hurt, too." The air was suddenly heavy with melancholy. He sensed it too. Breaking the tension, he took a bite from his burger. "So, tell me about yourself. I assume you work for the FBI because you work with Rhonda. Where are you from? What brings you here?"

I wiped away a few errant tears and said, "I'm from Kansas City. And, I'm working on a homicide case here."

"Oh yeah? Which one?"

I took a bite of my burger. If he was talking with his mouth full, so was I. "Bradley Cravens."

He nodded. "Senator Cravens's boy. I heard about that. So, why did they pull you from Kansas City?"

I shrugged. "They needed the best investigators and forensic staff, so they sent me."

He smirked. "You're the best, huh?"

I chuckled. "That's what I'm told. What about you, counselor?"

He continued to eat and talk around his food. It was too charming to disgust me. He had no intention of impressing me. I could tell he was just being himself. "Well, you already know where I'm from. So, from farm country to Marine Corps, I went. I served until I was shot in the leg while in Afghanistan. I was honorably discharged, so I came home to start a career away from the military. I was still really young, and my dad is an attorney. So, I figured why not? I grew up around this stuff. He never pushed me into this. He just told me to make him proud. So, I've been trying ever since."

I smiled. "That's sweet."

He rolled his eyes. "That's not what I was shooting for, but grannies always look for the sweetness in all things."

I laughed and nudged him with my elbow. "Keep going."

He let out a long breath. "When I got back, I got married to a really sweet girl. Beautiful girl. We had a daughter. God, she was gorgeous. Most gorgeous thing I'd ever laid eyes on."

He paused for several seconds as he fought his tears. I didn't. I let mine freely flow as he avoided my eyes. "What were their names?" I whispered.

He huffed and stared at the carpet. "My wife's name was

Arianna. My daughter's name was Haven."

He pulled out his wallet and fished for the picture that he handed me. He was right. They were gorgeous. As I stared at the two lost women in his life, he continued to speak, "My greatest pride was being a father. I was scared at first, but right when I saw her, I remember looking at Ari and saying, 'Let's do this.' I miss them. Every day."

I wiped my face with a scratchy napkin I pulled out of the bag that smelled like fries. "What happened to them?"

One word broke my heart for him all over again. "Murdered."

I sucked in a breath and I felt my food in my throat. I managed to whisper, "I'm so sorry."

Still looking down at my floor, he shook his head, leaning forward with his fingers laced together. "It's been a little over five years." He met my eyes. "They, whoever the illusive *they* are, say it gets easier, but I think the heart just gets hard. The pain seems to lessen. But, so does the happiness and the joy. Everything just gets turned off, you know? To not feel the pain, you can't feel anything."

He was exactly right. He spoke the words that explained exactly how I felt. I was so lost. I had strayed away from everything and everyone. I had lived in sadness and darkness, because I couldn't find the words, and didn't want to find the words, to say how I felt.

When he could tell that I could say nothing, he continued. "I could've rolled over. Died with them. But, I refused. I have dedicated my life to putting the bad guys away. I keep their pictures out, in my apartment, on my desk at work. I don't want to forget why I didn't die instead. It was to do this. To make them pay." He took several deeps breaths before he asked me what I had anticipated. "And, your husband?"

I sniffed and wiped my face once more. I couldn't tell him the truth. A truth so shameful. I could not let him know that I had failed my family, especially my son. That's what it felt like. I had failed him. In my own mind, I contributed to his death, by not making a ten second phone call earlier that morning.

"I lost him and my son in an accident." That's all I could say. That's all I could confess. I also could not tell him I had lost the new life growing inside of me due to my grief. Two children and a husband, all lost within a matter of days.

I was swept away with the tide, pulled into the deep, dark ocean. I had been towed so far from the shoreline, I knew in my heart that all was lost. Then, in the middle of the cold, dark night, this man who made sure I didn't die in my sleep after bumping my head, who brought me a cheeseburger just the way I like it, who made fun of my air freshener, who made me laugh for the first time in years, sat on my couch like a homing beacon, a lighthouse, guiding me back to the shore.

Unexpectedly, his watery eyes scanned my wet and ruddy face and he let out a hard sob. His composed face crumbled and he buried his face in his palms, sucking in hard, hitching sobs. I scooted until I was right up against him and reached out to run my fingers along his back. There were so many times that I needed comfort, times it wasn't obtainable or times I pushed it away. But, this...man's man, a man shaped by combat wounds and a father's heartache needed comfort. He shook his head and in a squeaky sob he spoke, "It doesn't get easier. Each day that passes is one day farther away from them. Some days I just can't stand it. I...don't understand why. I'm just so angry." His chest heaved until his breathing steadied. I ran my fingers up and down his strong back while he gained his composure.

He wiped his face and stared ahead, avoiding my gaze. "I'm sorry. I haven't lost it like that in years." He let out a breathy laugh of embarrassment. He glanced at me. His bloodshot eyes and flushed cheeks were so appealing. The blue of his eyes appeared even more crystalline than their normal sky blue.

I continued to stroke his back, just relishing in being a comforter again. The soother—my favorite part of being a mother. "Don't ever apologize." I could only speak around the hitching in my own breath. "At least you can look at their pictures." I shook my head. "I just can't. Not yet."

He finally looked at me again and smiled. "You will. Then you'll wonder why you ever put them away." One tear ran down his red cheek. "Don't keep them hidden, Evie. They wouldn't hide you."

"How do you know?" I asked quietly.

"Because *I* wouldn't."

CHAPTER TEN

RHETT

Mortified. That's what I was when I closed Evie's door that night. I felt complete humiliation for how I acted and how I lost it like my wounds were fresh. Needless to say, I didn't stick around. It took me about two minutes to finish my burger and fries and bid her goodnight.

And, *vittles?* What the hell? Just kill me now. I've never even said that word before. It's like Evie turned me into a blubbering, crying idiot. I don't know what happened to me and it pissed me off. My story. Her face. Her empathy for the heartache that I had desperately tried to cover up for years. I barely cried the day they were placed in the ground. I was so angry and fueled with hatred. For their killers. For my shortcomings. For the condition the world was in. I was mad at everyone and everything.

But, the night before, I finally felt the sorrow. She cried for *me*. Not for herself. Her own residual pain most likely traipsed in the recesses of her mind, but those superficial tears were for my losses. My wife and my daughter.

What a pair we made. If only it were an accident, I would say it was meant to be. But, she was sent to me for a purpose. An assignment. Even so, it was a relief. When my sobbing was nearly out of control, I concentrated on her fingers gliding up and down my back and followed her unfaltering movements. She showed no hesitation to touch, almost like she needed it as much as I did.

My embarrassment was still fresh the following morning. I didn't want to face her, probably ever again. I should have never volunteered that much information, much less bawled in front of her like the weeping widower I had become. As much as I wanted to, I knew I couldn't pull away from her completely. I had to focus on my mission, and that was finding out information about details of the Cravens case. But, I needed a break. Less than three full days in and I needed a break.

After dressing that morning, I checked myself out in the mirror and my damn eyes were swollen, almost like I had an allergic reaction to some bad shellfish. My face was puffy and raw, and I was not excited about going to work like this, stuffy nose and all.

I looked around my apartment and noticed how clinical it was. I had moved out of our family home about a year after Ari and Haven were killed. I felt like I was literally going crazy. I would try to sleep at night and could swear I heard little Haven's cries and Ari's lullaby-singing voice, slightly off-key. I knew that it was my own imagination or my vain hopefulness.

I laid in bed many nights, speaking into the night, hoping that they could hear me. I shed a few tears, but my fury had dammed my torments. I would tell them over and over that I loved them so much or ask Ari if she remembered random things about our short-lived time together. Each confession and declaration was only met with silence.

This apartment was not a home. I had walked away from the one place in which I felt like I belonged. A friend from law school purchased my home with the promise that if I ever wanted it back, he'd sell it back to me. I couldn't sell it to a stranger. I wouldn't allow a stranger to move in on my memories and replace all of my family with all of theirs. I sold it to a cousin of Evie's assistant, Rhonda. I was certain that even Rhonda wasn't aware of my connection to her cousin's home, but the question of why a bachelor needed a five bedroom house was always lingering.

Other than the pictures of my girls on display, there was nothing else personal about my living space. I think that in my mind I needed to keep it simple so that if I needed to pick up and leave, I could do it quickly. Hatred and fury aside, I longed for that permanence again. It hadn't crossed my mind until the night before, but I realized something while I laid on my bed and stared at the ceiling.

I wanted a home. I wanted someone to love again, and this time, I would do it right. I wanted children, more of them. I wanted joy and elation. I wanted laughter in my life again. I started thinking about the asshole that I had become. There were days when I was rude to random people for no reason. I was the biggest smartass known to man. I was bitter and livid toward random things, things that reminded me. I hated Christmas trees, even Santa Clause. I hated puppies and roses, cartoons, anything pink or purple, princesses and hair bows. I hated all of it. I loathed anything that reminded me of them.

Fortunately, I did not see Evie that morning. I wasn't ready. My hearings performed by my melancholy self had judges and defense teams trading looks. My speech was slower and more methodical than it had ever been. In my last hearing involving a juvenile being tried as an adult for theft and possession, I spoke directly to him and tried to convince him that he was better than his crimes, and I encouraged him to do something productive with his life and change for the better. He was in tears when I walked away from him two hours before the guilty verdict was read. He asked to address those in the courtroom and given the mic, he spoke the most inspiring words I'd ever heard spill from the mouth of a sixteen year old. As I sat in my office, I closed my eyes and relived it and let his words replay in my mind—the words from a rich white kid that everyone calls Slinky. I will never forget what Fitzgerald Coulter, III said on record that morning, through his tears and around his sobs.

"You know, my dad is in prison right now for killing my mom. He shot her right in front of me. I was nine. I remember him saying, 'Well, that's over with,' then we went out for pizza and he took me bowling. All the while, my mother was in the floor of our kitchen bleeding all over the new tile she was so proud of. I remember her screaming and begging him not to hurt her. I remember watching him and thinking to myself, 'I will never be this man…this monster. I will never hurt someone like this.' But, you know what? That's exactly where I'm headed. I'm following in his footsteps and I don't want to. I don't want to be a monster. I don't want to be feared or hated. I don't want to live out the rest of my days in a cell. I want to live in the sun. I want to laugh. I want to have a career, get married to a woman just like my mom. I want someone to be proud of me. But, who do I have now?" Then, he turned directly to me, tears drenching his face, reaching up to wipe his nose with his cuffed hands, and addressed me, "Mr. Trimble, I want to make you proud. I will make you proud. I promise to be better and purer." Then, a smirk crossed his face. "I'm going to take your job one day."

The courtroom erupted in laughter. He nodded twice, smiled, walked away and I called his name, "Coulter. I hope you do, son. I hope you do."

That night when I arrived home, I could hear rustling and banging next door which was clearly the sound of Evie putting her things away. As long as she was over there and not in my presence, I could attempt to forget about the night before. What I had intended on being light and pleasant conversation turned into a boohoo fest and I was in no mood to repeat it.

I had just changed out of my suit into a pair of basketball shorts when there was a knock at the door. *Shit*. Surely, it wasn't Evie. Maybe I could pretend I was not home. Like a teenage girl at home alone, I tiptoed to the door and peaked through the peephole. I released a heavy breath when I saw it was *The Queen*. I felt like I'd dodged a bullet and literally wiped my dry brow, opening the door. She greeted me with a huge smile. Likewise, I greeted her and invited her in. I reached out and squeezed her in a tight embrace.

When she stepped back, she still held onto my biceps and lightly squeezed. "Has Ms. Harrington seen you like this? Apparently not or she would be over here instead of next door."

I chuckled. "Actually she has. She has seen me in less, as a matter of fact."

"Is she blind as well?" she asked incredulously. "So, you've met her? How did it go?"

I gestured for her to sit down on my couch. "Besides the fact I was in my underwear? There's not much to tell, really." I didn't feel the need to tell her every little detail—or big details for that matter. I was doing what had been asked of me. That's all she needed to know.

"What's she like?"

I couldn't help but smile, eyeing her warily. "She's beautiful, like you said. She's also broken, like you said. She's suffered a great deal. I don't think she thinks she's ready for a friend, but I'm willing to reach out to her. She needs someone."

"Like you?" This woman knew me too well. It was almost scary.

I nodded. "Yeah. I need someone, too. I spent the evening with her last night and we," I drifted off, clearing my throat, "bonded. I realized some things last night—things I need to work on. We might be able to help each other…heal? If that's the right word." I shook my head. "I just don't want to hurt her and I feel like when all of this is over, I will be required to tear myself from her life. I just hope I'm strong enough for that." I paused and she sat silently waiting. "I feel a connection to her, almost like I'm certain I won't want to let her go. And, it may not even be about her specifically, but I thought maybe I could start dating again or try at a relationship. I spent hours with her and I miss that companionship—that knowledge that someone is there for me, even if it's just waiting for me at the end of a long day. I've exposed more of my…soul to her in the last three days than I have with anyone else in my thirty years of living. Even with Arianna, I was closed off to a certain extent. I never let her know about my demons and most of the time I told her half-truths. Half-truths that ended up killing her.

But, last night…I can't find the words to tell you exactly how I felt."

She smiled at me so sweetly. "That's good," she whispered. "I didn't expect things to go this well so quickly, but it is certainly a pleasant surprise." She patted me on the leg. "Get close to her, and if you feel like you need to keep her when your assignment is done, we will figure something out for you."

A burst of genuine laughter filled the air. "I don't think that's gonna happen, so don't worry yourself with our future living arrangements." She sat and stared for several long seconds, just smiling. "What?" I asked her, growing nervous over her gawk.

She shrugged. "I've never heard you laugh before. It's nice."

To my horror, I blushed like a redhead who had just been asked if the carpet matched the drapes. "Yeah. It's happened a lot these past couple days."

"That's good," she repeated. She patted me on the leg again. "I better get going. Keep up the good work, and just so you know, this will be your only assignment until this case goes…*cool*. As soon as that happens, you're off the hook."

We reached the door, and when I opened it, Evie stood with her fist held up as if a good rapping were to come.

She dropped her hand and smiled. "I'm so sorry. I didn't know you had company." Her sweet voice washed over my body like a clean, summer rain that had come to wash all of my sorrows away.

I stood there like a gaping idiot, looking between her and *The Queen*. I looked down and Evie balanced a casserole dish in one hand. Her beauty nearly knocked me on my tail every time I saw her, but tonight, she was exceptionally gorgeous. I smirked slightly when I realized…she dressed up…for me. Pretty sure. I knew she hadn't worked and I was pretty certain that women don't dress up to clean house. I could be wrong, but I would put money on it. She painted her eyes to appear enormous and styled her long hair to look like a sexy case of bedhead. Her jean capris and tight flannel shirt had me tingling below the belt…or elastic band, rather. "I can come back," she said before quickly turning to leave.

The Queen called out to her. "No, please stay. I was just leaving." Evie turned around and gave a shy smile. She held her hand out to Evie. "I'm Nora. A friend of Rhett's family. I was just in the neighborhood and thought I'd stop by." She turned to look at me and winked, then turned back to Evie. "Had to make sure he stayed out of trouble." She leaned over and kissed me on the cheek. "I'll talk to you later, sweetie," was all she said before she walked away from me. I stood and watched her for a couple seconds wondering if Nora was really her first name. I don't know why it mattered, but she was always such a mystery, and sometimes I was curious.

I turned back to Evie and grinned. "Whatcha got there?" I asked, leaning over in her direction, attempting to lift the foil. She pulled it out of my reach and smirked.

"It's just a little something to pay you back for dinner last night."

I shook my head, "I didn't do it to be paid back. I was trying to be nice...and neighborly. What is it?"

"Terrible, most likely." She chuckled. "I haven't cooked in a really long time and I just made this from memory."

I stepped back away from the door and asked her in. She gingerly followed me and put the casserole dish on my table. I was still only wearing my shorts, so I offered her a seat and went in search of a shirt. I slipped on the first one I grabbed which happened to read *Harvard Law* in huge letters. Under it, it read, *Just Kidding*, a gift from Adam. When I came out, Evie snickered. She pointed at it and said, "That's funny."

I smiled. "You wouldn't believe how many people don't see the *Just Kidding* part. I'll be in the checkout line at the grocery store and some goon will ask me, 'What year did *you* graduate from Harvard? I graduated in 2000!' I usually pull a random year out of my ass, usually in the 1980s and they still don't get it. I really hope I'm never that clueless. I feel like people, in general, are getting stupider. Don't you think?" She didn't answer and I looked at her, staring at me, seemingly oblivious to what I was saying. "Evie?"

"What?" she answered, after blinking twice and shaking her head slightly.

"What do you think?" I repeated.

"About what?"

"What I just said."

She tucked her plump bottom lip between her teeth and bit down, which caused my manly parts to stir. They hadn't stirred in so long, the feeling was foreign to me for a moment. Sure, I punched the clown in the shower every once in a while, but it had been so long since the infamous swell was caused by an outside source. Instead of embarrassing either of us, I just repeated my question. "Don't you feel like the people of the world are getting dumber?"

She recovered from her fog quickly. "Yeah. It scares me sometimes. A few weeks ago, an intern was out in the parking lot and told me something was wrong with his blinker, so I told him that he needed to check his blinker fluid. He was out there for an hour and a half with the hood up looking for his blinker fluid reservoir."

I couldn't help it. Laughter burst from my chest. At first, she just smiled and shrugged, and the more I laughed, the more she laughed. Within a minute or so, my eyes were watery and I was struggling to breathe.

As she ran her fingers under her eyes to clear away any running makeup, she said softly, "I didn't even laugh when it happened. Everyone should know you just change the bulb. There should be no inquiry. I was being kind of bitchy, I suppose."

I shook my head, still recovering from my laughter. "No. He deserved that. I can't imagine bitchiness coming from you. Seriously."

"Trust me. I can be. I have been." She lowered her gaze and picked at the hem of her shirt with her delicate fingers. "I've shut everyone out and pushed them away. That's so unlike the person I was." Her teary eyes met mine. "I miss her." She nodded. "Being with you these last few days—I feel like my old self, in a sense anyway. It's nice to be in the company of someone who doesn't look at me like a wounded puppy or something damaged beyond repair. You lost something irreplaceable. Just like me. I lost the best parts of myself just as you lost the best parts of yourself. You know *exactly* how I feel. I need a friend like that."

I reached over and took her hand. "I'll be your friend."

"Good," she whispered. She glanced around my apartment and I witnessed the moment she saw the picture on the end table. She pulled her hand from mine, twisted her body away from me, and reached for it. I had no apprehensions or shame as I watched her. I was proud for her to see my family. Watching this beautifully broken woman caress the face of my deceased wife caused my heart to thunder in my chest. I watched silently as she reached up to cover her mouth with her hand and tears seeped from her gorgeously painted eyes. "Oh God," she whispered. "Rhett…they're so beautiful, it hurts."

Fighting my own tears, tooth and nail, I whispered the only response I could collect, "Thank you."

Tears ran down her face, and this time she made no attempt to stop them. "Who took them from you?" she whispered.

I leaned forward, running both hands through my hair and resting my elbows on my knees. "I don't know. The case was never solved. Investigators concluded that it was some type of gang initiation or something, but the manner of their deaths…it wasn't random. It was vengeful. There was hatred in how they died."

"Tell me. Please," she begged.

I shot her a quick glance. "Can you just read the file? I'm sure Rhonda can get it for you." I smirked. "She's pretty…resourceful."

"I'd rather hear it from you," she said softly.

I nodded. "Okay. But, if I tell you this, you have to tell me about your husband and son. Friendships aren't usually conditional, but we cannot have this mystery between us. Okay?"

"Okay," she whispered.

I had not told my story aloud. I didn't need to because it was all over the news for weeks. I wasn't sure I could make it through it.

But, the anticipation of hearing the details of what had broken her drove me to propose the complete exposure of our losses. I still had an assignment to do. This was the best way. Get personal. Be relatable. Appear vulnerable.

That's what I kept telling myself. But, in reality, I *wanted* her to know my story. I *wanted* to be bared to her completely. She intrigued me, and she made me want things—things I didn't think I ever wanted again. So, I told her everything, detailing their horrendous deaths.

"It was the end of October 2009. The day before they died, I had picked up a Halloween costume for Haven. I was excited to take her trick-or-treating. She wouldn't remember it, of course. But, I would. She was only fifteen months old, but I was so thrilled. I had found the cutest cow costume, and I knew she would look adorable in it. Her Halloween party was the following day, so she wore it to daycare." I closed my eyes and took several deep breaths. I could still see her sitting in the backseat of my wife's car, grinning at me as I leaned down to kiss her goodbye—dressed like a cow. I cleared my throat and took several unsteady breaths. "When I arrived home, she and Arianna should have been home for at least an hour. And, she wasn't. I called her work. Her boss said she had left around two that afternoon, which was odd, because she always left at five. Her boss said that she had gotten a call that I was in an accident, and she left. Right then, I knew something was definitely wrong. I called the daycare owner, because the daycare was closed, and she told me that there was no record of my daughter being checked out of daycare, but she knew she was there because she saw her around lunchtime. When I told her that my wife wasn't home, she started to worry as well. So, I called the police. The police gave me the twenty-four hour spiel, but I knew something was wrong. So, I called Rhonda. Her cousin was a good friend of mine in law school, and Rhonda worked for the police station then. She was just a dispatcher, but she had connections.

"Her husband, who was a police officer called me. I told him what was going on, and he called in a few favors. He asked a couple of officers who were off-duty to check things out in and around St. Louis." I paused and tried to blink back my tears, not that it was any use. Then, I continued. "The police station received an anonymous tip. It was written on the back of the daily report my daughter's daycare hands out. On the side with the report on it, her name written at the top, was everything she had eaten and every diaper change she had received that day. The words *Afternoon Snack* were marked out, and written above it, it read, *Last Meal.*" My breath hitched and my chest filled with fury and tears poured down my cheeks.

"Last. Fucking. Meal. What kind of sick fucking bastard writes that about a baby? Prisoners get last meals. Criminals are offered last meals." I shook my head and whispered, "Not babies. Babies don't get last meals. They get kisses and warm bottles and assurances that daddy's gonna make everything okay. Babies don't get last meals. They get broken fucking promises."

As I cried, my body rocked slowly back and forth. "You can stop," Evie whispered.

I looked at her and her makeup was a lost cause and her face was blotchy with anguish. I kept going. I had to tell her.

Taking in a shaky breath, I continued. "On the other side was the location of her car. It was in the river. I got the call and I went to the location where I was told it was. I was instructed not to show up, but I couldn't not go. I got there just as they were pulling her car out of the water. I ran to them. I ran. As fast as I could." I wiped the tears from my face, only to be defeated by more tears.

"I saw them first. I got there before anyone could stop me. I fell to my knees when I saw their pale little bodies. Arianna had been shot in both legs and she had been duct-taped to her seat, sideways, facing the passenger seat. She was twisted up like a pretzel. Obviously beaten. And little Haven…" I sucked in deep breaths, my entire body racking with sobs. I felt Evie reach her arm across my shoulders and tug me close. I collapsed against her. On instinct or something else, I pulled my legs up on the couch and laid my head in her lap. I didn't ask permission and she didn't fight it. She even leaned back to accommodate me.

Tucking my hands under my cheek, I closed my eyes and relished in the affection and comfort that came with Evie's fingers pushing through my hair.

I finally finished, but only in low whispers. "Haven, still in her car seat, was taped to the passenger seat, facing her mother, still dressed like a little cow. They both drowned. Haven was otherwise untouched, but Arianna—she was badly beaten, but alive when her car hit the water. She tried to get out, but…they forced her to watch our daughter die, leaving her absolutely helpless."

I was physically and emotionally drained. I felt exhausted, and my body was completely wilted. But, I felt relieved. I felt like a weight had been lifted from my chest. This woman, who I was supposed to be breaking down, was tearing me down so quickly that I couldn't even hear the walls crumbling.

I only focused on the sensation of Evie's fingers brushing through my hair, and before I knew it, I had fallen asleep.

CHAPTER ELEVEN

Evie

I thought I had experienced the worst heartaches. After hearing Rhett's account of what had happened to his wife and daughter, I was certain that he had lived through the worst pain the human heart could ever feel. An accident and Dash's claim of responsibility paled in comparison to a man's family being torn from him in the most brutal fashion.

I was already heartbroken for him, but the innocence of his daughter in her little muddy costume that made this brute of man ball up like a frightened and broken child, made me feel like my heart was being ripped from my chest.

I had known this man less than a week, and I felt closer to him than I had felt to anyone in two years. We were two lost souls who weren't exactly lost anymore. We had each other, if only for this.

He whimpered in his sleep. It was charming and heart-wrenching at the same time. As he slept in my lap, I rubbed his head with one hand and traced the tattoos on his arms with the other. From afar, they looked like a jumbled mess. Beautiful, but a mess. There were several graphic tattoos covering both arms, demons and angels. There were symbols and words that were clearly different languages, covering both arms. I traced them with my fingers over and over as he slept. He was out for four and a half hours. I had fallen asleep for a couple of hours in between and when he stirred, it was nearing midnight.

I continued to run my fingers over his skin as he stirred awake. He turned his body slightly, and his red, puffy eyes met mine. In a husky voice, he answered the question which I had not asked.

"They say, 'Vengeance is mine; I will repay, saith the Lord' in ninety-three different languages."

"Ninety-three?" I felt my eyes go wide with shock. "Do you still believe that? That God will avenge you?" I asked with complete seriousness. I needed to know what he believed.

"Absolutely. Do I think God is going to come down here and kill them back himself? No. Do I think God uses man to do the dirty work? Yes. When he blesses us with that opportunity."

His words were serious and cold and caught me off guard. However, I continued to push. "So, if you had the chance to kill whoever killed your family, you'd take it?"

He didn't hesitate. "Without a doubt. I know how our justice system works, and it's not like I've never killed anyone before." He smiled. "Before you freak out, remember that I was a Marine for several years and was overseas. It kind of comes with the job."

I smiled back at him as he continued to lay in my lap, making no attempt to move. "I guess you felt me tense up, huh?"

He chuckled. "Yeah. Freaker-outer." He rolled over to face me, lying flat on his back. "Why do we always start out by having a good time and it turn into a boohoo fest pity party?" We both laughed. "This is the second damn day in a row that I've completely turned into a wailing woman. What are you doing to me?" he finished softly.

The closeness to him and the intimacy was too much to bear. I patted him on the arm. "Jump up. The lasagna got cold hours ago. Do you want some? I know it's kinda late."

He stood slowly, stretching when he stood upright. "Yes, please. I'm starving. You brought lasagna, huh? Did you call my mother or something to find out my second favorite meal?"

I smiled. "Second favorite? What's your first?"

He shook his head. "That's confidential. I'm sure you

understand."

"Ah. Definitely understand. So, mother, yeah? Tell me about her. Other family?"

He smirked. "I love my mom. She's an amazing woman." As I turned his oven on and placed the dish on the rack, he continued to talk. "She's a kindergarten teacher, so of course she talks to me like I'm five, but it's all good. She so positive and encouraging, constantly asking if I need to use the bathroom." I laughed. "Nah, she is great. She started teaching the year before I was born and hasn't stopped. My parents are still married, have been for forty-two years, I think. My dad is an attorney. He's just as awesome. He will talk to anyone and everyone. Just genuinely kind. Well, used to be. We are kind of on the 'outs' right now. They're hardcore Baptists, which I just love. They reared me right, no doubt."

He took a deep breath. "I have two brothers, Jonah and Luke, they're older than me by two and four years. One's on the east coast, the other's on the west. Then, my little sister, Macy, lives five blocks away, also a teacher, but teaches high school."

"Wow. You have a large family. Any nieces or nephews?"

"Uh. Yeah. Jonah and Luke each have three boys and Macy has two boys, and she is expecting a little girl in December," he finished, almost on a whisper.

Eight grandchildren for his wonderful parents. Nine in a few months. His little girl was on the list of grandchildren until she was stolen from this wonderful, but wounded man. Looking at him now, completely disheveled and ruddy-faced from his grief, he looked…lonely. This was the first week in a long time where I did not feel alone. His broken presence was calming to my rapidly beating heart and unsteady hands. My nap that had lasted only a few hours, in which his head rested in my lap, was the best sleep I had gotten in two years.

I had come to him only to pay him back for the meal he bought the night prior, but once again, he had given me something which I felt I could never repay. The raging storm that battered me day in and day out was calmed by his smooth voice and rumbling laughter.

I had picked out my simplest outfit and put on a little makeup, like I used to. It had been a long time since I wanted to be beautiful for someone. I didn't want Rhett to see me as a woman in eternal mourning. I wanted him to see *me*. I wanted it to look like I was holding it together, even though I was fraying at the seams.

The small talk lasted through our reheated meal and was enjoyable and something I desperately needed. We discussed simple, but personal, things. Our favorite things, things we hated, things we hoped to do and see one day. It was nearly one in the morning when our conversation came to a close. For the first time since I arrived, there was an awkward silence. I was just about to bid farewell and escape what I knew was going to come, when he called my name.

"Evie," he said quietly from across the kitchen.

I didn't fight the tears. My face drew up with heartache and I closed my eyes. I didn't want to tell him. I hadn't told anyone who didn't already know. But, he stripped down every wall around himself and wept like I had only seen one other man weep in my lifetime.

Rhett turned to leave the kitchen and sat on the floor in the living room, leaning against the couch. I followed suit, but propped myself up against the recliner. Having noticed my fidgeting hands, he handed me a throw pillow to use the edges to keep my fingers busy and act as a slight distraction.

Without delaying any longer, I gave in, not holding back my emotion for it was pointless.

"I..uh...met Dash at work. He stole my heart the moment I saw him. I was instantly in love with him," I said, smiling, remembering his absolutely boyish charm. I took a deep breath and just let my tears roll down my cheeks, licking them away when they reached my lips. "He was...incredible. If you take everything wonderful and beautiful in this world and rolled it up into one man, that was Dash. He was kind and sweet, and he made me feel so...beautiful. We dated for seven months, and he asked me to marry him on the bank of a pond we would have to trespass to swim in." I chuckled, remembering how young he made me feel, young and law-breakingly free.

"We tried to have a baby right away. Every month would go by and…nothing happened. We never had a positive test, ever. I was the problem. I wasn't ovulating like I should, and after several failed fertility treatments, we just gave up. We decided that maybe it just wasn't meant for us to have a family, you know? So, we quit trying. I was absolutely heartbroken, but I did not let it change me. I would be strong for him and for me. It was hard, but we poured everything we had into our marriage. We started going on trips and stuff. We just…lived," I whispered. "We. Lived. And, it was wonderful.

"We were in Hawaii for our fifth anniversary, and I was sick every morning for the entire week. I was so mad, but Dash was…hopeful. I had just woken up from a nap when I found him sitting beside me on the bed with a test. Without a word, I took it and we stood and waited. It didn't take twenty seconds for that positive sign to pop up." My breath hitched with a single sob. "He literally fell to his knees and wrapped his arms around me, and just…cried." I reached up to wipe my face with my shirt, my fingers going back to pluck at the tag on the pillow.

"Sure enough. I was pregnant. I never had any problems; it was a dream of a pregnancy. I couldn't have asked for anything more wonderful. I loved the feeling of him moving around, tossing and turning. There's nothing like it in the world." I paused, only to prepare myself for the hardest part.

"After he was born…that was the best ten months of my life. I was finally a mother. The only thing that I'd ever wanted to be." I stopped for several minutes, staring at the pillow on my lap. I knew he was watching me, but I couldn't look up. I couldn't look at him.

"The morning he died…uh…I had a doctor's appointment. Dash agreed to take him to daycare. My appointment was early because I was so excited, I couldn't wait. I had taken a pregnancy test a few days before and I just wanted to make sure. Baby number two was a surprise, but a pleasant one. I didn't want to tell him until I had seen the doctor. So, I went and found out I was about six weeks pregnant." I smiled. "Noah was so young, but I wanted to have as many as God would give me, and I was thrilled. Absolutely thrilled. I was going to tell him at lunch when I saw him."

I blew out a long breath. "I always called him from my desk a couple of times in the morning before lunch, just to hear his voice. But, that day—I didn't trust myself to not tell him the news, so I didn't call." My bottom lip quivered so hard that I bit down to tame it. "I didn't call," I whispered. "I should've called," I cried.

"When I called him at lunch, he answered. I said, 'hey, you.' All he said was, 'oh no,' and hung up." I shook my head. "I knew. I just knew. I felt it in my heart." I paused. "He forgot to drop him off. It was a hundred and two outside that day," I whispered.

I finally gained the nerve to look up at Rhett. Tears rolled down his red cheeks and his lips were tucked between his teeth. He opened his mouth to speak, but I cut him off.

"When I reached the front door, I could see him beside our car in the parking lot, on his hands and knees. He was...w-wailing. My heart sank to my feet, but I ran. I ran as fast as I could to get to my baby. But, it was t-t-t-too late," I stammered around my sobs. "While Dash was down on the ground, I pulled Noah from his car seat and tried to resuscitate him, but he'd been dead for hours. So, I picked him up and kissed all over his little face and r-r-rocked him. I told him that I was so, so sorry that mommy didn't help him. Didn't come for him." More to myself, I whispered, "He cried. And, I didn't come."

I wasn't finished. I had to keep going. I had to say everything. Once I started unloading, I couldn't stop.

"It was an accident. I was not angry at Dash—not for that. I was absolutely broken, but I didn't blame him...didn't hate him. My son was gone and it destroyed me, but Dash—we were supposed to help each other through it. That night, we both went home and I knelt beside the bed, and I begged God to tell me why. Tell me what

I had done to deserve that. Dash hadn't spoken a word to me. I couldn't muster any words to speak—not even to him. He was obliterated. He hated himself so much. He knelt down beside me and wept. The only thing he finally said was, 'I'm so sorry, baby. I'm so sorry.' I should've told him that I didn't blame him, but I said nothing. I didn't even acknowledge his plea for my forgiveness. I just sat there with my eyes closed, scared to look at him." I ran my fingers over the smooth fabric of the red pillow, tracing the little designs stitched in intricate patterns.

"I fell asleep on my knees, right there by the bed. I woke up in the middle of the night and went in search for him. I found a note on the table. I remember every word because I've read it a thousand times. It said, 'I'm so sorry, baby. I've destroyed everything. I love you more than anything in this world, but I cannot live with this. I can't live knowing that I've probably killed you too. Don't go to the barn. Just call the police. I love you.' I didn't heed that warning. I ran to the barn and that's where I found him. He had shot himself."

I looked at Rhett whose tears had not relented since the last time I met his eyes. Before I realized what I said, I asked him between hitched breaths, "Why would he leave me here? Alone? Why did he do that to me?" He had no answer. He only stared. "I dropped to my knees right beside him. There was blood everywhere, but I didn't care. All of that beauty and all of that goodness snuffed out by forgetfulness." I took a deep breath and looked at Rhett once more. My face was red and sticky. My chest felt heavy and my throat was sore, but I had one last thing to tell him. Completely and utterly exposed. "I lost the baby the next day. I never got the chance to really tell him. There are so many things that I should have done differently. I should've been patient and made a later appointment. I should've called Dash that morning and Noah may still be alive. I should've told him that I'd forgiven him and that I loved him. I should've considered the life inside of me and stayed strong for him…or her. But…I did none of that. I did everything all wrong."

Rhett finally spoke, only able to conjure a soft whisper. "I'm so sorry, Evie. Please, please don't blame yourself," he begged. "None of it is your fault."

I met his gaze, completely incapable of believing his words. "Isn't it?"

He shook his head. "No."

I stood quickly and headed for the door, leaving him on the floor. "I have to go."

Before he could stop me, I quickly made my way next door. As I laid in bed, I heard a light rapping on the wall just on the other side of my head. I heard Rhett say through the paper-thin walls, "Goodnight, Evie."

I wept until I fell asleep while hopelessly seeking comfort in a dead man's blue shirt.

CHAPTER TWELVE

RHETT

Guilt. She lived with it every single day. In my own way, less comforting than *The Queen* had been, I tried to convince Evie that the heartbreaking things in her life were not her fault.

Shame. I saw it in her eyes when she finally looked at me. She was ashamed of herself for making the wrong choices, only wrong in her eyes. Had it not been the heat and the gunshot wound, her family would still be gone one way or another. But, it is easier to see that in someone else's life than in your own.

Brokenheartedness. A father's heart aches in ways a woman could never understand. But, a mother's broken heart is something that a man could never bear. I could not imagine growing another life inside of me. A mother feeds her baby before it takes its first breath. She feels her baby move and kick and hiccup long before a father ever sees it. Her baby knows the sound her heart makes when she's calm or excited or scared. Her baby knows her voice before he or she even sees the true light of day.

Then, when that baby is born, his or her mother feeds, changes, bathes, cuddles, and rocks them. The mother puts in the time and the sleepless nights and the hours of worry.

All of that time devoted to a life, only to have that life taken away, carries tremendous devastation and utter hopelessness.

There are so many days that I wish it was me who died instead.

But, if Haven was gone, Arianna wouldn't have it any other way. She would rather die than bear the heartache of living without our daughter. I know that for a fact because I knew Arianna, and I knew that she was a wonderful, selfless, and loving mother. And that, my friends, is just how loving mothers are.

Children are not supposed to die before their parents. It is some unwritten rule or understood law of the universe. But, the Maker doesn't live by those rules or laws.

He does what He wants to. On His own time. I was raised to believe in a God full of loving kindness and mercy. The Santa Clause of the heavens is how I saw Him, about like everyone does these days.

After my family was murdered, I questioned His existence and tried to find fault in the gospel I believed in. But, to hate Him, I had to believe He was real. It wasn't until *The Queen* taught me that he was also jealous and vengeful that I saw Him as something I could relate to. I'm not sure how I will be held accountable for the deeds I see as good. I carry out justice the way God himself told us to take care of the worst violators. I only deliver death as we are instructed to do.

Evie's husband was a coward. Checking out early was never even an option—not because I was scared or didn't deserve death. Death didn't deserve me. How could anyone walk away from someone so beautifully broken and incredibly perfect? I'll never understand this man that she misses so much—this man who was not worthy of her forever. What he had done was not intentional. It was a mishap. I can't help but wonder if they had gotten into an accident and he survived, but their child didn't, would he still have made the same decision? Would he still have taken his life—the most desperate escape?

It took every ounce of willpower not to reach out and touch Evie. I'm afraid if I started, I wouldn't have stopped. I wanted to kiss her tears away and hold her close. I wanted to be the man her husband could never be. On a night where she had lost everything, he made her go to bed alone. My life was different. Arianna hadn't chosen to leave me. She loved me desperately. I can't help but doubt that Dash had loved Evie with that same desperation. I'm not accusing him of a floundering, superficial love. But, I can't stop myself from wondering.

My bond with her was scary and thrilling at the same time. I wanted to be near her. I wanted…her. There was no point in denying it. She was lovely and lost, and when she looked at me, I could see the need. I didn't even see desire or want, only her desperate need for a friend. Someone who was in the same boat. Someone who lived with a similar misery.

I sat on my bed and listened to her soft cries. After she bailed, I leaned against my bedroom wall resting my weight on my forearms until I told her goodnight.

I couldn't stand it any longer. I stood up and my body moved on its own accord until I was standing in front of her door. I stood there for at least a minute, willing my heart to tell my brain to walk back to my apartment and go to bed. My heart told my brain to just knock on her damn door, and I lifted my hand and knocked loudly.

I stood there for two solid minutes before turning away and walking back to my apartment. As I reached it, her door opened and she stepped out. Her face was free of makeup, but red and chapped, and her hair was pulled up on top of her head. All I could see she wore was a familiar blue shirt that swallowed her completely.

I wanted to bury my hands in her hair and pull her pink lips to mine, but I fought that urge. So, I did the only thing I knew to do that wouldn't push her way. I wanted to give her something she didn't even know she needed. Little did I know, I needed it too.

I walked up to her, in a rush, and put my arms around her waist and lifted her off of her feet in a tight embrace. Instantly, her arms went around my neck and she clung to me. She buried her head in my neck and cried. She wept as I held her suspended in the air.

My grandfather told me years ago that hugs go a long way, 'sometimes beyond making love. Sometimes a woman just needs to be held.' That's what he'd say.

Evie…needed a hug. She held onto me so tightly, I felt like I was suffocating, but I said nothing. I just held her as she fell apart. I quit being a crying pussy for five minutes and just held my composure for her. My throat was thick and my neck was hot, and my heart was pounding out of my chest to the same rhythm that the blood pounded in my ears, but I held strong for her.

While her sobs softened, I ran my hands up and down her slender back, feeling the soft cotton underneath my fingers. I quietly shushed her cries, running my lips along the shell of her ear.

"I've got you," I whispered. I didn't know what else to say, really. I would stand here all night long if she needed me to.

She spoke softly and her breath was wet against my neck, "I want to believe you." She paused. "That it's not my fault. I just don't…" she trailed off.

"You should believe me. I'd never lie to you." I felt like the worst kind of asshole. I had lied. I was not completely honest with her about who I was, but I made up my mind a long time ago that omissions out of necessity were not lies.

After holding her for several minutes, I set her feet on the floor and lifted my hands to brush the sopping wet hair from her face, tucking the strands behind her ears, and pinned her face with my hands. Her eyes were red and puffy, and her lips trembled with agony. As I leaned down, she closed her eyes, and I pressed my lips against her forehead and held them there before finally pulling away.

In those wee hours of the morning is where my own healing began. It all started with a simple proposal.

I smiled at her and she attempted to smile in kind. "Have supper, or dinner…most people call it dinner, with me. Every night. For the next few weeks while you're in town. We can eat, play games, watch TV, and…live. We'll try not to talk about things that depress the shit out of us. We'll try not to cry. Let's not regret. No more thinking back, attempting to justify or be guilty over the past. If we need to talk about something to help us deal, we'll talk. But, for the most part, let's just have some fun together and not feel bad about it. What do ya say?"

I gave her my most charming smile and stepped away from her. I don't know why I was surprised, because I can be quite convincing, she agreed. She nodded. "Okay."

I felt my eyes go wide. "Really?"

She chuckled. "Yes. I'd like that."

"Okay then. It's past midnight, so dinner, my place, tonight. I'm cooking."

I started walking back to my apartment backwards, not ready to let her out of my sight. She nodded. "Sounds good."

I fired at her with my pistol finger, thumb in the air and winked. "Hope you like chili dogs." She laughed and I turned to open my door before giving her one last smile. "Goodnight, Evie."

She smiled and shook her head, "Goodnight, Rhett."

I shut the door behind me, walked to my bed, and fell asleep with a fucking smile on my face.

***

I called my mom at lunch to ask for her chili recipe. Shit chili from a can would not impress my dinner guest, and that was my intent. I was going to try my best to astonish the shit out of her. I was a pretty good cook, but I called my chili cook-off winning mother for her prize winning measurements.

I talked to my mother every few weeks, but I had not seen her nor my dad in a year or so. I had seen my dad, but he had not spoken to me in several years. I felt bad about it, really bad, and had vowed to do better. Nonetheless, I called her up and she answered on the second ring.

"Hey, Harrison. How are you doing?" My mother has always called me by my middle name. The old classic movie (with that one guy…what's his name? Oh yeah…Rhett) has always been my mother's favorite movie, and according to my dad and both sets of grandparents, she threw a bitch-fit when dad didn't want to name me after Clark Gable's character. She won that battle. But, unless I was in trouble, she never called me by my first name. My dad did, however, just to spite her refusal to use the name *she* fought to give me. I was Harrison to her and nobody else.

"Hey, mom. I'm good, how are you doing?" I tried to hide the happiness in my voice, but my mother, the all-knowing, well, she knew.

"You're smiling. I can hear it," she chuckled.

I laughed. "Yeah. I guess I am."

"Did you win a big case or something? My boy, putting the bad guys away."

"Nope. That's not it." I let out a hard breath. "Listen, I can't really chat for long, I just have a few minutes left for lunch, but I need to get your chili recipe," I said in a rush.

"Hmmm. I don't know," she teased. "That's kind of a secret family recipe."

"Uh. Pretty sure that we're related. Pretty sure you can give it to me." I laughed.

It took her forever to find her cookbook and spout the recipe off to me. By the time she was finished, I was cross-eyed with irritation and had my forehead resting on my fist. It reminded me of being at my wedding and I thought I would reach my eightieth birthday before she was done taking pictures. By the time she finished, half of the guests had left and my dad was asleep under a pew. Yes, under it.

"So," she began, "are y'all having a cook-off at work or something?"

I paused. I didn't want to tell her much, but she worried about me being alone so much that she sent my sister and Adam to check on me often. I was pretty sure my mom had a little crush on him. She'd loved him since my wedding day when he convinced her that I was good enough for his sister. Sadly, I wasn't. But, I wanted to tell someone about Evie. I trusted my mom. I loved my mom. And, if I needed help discovering my feelings, she would be the person that I would go to. That's just how it was. My dad, when he spoke to me, was truly the best man I knew, but slightly cynical. My mother, on the other hand, was a hopeless romantic. Sometimes, I liked to hear what she had to say. It made me feel warm and fuzzy inside and I needed that sometimes.

When I found out Arianna was pregnant and I told my parents, my dad just huffed and left the room. My mother bit the bullet and talked me through it. She convinced me to marry the mother of my child and, to date, it was the best decision I had made, although it was the worst for Arianna. It was a decision that ended up killing her, but not even fear of death would have stopped that girl from loving me. My mother told me that Arianna loved me long before Ari even spoke the words to me. She looked for the positive in all things. A terrible tragedy strikes and she is the one thankful for the survivors while the entire world is angry over the losses. My mom—the eternal glass half-full person.

I ran my hands through my hair. I knew my secret life would eventually cause me to lose my newfound friend, who should be just a job but was so much more. I wanted to give my mother hope. Maybe I wanted to give myself some hope.

"I met someone. I'm cooking dinner for her tonight."

My mother gasped—whether it was shock or chest pain from a mild heart attack—she freaking gasped. I smiled at her surprise. Boy, she really thought I was a hopeless case.

Out of all the questions in the world she could have asked, the *someone's* name, her job, what she looked like, that sweetheart I call my mother asked, "Does she like chili, son?"

I laughed—not a little laugh, but a full-blown belly laugh. "That's all you can ask me? Seriously?"

Silence. I was met with absolute dead silence on the other end of the line. "Mom? Mom?" My heart began thumping the inside of my chest. "Mom?"

Then, she sniffled. "Oh, Rhett." She paused for a really long time. "I didn't think I'd ever hear that sound again."

She was crying. I could tell. I took a deep breath and tried to lighten the air a little. "You scared me. You called me by my first name. I thought I was in trouble."

She chuckled. "Well, if you don't bring her down here and let us meet her, you will be."

I was certain that would be impossible. So, I made a blanket statement that would appease any future requests. "Well, we'll just see how this goes, and I'll let you know." I chuckled. "But, since you asked…" my everlasting sarcasm kicking in, "her name is Evie." Like every other *girl* in America, my voice softened when I talked about the one who had unwittingly struck my fancy. "She is beautiful, smart…a little shattered. But, totally and wonderfully remarkable. And yes, she likes chili."

She chuckled. "That's good. I'm happy for you, Harrison. Really happy for you." Her voice turned motherly soft and soothing. I knew what was coming—her blessing, her own willing for me to forgive myself. "You deserve this. Someone good."

I shook my head, my own silent denial. I didn't deserve Evie, not by a long shot. I was lying to her. I was being so deceitful. But, at the same time, she was opening up the well of emotion inside of me, seeing me in my truest nakedness, reaching into my cold chest and stroking my bitter and broken heart with her delicate words and altruistic tears. She was changing me. From the moment I laid eyes on her, the change inside of me began. The shifting of the asshole gears in my brain and the sweetness on my tongue of bitterness and hatefulness all started when Evie banged into my door a week ago.

I didn't want her to be a job anymore. I wanted her to be mine. Only mine. I would not call it love. Not yet. But, it was something that didn't have a name. It was a mix of hope and longing, excitement and dread, fear and shame, conditionally unconditional, if that even made sense. It was all of those things rolled into one emotion.

My mom interrupted my thoughts. "Shattered?" she asked. "You said shattered."

"Yeah. She lost her family a couple years ago. She was married and had a son. She lost them both under terrible circumstances." I paused. "She needs me, mom. And…I think…am certain…that I need her, too."

***

Evie showed up an hour late for chili dogs, but she showed up. That's all I could ask for. She said she had accidently fallen asleep because of her pain medication. She was tired and rumpled, but she was still just as gorgeous as any other time I'd seen her. When she arrived, she knocked on the door as she was walking in and caught me stirring the chili in my boxers. I wasn't expecting her to just walk in, and she scared the shit out of me again. I heard the knock and looked behind me and saw just her head peeking around the door.

I literally jumped backwards and yelled, "Holy shit!" and dropped the chili spoon. I looked down to make sure I didn't have to clean chili and piss off of the floor.

She made the apologetic face that says, 'I'm stretching my open mouth in a straight line to hide my smile because it's taking everything I have to not bust a gut right now.' You know the face I'm talking about. The 'I'm sorry but I did it on purpose' face.

My mom's champion recipe was a hit. I knew it would be.

After eating, after I put some shorts on of course, we sat on the couch just to hang out.

We engaged in light conversation while we were eating, which included her complimenting the meal about twenty times. When we sat down to relax, the commending continued.

She rubbed her belly. "Oh my gosh. That was so delicious. That was the best chili I've ever had in my entire life." She laid her head on the back of the couch. "Oh, I'm miserable."

"Me too. I'm so glad I'm wearing elastic, because I would totally find it necessary to unbutton my britches right now."

She laughed out loud. "Britches? And I'm the granny?"

I shot her a narrow-eyed look, but managed to lose my serious glare trying to stifle a smile. "So, how's the case coming? I talked to Rhonda today about a different case, and she said she talked to you today. Was it about the Cravens case? Any leads?"

She shook her head. "You know I can't discuss that with anyone."

I shrugged. "Thought I'd give it a shot. I'm…," I searched for a word, almost coming up short, "nosey."

She smiled. "It's okay. I just can't talk about it." She smoothed her long hair back away from her face. "So, did you put any criminals away today?"

This thing we were doing—talking about our day—this is one thing I missed. Carrying the weight of daily hardships, although minimal at times, builds up, making them unbearable. I missed having a person that I could unload on and she would help me carry it or tell me to bury it.

I still needed to gain her trust, so I would tell her things, things I shouldn't tell anyone. I wanted her to believe she could confide in me. I still needed to find out how close she was to discovering that I had killed a beloved do-gooder, a model citizen, a senator's kid.

He was a worthless piece of shit. A kidnapper and rapist. A sorry excuse for a human being. Someone who deserved something worse than hell.

On this night, I told her about the Coulter kid. I told her the good things about my job, some of the shitty things about my job. I told her about Jimmy Reynolds, a fifteen-year-old kid who strangled his grandfather who had molested him for years. I told her things that were not public record. I told her secrets of the courtroom.

At one point, she smiled and said, "I really don't think you should be telling me all of this."

I answered, "This is what friends do. I trust you. I know we agreed to not talking about heavy shit, but I think this little unloading session may be good for us. Maybe we could reserve a few minutes to talk about shit that's bothering us that day. Then, we'll resume, what I'm calling, *Operation MLC*." This was a split decision, creating this made-up thing to break her down. Not only that, I was hoping that she would be willing to spend bookoos of time with me.

Her forehead creased with confusion. "What does that mean?"

"Misery Loves Company," I said with the straightest look on my face.

She bowled over with laughter. "I like that. Certainly not what I would have chosen, but it works."

I smiled at her and leaned forward, placing my elbows on my knees. "Oh yeah? What would you have called it?"

"I don't know, *Operation Smiles* or something like that."

I shook my head and laughed. "We're not maxillofacial surgeons. Pretty sure that's the name of a *real* mission. They're really helping people."

Her face sobered slightly. "Well, I think *Operation MLC* will be helping people, too."

I agreed, "Yeah. I think you're right."

After that, I moved to my recliner and she stretched out on the couch. We talked a little about our childhoods. I told her a little bit about my tours overseas—just the light stuff or funny things that happened. Or stories about people we helped.

She told me she played the cello, or did. She also told me that she played Dorothy in her high school production of *Wizard of Oz*. She told me that she was terrified of elevators which led to her reading me a list of annoying things to do in an elevator. I laughed so hard, tears rolled from the corners of my eyes, and I vowed to do one of those things on the list every time I rode an elevator from that day forward.

"Read that one again," I insisted.

She held her phone up above her face and read, "It says, 'when someone enters, ask if you can push the button for their floor and push the wrong one."

I started to laugh when I heard her gasp and screech, "Oh, thit!"

I sat up from my reclined position quickly. "What happened?"

I stood up and made my way to her. She held both hands over her mouth and her eyes were red and watery. She managed to speak. "I dwopped my phone." She took her hands away from her face. "It hit me in the mouf."

I knelt in front of her. "Holy shit," I breathed. "Are you okay?"

Blood poured from inside Evie's mouth. Her teeth were covered in blood and it was seeping from the corners of her mouth and it covered her bottom lip. "I fink fo. I bith my thung, thoo."

The first time that I touched Evie's mouth, it was covered in blood. It was definitely something I'd never forget. "Let me see." I carefully peeled her top lip up and sure enough, there was a small gash on her gums and both of her lips were busted. "Shit, Evie." I took my hands away. "Do you want the good news or the bad news first?"

She didn't smile. I'm certain she wasn't able to. "Bad newth."

I clamped my teeth together and sucked in a breath, "You got blood on your pretty white shirt."

She looked down, "Thit! I luth thith thirt!"

I laughed. "Good news? I think you're gonna make it." She huffed. "I know. I know. It was touch-and-go there for a minute, but you're gonna live!"

She started laughing. "Don'th make me laugh!" She shoved me and I fell to my ass in front of her. "I gotta go."

"No!" I said loudly, still laughing. "Just go rinse your mouth out. I need to keep an eye on you to make sure you don't bleed to death. It's only eight, granny. It's not bedtime!"

She gave in. It didn't take any more convincing than that.

By the time eleven o'clock rolled around, we were both struggling to stay awake. My face was sore and my stomach felt like I had done a thousand crunches that night. Laughter was good, even though I felt like I had been doing aerobics.

When I walked her to my door to see her out, I leaned over her and hugged her once more. She was so warm and soft, and when she hugged me back, I could feel her body relax against my chest.

"Thank you for tonight," she murmured.

"Thanks for coming. I enjoyed this. A lot."

"Me, too," she whispered. She was still hugging me when she

continued, "This helps, you know?"

"Which part?" I whispered against her ear.

"All of it. The smiles, the laughs, the cries. Even the hugs."

She pulled away from me and it felt too soon. I had to agree with her because she was right. "Yeah. It helps me, too."

She ran her hands up my arms quickly in a friendly, comforting gesture. "See you tomorrow night?"

I nodded. "And the night after that. Give me your phone." She handed it to me and I punched my number in and sent myself a text. "There. Now you can call or text before you get here and I won't have heart attacks when you walk right in." I laughed and she just smiled.

She turned and opened the door, looking back at me. "Goodnight, Rhett."

"Goodnight, Evie."

Despite the battle between my head and my heart, I held onto this idiotic hope that *Operation Misery Loves Company* would make her mine. In the end, I knew it was an impossibility, but the war was raging.

And with that, I went to bed alone but found comfort in knowing that she was sleeping on the other side of my wall. Her stories and her allure and innocence and her infectious laugh and gorgeous smile got to me that night. When she walked away from me, my chest felt lighter. And, I could only come up with one explanation. Whether she realized it or not, that night when she stepped into her apartment and the door latched behind her, she took a little piece of my heart with her.

CHAPTER THIRTEEN

Evie

When I closed the door that night, my entire body just slumped against it. I was exhausted and my mouth was throbbing, but I still found it in my heart to feel relief. I closed my eyes and smiled. He felt so good against me. Strong. So…there and alive.

He was so handsome it was painful just to look at him. And, he stared at me. A lot. It was a bit unnerving at times. I'm nothing special. I have never thought of myself any differently than any other woman. But, he looked at me like I was…beautiful.

He was also not at all as people had described him…an unforgiving, angry asshole. Rhonda had said it. And, after I went back to work, I heard it around the office. No one ever wanted to talk to him. It was funny to sit back and watch people fight over who was going to call his office about different cases. He was always sweet as pie to me. Maybe he just felt sorry for me. That's what I constantly told myself, but he seemed too genuine for that, and he didn't act like the type that felt sorry for anyone or anything.

I had dinner with him every night. We alternated cooking nights and we washed dishes together. It was very domestic. I was so comfortable that it was worrying me. I was terrified that if I let someone in, I would have to let something go. I wanted to let the pain go that came with losing my family, but I wasn't ready to let go of their memories. It hurt to think that I was pushing their memories out to make room for new ones. But, I was hell-bent on enjoying myself.

So, this thing Rhett called *Operation MLC* began.

***

Rhett pulled a popsicle stick from a can and read it out loud out loud, admitting that he purposefully chose that one specifically. "Do something that you used to do."

I looked at him with a furrowed brow. "Like what?"

He shrugged. "Well, like anything."

"What can we do tonight? It's already eight o'clock. We'll need to figure it out and do it later this week."

He smiled sheepishly. "I kind of…already…" he trailed off.

"What?" I asked impatiently.

"Let's go. You're driving. I don't have any gas." He grabbed my hand and led me out the door and directed me to a music store a few blocks away from our apartment.

"What is this?"

He pointed at the building. "A music store?"

"Yeah. I see that. What are we doing here?"

He grinned. "I know the guy that owns the place, and you my lady, are going to play a song for me."

I shook my head. "No way."

"You have to. I said so."

"You are *not* the boss of me."

He laughed. "And you are *not* six, so don't ever say that again. You're playing. You said you would do this, so you're doing it."

I conceded. I went inside of that store, sat behind a cello that had been set up for me and I played from memory. I didn't play one song. I played four. The feel of the strings underneath my fingers and the pull of the bow in my right hand were all so familiar. My left hand moved quickly and never faltered. I kept my eyes closed as I played. I knew Rhett was sitting in front of me, watching me, but I could not bring myself to look at him.

After I played the last note, I stood and walked away from him and out the door. I was panting when I reached my car. Rhett did not know that I played up until Noah died. On nights he was restless and inconsolable, I played for him until he fell asleep. I was sucking in heavy breaths when he reached me.

"What happened? What's wrong?"

"It's just hard. Everything I do reminds me of him." I turned away from him and braced myself on my car.

"I know," he said softly. "That's why we're doing this. So, you can do things—things you used to love but hate now, things you can learn to love again. Things that make you remember what life is about."

I was suddenly angry. At the world. At him.

"Who the hell do you think you are anyway? You planning on saving me or something? Is that it?" I was panting with fury. "Well, guess what? I don't need to be saved. I need to be left the hell alone!" I pulled the car door open and sat down and started it.

By the time I looked back up, he was pulling the passenger door open and was leaning in the car. "I'm not leaving you alone. You can run away from me. You can hide. But, I promise you this: I will come after you. And, I will find you. So, just give it up right now." He sat down and slammed the door. "Evie," he took a deep breath, "you have so much to live for."

I snickered. "Oh really? Like what?"

He turned his head and glared at me. "Quit acting like your life is fucking over. Hell, it's barely started. You're what twenty-seven? Twenty-eight?"

"Twenty-nine," I answered.

"Okay then. How I see it, if you live to be eighty, you have another fifty-one years to live for something. If you're gonna waste those years shutting everyone out, rolling over and dying, what the hell are we doing here?" His voice lowered. "You promised you would try this. I need this too. You're not the only person who's lost someone, Evie."

"I know that."

His eyes narrowed on me. "Then quit acting like it. I have my own shit to deal with. Do you know how angry I get some days?" I shook my head. "Just think about it. How angry would you be? I live with that every day. I grieve. I'm pissed. I hate. I'm an asshole." He took another deep breath. "I need this too, Evie. I need to know what it's like to live again. To have fun again. To smile and laugh and not feel guilty." He looked at me and his eyes bore into mine. "You are the only person I've ever met who knows almost exactly how I feel. I can't talk about it to anyone. I can't put into words how it makes me feel. But with you...with you, I don't have to say the words. I don't have to tell you how I feel, because you already know. You *already* know." He took his eyes off of mine and faced forward. "We are going to do some fun things, but I'm just warning you, we're going to do some tough things. Don't you want to face your fears, change your heart, and let the sun shine on your face again? Don't you think Noah would want that for you? Because I know...I know Haven would want that for me. I want to make her proud. How can I make her proud if I'm an unhappy, good-for-nothing asshole?" He looked down at his fingers that were twisting slightly in his lap. "It would make her proud if I could help someone...I mean really help someone."

My anger was fleeting more and more by the second. "And, you think that someone is me?"

He met my eyes again. "I *know* that someone is you. Just trust me, okay? Do you trust me?"

Everything inside of me was screaming no, only because I didn't want to leave my zone of loneliness that I found strangely comforting. But, he was getting to me, and he was sincere.

So, I nodded. "Okay. Yeah. I trust you."

CHAPTER FOURTEEN

RHETT

So, *Operation Misery Loves Company* really began. I thought of everything I could that would open her up—from simple Q&A to some really tough shit for her to face. But, I didn't leave myself completely out. I meant what I said about needing this in my life...adding *living* to my life, but I was mainly doing it for her. I was an idiot when it came to her. Some days I forgot the real reason I was with her. She quickly turned from a job into a confidant. I didn't want to think of her as a project for that was so unfair to her. But, I truly wanted to help her and get on with my life as well.

So, I tried to think of everything possible. I took all of my ideas and wrote them each on colored popsicle sticks. I shoved the stick down in an empty can of green beans (that I had washed) and set them on my coffee table. Every week, sometimes twice a week, we would pull something from the can and do it—without discussion, without thinking twice.

I had already forced Evie to do something she used to do, so I decided I would do something I used to do. So, on a Saturday morning, I asked Evie to accompany me to Creve Coeur Lake to go fishing.

Much to my surprise, Evie could bait her own hook and even take her own fish off of the hook. I complimented her constantly on her patience and her lack of nasty-niceness.

We fished in silence for the most part as the wind blew the boat slowly across the water. I would look up every once in a while and catch her lost in her concentration and her thoughts. The silence was deafening, until she spoke. "So, did you go fishing all the time?"

I smiled. "When I was a kid, yeah. All the time. As I got older, started working and stuff, recreation became a thing of the past. I started fishing a little bit again after I got married." I figured if I was with her and we were doing this, I would be completely honest. "I did it just to get away sometimes."

"Get away?"

"Yeah. I felt like I was suffocating half the time. I would come out here and fish for hours and just enjoy my time alone."

"While she waited for you at home?" I nodded. "So, you came out here to have space?"

I nodded again. "I was excited, but I was terrified of being a father. When I was around Arianna, it was this constant reminder that my life would never be the same. So, I did this so I could keep a little piece of who I knew I was. I had this just so I could get away from her." I chuckled while I reminisced about my old life. "The last time I came out here, I actually invited her. Macy watched Haven while we enjoyed a quiet afternoon of fishing. It was a great day. A really great day." I closed my eyes for a second and for a moment I could see Arianna smiling at me. She wore a huge floppy hat and she smelled like bug spray. She was definitely the reluctant outdoorsman. I sat and watched her watch her bobber for hours. We stayed out there until the sun went down. That was the most beautiful sunset I had ever seen. I almost told her that night that I loved her, because I did. And, I knew I did. We didn't say much to each other at all. She said that she liked the quiet, even if the crickets and cicadas were going crazy.

"When was that?" Evie asked interrupting my reverie.

"Three days before she died." She just nodded because there was nothing left to say. I felt a tug on my line. A hard tug. "Shit," I said and yanked. I started reeling in my line. "Got one! Yoohoo!

Alright," I said. "Come to daddy." I looked over at her. "Sorry. I get all dorky when I catch one."

She laughed. "Hmm. Could've fooled me. I thought you were dorky all the time."

I pulled in my fish and threw it in the live well. "That was mean as hell, Evie. Mean as hell."

Our very own fishing derby ended just before sunset. I didn't want to tell Evie, but I wanted to beat the moon. I wanted the sunsets there to belong to Arianna forever—in my heart, sunsets on that lake would always belong to her.

We loaded up in Evie's car, after returning the boat, and headed home. We always took her car, no matter what we were doing. She told me that she liked to be in control behind the wheel and riding shotgun gave her "nervous belly." So, she drove and I didn't care. I'd kick back in her sedan and let her chauffer me around. And, I kind of loved it.

After that, at least once a week, we started pulling popsicle sticks from the can.

Conquer Your Worst Fear

As we stood in line to ride the biggest roller coaster in the theme park across town, I thought Evie was going to lose it.

"Are you crying?" I asked her.

"A little," she responded. I died laughing. "Stop laughing! I am so scared right now." Evie had her hair tied up in a messy bun and she wore shorts and a t-shirt. Simple. And beautiful.

"You know, someone died on this ride last year," I said with a straight face. She started walking away and I grabbed her arm. "I'm kidding! Get back here."

We rode that roller coaster eight times before the end of the day. After the first time, she laughed and laughed. She held her hands way up in the air and screamed every time the bottoms dropped out of our bellies. It was refreshing to watch her. When we climbed off the last time, she reached up and hugged me. When she looked up at me, I saw it—that little bit of life flicker in her eyes.

My worst fear is one I share with ninety percent of America. When I told Evie, in all seriousness, that I was terrified of clowns, she laughed so hard she choked on her chicken noodle soup. I was a little offended to be honest. I threw my hands in the air. "Don't even act like I'm in the minority here."

After she was cured of her giggles, she arranged and even bought tickets to a circus that happened to be in town. As we walked in, I counted five clowns. Trust me, I was flipping out a little bit. How can kids seriously like this crap?

When three of the clowns were out in the center of the stadium doing their act, and my name was called over the loud speaker to "come on down," I was livid…and scared to death.

I looked at Evie. "Are you freaking kidding me?" She just covered her mouth and stifled her giggles. She was laughing so hard, tears were streaming down her face.

I walked down to the center and one of the clowns walked up to me and touched my arm. I yanked it away so fast, he jumped back dramatically. "Don't touch me," I warned him.

I didn't even really do anything. I literally stood down there like an idiot. They asked me to act like I was riding on a bus or something and I was so irritated and embarrassed by the time I got back to my seat that I couldn't even look at Evie.

"Why are you mad?" she asked me when we climbed into her car.

"I'm not mad. I'm terrified of those things. Just seeing them was bad enough. I didn't need to climb on an imaginary bus with them."

She was laughing so hard she couldn't breathe. "Well, I don't really know if you conquered that fear. Maybe we need to come back tomorrow."

I huffed. "Screw that. Okay. I'm not scared anymore. Fear. Conquered."

Go to a Winery…or a Brewery

"This wine tastes like shit," I said. "It tastes like I'm sucking on a nut." Evie froze with her test tasting glass in midair. "I mean…like a hazelnut. Not a… Nevermind." Wine spewed across the table and rolled down Evie's chin. "Shut up."

"I didn't say anything," she said, wiping her chin off.

"Do I hold my pinky out like this or what? You're not holding your pinky out. Am I supposed to? Do you cup it like this? Do you turn it up from the bottom? What?" She just laughed, not answering my questions. I looked at the woman standing next to us. "Do you know?" The lady literally turned and walked away without answering my question. I watched her prance away from me with an upturned nose. "What a witch," I murmured. I looked at Evie. "Is it because I'm wearing boardshorts? Is that why no one's taking me seriously?"

"Either that or the fact that you're wearing a tank top."

"Men don't wear tank tops. This is a muscle shirt."

"Okay. Well, your tattoos make you look like you just got out of prison."

"What if I did? Personally, I'd be a little nicer to someone who looks as fierce as me. What? You don't like my tattoos?"

She actually blushed a little. "I like them. A lot. They're beautiful. And, because I know what they mean to you, they're even more beautiful to me."

The winery was fun and Evie actually bought some. She asked me if I wanted some and I just shook my head. "No spanks. Swing me by the liquor store. I'm getting some beer."

Evie drank her wine that night—a little too much wine. She laughed and was acting so…silly. When she started scooting a little closer to me on the couch, I decided it was time for me to go home. She hugged me goodbye and her embrace lingered. She felt good. Really good. But, I broke the hug when I reminded myself that she was my friend but also a job. Earn her trust. Find out what she knows. With that reminder, I bid her goodnight.

Go to a Painting Class

"What. The. Hell. Is. That?" Evie asked me pointedly.

I pulled my paintbrush away from the canvas and stared at her with narrowed eyes. "Why do you look like you're going to throw up?"

"That looks awful, Rhett. What is that?" she asked as she began to laugh.

I shrugged. "What do you think it is?"

She shook her head. "I have no idea. She is showing us what to paint. It couldn't be any easier unless it was a 'Paint by Numbers' class. You need one of those coloring books. You know, where you just put water on the pages and the color appears?" Her laughter became louder. "I can't even..."

Slightly annoyed at her ridicule, I looked over at her canvas. Of course it looked like something Rembrandt painted. "So, do you always do this?" I asked her.

"What?" she asked, her smile fading.

"Make fun of people to make yourself feel better?" She smiled and gasped at the same time. I pointed at her. "You're a bully."

"I am not!" she exclaimed.

"Yes, you are. I can't believe I've never noticed." I said softly. "All this time, I've thought you were this sweet, picture-perfect, adorably beautiful woman."

"And now?" she asked, chuckling.

"Well, I still believe all of that...except the sweet part. I almost feel like you would beat me up and steal my lunch money." I started rubbing my back pocket. "Where's my wallet?" I paused. "Oh. There it is. You're not getting it today, you junkyard dog," I teased.

I laughed and looked away from her. I never saw it coming...not until my face, hair, and shirt were splattered with yellow paint. At the contact, my eyes closed and I sucked in a hard breath.

But, I gave it back to her in *blue*. Before I knew it, we were both covered in splatters of the rainbow.

"Is there a problem back here?" a weak voice interrupted.

We both froze. I looked at the little old lady and gave her my most dashing smile. I pointed at Evie. "She started it."

Get Dressed Up and Go to Open Houses

This was probably one of my most favorites. I spent all afternoon on the phone with a realtor, insisting that I would not live in anything under two million dollars, so it would be preposterous to even show me anything less than that.

I called Evie. "Get dressed up. I'm talking, you better wear a dress. Some heels. Updo and the reddest lipstick you have."

Walking through four and five million dollar mansions with a straight face was one of the most difficult things ever.

"This is nice, but we were thinking something much larger. Weren't we darling?" I looked at Evie. To my surprise, she played along.

"Yes. And we would really like to have a fountain in the foyer." She looked up at me. "If that's possible."

I had to turn my head and cover my laughter with a cough. The realtor looked at me with wide eyes. "*In* the foyer?" I nodded.

"Yes. Maybe a stream with some goldfish in it as well?" I asked.

"Sir, I really don't think I know of anything on the market like that. That will probably be something you will have to add later to a home that closely meets your requirements."

"Okay. Well, let's move on to the next one."

The next one was gorgeous. I could definitely live in that monstrosity of a house. While Evie walked with the realtor, I slipped away unnoticed and hid in a closet in one of the thirteen bedroom suites. I timed it. It took them twenty-six minutes to find me. Well,

I actually found them. When they finally entered the room, I scratched on the door until they neared it. When they approached the door fully, I pulled it open and yelled, "Boo!"

No lie. The realtor sharted. Yes. Sharted. She excused herself to the restroom and Evie and I ran downstairs and jumped in her car and sped away.

I was laughing so hard, I started coughing and couldn't stop. Evie looked at me, her eyes watery with happy tears. "She shit herself! Like, you literally scared the shit out of her!"

And that, my friends, was the hardest I had laughed in years.

Tell Me a Secret

My life is full of secrets. It was hard for me to choose just one. My military career is basically one big secret. I was never allowed to talk about the things I had done or seen while serving to anyone outside of the military. I didn't think she wanted to hear anything related to my career anyways—then or now. And, if she was going to trust me, I had to make it personal. But, as always...ladies first.

After dinner one night and after we washed dishes, she sat on the couch and I sat on the floor in front of her recliner. We said nothing for almost an hour. We sat in a silent room, not saying a word.

Finally, she broke the silence.

"I have two. Two secrets. I have a shirt—it's not mine. It was Dash's. I go home on days where I feel so lonely and put it on. I strip down and put on that blue dress shirt. He wore it the day he died. I wear it on days that I allow myself to fall apart." Her lips began to quiver. "I feel like his arms are around me when I wear it. I can't explain the comfort I find in it. I feel pathetic—like some pitiful widow. I loved him so much and some days, I still need him." She dropped her chin to her chest. "He made love to me while I wore that shirt once. I was wearing it again the day we found out I was pregnant. It was there in our finest moments. It played a part in the best day of my life. And, the worst. I can't let it go. I don't know how." She sucked in a breath and cleared her throat.

Then, she looked me right in the eyes. "I didn't cry at the funeral." She balled up her fist and put it against her mouth. "What kind of wife doesn't shed a tear when her husband is lowered into the ground? What kind of mother looks at her son's coffin with such an emotional disconnection that she can't even cry over him?"

"You were in shock, Evie."

"Maybe. I still feel like the worst wife and mother in the world."

"We both know that's not true."

She just nodded. After she took a minute and regained her composure, she looked at me. I wasted no time. It's almost like what I was about to tell her had been tearing at my heart for so long—trying to get out. So, I told her a secret that I had kept all to myself all these years.

"I never told my wife I loved her…until it was almost too late. I'm not going to lie—I was an asshole to her. All the time. Luke gave me shit about it every time I saw him. He told me on several occasions that I was a worthless piece of shit." My lip turned up on one corner. "He was right. No one knew that I never told her that, though. I didn't tell anyone and I know she wouldn't have. It hurt her too much."

I blew out a hard breath. "I met her at a bar and took her home with me. She was sweet and kind and so innocent and too young to be at a bar. I shouldn't have touched her," I smirked. "She didn't tell me she was a virgin. What's bad is that I couldn't tell she wasn't. I was so wrapped up in her. She was a quiet beauty. Shy, didn't have much confidence. I think that's what drew me to her.

"She was a one-night stand. Or was supposed to be. We didn't exchange numbers, but she knew where I lived. Eight weeks after our night together, she was waiting for me on my doorstep. I knew when I saw the tears and her suitcase that she was pregnant. I didn't even really know her, but I married her two weeks later. I was noble, like that. She was nineteen; her parents kicked her out and cut her off. I was all she had. I didn't love her," I whispered, "but I promised to take care of her." I let out a hard breath. "She loved me that first night we were together. There was no question. There was *never* a question. She told me all the time that she loved me. I would only say, 'Okay' or 'I know.' Sometimes I wouldn't say anything at all. One time, I even rolled my eyes at her." My nose burned and my tears began to escape a little. "She saw me. It hurt her and I knew it. But the more time I spent with her, the more she grew on me. She was always so positive and so happy and so warm to come home to every day.

"I starting loving the little things. Like how she always wore socks to bed," I chuckled. "She could be butt-ass naked in bed, still wearing socks. The way she put on her mascara. The way she shimmied out of her jeans. The way she looked at our daughter while she breast-fed.

"I didn't realize how much she meant to me. I had tried to keep my distance, but after she had Haven, I just...." I drifted off before huffing, "looked at her differently. Purely. Fondly.

"I had a dream one night that she was killed in a car accident. It was so real. So vivid. In my dream, I saw her in the car and as I neared her, she disappeared. I couldn't find her anywhere and I was screaming for her, searching for her and she was nowhere to be found. I woke up in a panic, in tears, and I look over and she's sleeping right beside me. So peacefully. So beautifully. Breathing in and out so deeply. I woke her up and made love to her over and over and over. And, I finally said it. Those three words that I had withheld from her. I said them. Over and over. And, it felt so good. I told her that I loved her a hundred times that night.

"The next day when I left for work she gave me the sweetest goodbye kiss. The last thing she said to me was, 'There's more where that came from.' And she winked."

I looked at Evie. "I walked away from her not knowing that little wink was the last piece of love she would ever give me. I had finally told her that I loved her in the wee hours of the morning I lost her."

I blew out a shaky breath. "I've never told anybody that."

Exchange a Gift

I knew what I wanted to give Evie, but I had no idea what she had planned to give me. Naturally, she opened hers first.

When she took the lid off of the box and separated the layers of tissue paper, she looked up at me and smiled.

"I don't want it to replace what you have, but maybe you'll find a different comfort in this." She reached in and pulled out a purple, long-sleeve button-up that was much too big for her. "I was wearing that shirt the morning after the first night I met you. Remember that?" She nodded and lifted my shirt to her face and inhaled. That little act made my chest buckle a little.

"Your turn," she said softly.

I picked up the small box and opened it. It was a copper wallet insert card with an inscription. It was a scripture. Before I read it, she said, "I thought since you're covered in them, you might appreciate this one."

I read it aloud. "Two are better than one; because they have a good reward for their labour. For if they fall, the one will lift up his fellow: but woe to him that is alone when he falleth; for he hath not another to help him up. Ecclesiastes 4:9-10." I looked up at her. "That's beautiful."

She smiled and shrugged. "I thought it sounded like us. Two of us. Trying to help each other up and keep each other from falling further."

"I love it. Thank you." I could not take my eyes off of her. My feelings for her were starting to whirl out of control. I fell for her a little more each day. I was falling fast. And hard.

Go to the Zoo

"Are those turtles doing what I think they're doing?" Evie asked me.

"Yep," I said. I looked to my right where a kid that couldn't have been any more than six was standing beside me.

"Daddy, why is that turtle jumping on the other one?" he asked.

I looked over at the kid's dad who looked at me at the same time, his eyes wide. I just smiled at him and shrugged. I heard the boy's dad say, "Come on, son. Let's go find the elephants."

"But I want to watch the turtles," I heard the boy say as they walked off.

Evie looked at me and laughed. "Poor guy."

"What would you have said?"

"I would've told him that those turtles were having sex and we should give them their privacy."

I felt my eyebrows crawl up my forehead. "To a six year old?" I asked loudly.

She laughed so loudly that it ricocheted off of the buildings around us. She never answered me.

The bird exhibit was a completely different story. I never had a fear of birds until that day when I was literally attacked by a toucan. I ran out of there as fast as I could. Once again, Evie could not contain her laughter.

"Is my neck bleeding?" I asked her. I was feeling around for the blood I was certain covered my neck.

Evie snickered. "No. Oh, wait." She touched my back right below my collar. "Yeah. A little."

I swiped my hand across it and pulled it back. It was covered in blood. "A little?" I asked her. "I think I need stitches!"

"Oh. It's a scratch. Quit being a baby."

"How about you get attacked by a deadly bird and see if you don't feel like you're going to bleed to death?"

Evie's laughter had awakened something inside of me. I loved hearing it. It made me laugh. Her eyes were always so alive now. She looked bright and refreshed. In the beginning, her face looked tortured. I stopped seeing that side of Evie. She was fun-loving and gorgeous and sweet.

I loved watching her with strangers. Everyone was drawn to her. Once she started smiling, she was like a magnet for every old man and single dude we came across. It ticked me off a little, to be honest. I could feel jealousy rearing its ugly head often. There were times I caught myself tucking her under my arm and guiding her with my hand on the small of her back. I loved touching her—more than I should have.

Once she came alive, she became a completely different person. I was standing in line to buy a corndog for each of us when a man a little older than me, but good looking as hell approached her. She held out her hand to meet his. I was close enough that I could hear when he asked her what her name was.

"Evangeline," she answered.

Evie was starting to feel like mine, and I didn't even know her first name. I glared at the bastard who still hadn't released her hand and who knew more about Evie than I did, it felt like. My blood was pounding and my fingers were twitching. I won't lie and say that I wasn't a little pissed.

She looked over at me and waved. I shot her a peace sign back. *A peace sign? What the hell?*

I could still hear the douchebag that stood way too close to my Evie...or Evangeline, I should say. "Is that your boyfriend?"

She shook her head. "No. He's just my friend."

I couldn't take anymore. So, I spoke loudly, "Hey, baby! Come over here a sec, will you?" and waved her over to me.

She nodded and let the douchebag off with a shy goodbye. "Yeah?" she asked when she approached me.

I had to make up something. And quick. "Did you say you wanted ketchup?"

She shook her head. "No. Just mustard." She stood there for a few seconds, then turned to me. "Did you call me baby?"

"I don't know. Did I?" I lied. She nodded her head and I shrugged. "Hmm." I did call her baby, and it felt damn good.

Our weeks went on like that. Sometimes up to three times a week, we would pull a stick from the can and tackle something together. We were conquering things together; we were making memories. We were living.

We did all kinds of things.

Go to an Outdoor Concert
Test Drive Your Dream Car
Game Night (We did this all the time.)
Pretend to be a Tourist (Funniest thing ever!)
Tandem Bike Ride (So weird…and dangerous.)
Ride Go-Karts
Q&A
Watch Your Favorite Movie
Go to a Pottery Class
Share Your Dream Vacation Destination (Mine was St. Lucia. Evie couldn't make up her mind. She literally named fifty places.)
Get Matching Outfits (My parents still do this.)
Get In Trouble (This happened a lot.)
Build a Blanket Fort
Go to an Arcade

Evie smiled and laughed all the time. There was rarely a time when melancholy pulled her under. Even if it did, it didn't hold her for long. I would reach right in and pull her out.

Not all of it was fun and games. It was challenging. We had to face our greatest heartaches. We needed to heal. The laughter helped, but the tears did too.

Share Your Favorite Memory of Your Child

Tell Me Why You Loved Being a Parent
Write a Letter to Your Child
Write a Letter to Your Late Spouse
Write a Poem to Yourself
Lie on Your Back under the Stars and Speak Out Loud to Them
Go to Where They Rest and Take Them Flowers

In the midst of it all, there was a sweet mixture of the fun and the heartache. It was like looking outside and the rain is pouring down, but you can still see the sun. It was like a heat shower in the summertime. The sun felt good on our faces, but so did dancing in the rain.

One of the most difficult tasks was strictly meant for Evie. It was something that was not necessary for me to overcome. My heart broke for her. My eyes welled up right when she pulled the stick from the can. I knew it would be hard, but I would be there for her.

Look at Their Pictures. Be Proud and Show Another.

Evie looked at me with a tortured face. "I can't," she whispered. I nodded. "You can."

Conveniently in her apartment, I went to her closet and took down the large suitcase that I knew held her photo albums.

She stood in the doorway and watched me. She was shaking her head and she began to sob. "Rhett, please. Don't make me. Please don't make me."

Instead of dragging her over there and forcing her, I unzipped the suitcase and retrieved the album on top. I sank to the floor and stretched my legs out.

I opened to the first page, and a beautiful baby boy with blonde hair and huge blue eyes stared back at me. He had a chubby face and ruddy cheeks. He was smiling at me with a toothless grin.

"God, Evie. He's gorgeous," I whispered.

She started to sob. She knew how gorgeous he was. She also knew how *gone* he was.

I stared at her for a minute. She wouldn't look at me and she just stood frozen in the doorway. "Come here, baby." She shook her head. "Evie, look at me." It took her a minute, but she finally did. "He may be gone now, but he lived, baby. He lived. You know, sometimes I forget what Haven looks like," I shrugged. "I can't just close my eyes and really see her. I have her pictures, and I have to see them to remember. Do you remember what he looks like?"

Her face was wet and her cheeks were raw. She spoke so softly, "I forgot what he looks like. I mean, I have an idea of what I remember, but I forgot the small details…mainly because I think my heart wanted to forget him."

"Come look at him. Come see how beautiful he was. Refresh your mind. Remind your heart. It's going to hurt, but I promise…I swear you won't regret this."

I flipped through a few more pages before she moved toward me and lowered herself to the floor beside me slowly. The instant she turned her eyes to the page I had opened, she let out a hard sob. Baby Noah was asleep beside Dash in the bed. Both boys had their arms thrown over their faces, sleeping in the exact same position. It was adorable. And, adorably sad.

She reached over and ran her delicate fingers over the picture before turning and pressing her face into my back. I fought my tears. I had to stay strong for her.

"They always sleep like that?" I asked her. I felt her nod into my back. "Sit up, baby. Look at this one." Noah, in his newborn pictures, lie asleep inside of a baseball glove, his tiny hands clutching a baseball. I smiled at the tininess of that baby. He was the prettiest little boy I had ever seen.

When she sat up, I gingerly placed the open album in her lap. She took both hands and ran them down the pages reverently. Then, she looked up at me. "I miss him. So much. Every," her breath hitched, "day." She turned the page and stared at the pictures. I balanced my time between looking at the pictures and looking at Evie. When she turned to the next page, her lip turned up on one side. The picture was just a candid shot of her and Noah. Her hair was everywhere and she was grinning at the camera while Noah stared at her, enchanted by her, I'm sure.

She turned a few more pages before she started telling me about him and the history behind each picture.

"He was the sweetest thing," she whispered. "I took this one the day he started walking. Nine months old, my boy." She continued to talk about him. "Dash could never put him to sleep. I had to sing to him every night. I rocked him and I would sing any song I could remember the words to." She chuckled. "Some of them were inappropriate for a child his age, but I sang my heart out to him." She pointed at a picture. "Here he is with my mom and dad. They adored him. I asked them to keep him over the weekend one time, and let's just say that I was surprised that I showed up and they had not bubble-wrapped him. They treated him as if he were made of glass." She smiled. "I guess he kind of was."

We sat at the foot of her bed for three hours looking at pictures of her baby and late husband. She cried. She sobbed. She smiled. And she laughed.

I pulled out my favorite, a picture of Evie and Noah, most likely taken by Dash. Evie lie asleep on the bed while Noah, who was wide awake, smiled at Evie. She made him happy. Even when she wasn't aware.

"I'll be right back," I told her. I went next door to my apartment and grabbed an empty frame from my closet. It was pretty pointless to ask Evie for one. I took the picture and placed it in the frame.

When I entered Evie's bedroom, she still sat with the albums spread around her. "What did you do?" she asked me sweetly.

I put the frame on her nightstand. "I went and got this."

"Rhett, I don't know if I can…"

"Just…just try it. Okay? Don't put him away. Don't act like he didn't exist. I can understand your anger toward Dash. But, don't take your anger out on that baby boy." I pointed at the picture. "Look at him. He was this tiny little person—couldn't speak for himself, couldn't fend for himself, but he already knew how to love. Keep him out and love him."

I then bid her goodnight and tapped on her wall like always before I went to sleep.

I noticed something in those weeks. When I first laid eyes on Evie, I felt the earth shift beneath me. However, being in her presence every day was shifting everything I had come to believe and change everything I was living for.

Before I woke up every morning, my sole purpose for getting out of bed was to hate. I wanted vengeance. I wanted to kill.

With Evie, I felt none of that. I wanted to smile and laugh. I wanted to be a difference maker. I wanted to live too.

And, I wanted to love.

CHAPTER FIFTEEN

Evie

Four months went by. In addition to our goals and activities laid out for *Operation Misery Loves Company*, we continued our nightly shared meals. And, we were growing closer. He made me laugh like crazy, and forced me to face my heartache head-on.

Rhett was a woman's dream, the ultimate trifecta. He was gorgeous, open, and an incredible cook. He really made my hot pastrami sandwiches look like potted meat. He was meticulous about little things. I turned all of his canned goods with the nutrition labels to the outside just to tease him. The night before, he had opened his cabinets and mumbled, "What the hell? I seriously think I have a ghost. These damn things keep getting turned around." He was utterly confused and it was…adorable.

Every single day, my heart felt a little lighter. We joked, teased, argued. Needless to say, I lost most arguments—sometimes because I didn't know what I was talking about and other times he turned everything I said around to the point where *I* didn't know what point I was trying to make. After our argument about red velvet cake's true identity—chocolate cake with red food coloring—he looked at me and grinned, "You really shouldn't argue with an attorney, Evie. Especially when you don't know what the hell you're talking about. *And,* especially, *especially,* when you've never made a red velvet cake."

"Oh, and let me guess. You have?"

"You're damn right I have. My mom made wedding cakes for

extra money while I was growing up. I could make all kinds of cakes in my sleep, with both arms tied behind my back…without a recipe."

The man had lived a thousand lives it seemed. He had done all sorts of things, seen all types of wonders and traveled to different places. Sometimes I would just lay on his couch and listen to him speak. His voice was deep and steady and calming. I would close my eyes and listen to the deep inflection, his low voice always so thick with emotion.

He smiled a lot. He laughed a lot. His laughter was the cure on days where I was almost losing it. I realized the night before that I had not put on Dash's shirt since the night of my first dinner with Rhett. Usually, I would resort to it every other day or so, but the truth is, putting it on didn't cross my mind on the nights I spent with Rhett.

To top it off, the man never put on a shirt. We had breakfast for supper one night and he refused to put one on while he was cooking bacon. He would jump back and scream "shit" every time the grease popped him. He told me to hush and tried to convince me I was enjoying the show.

I was trying to fight my attraction to him. I wasn't ready for a relationship and this felt *too right*. I just kept waiting for the other shoe to drop. I could feel the dread in the pit of my belly. He was too perfect. The timing was too impeccable. His circumstances were too coincidentally close to mine. The bond was too strong. Too flawless. His story checked out completely. I read a couple things, just glancing, in his wife's file. Every detail he told me was true. Everything he said was substantiated. Maybe I was being too distrustful. Maybe I was trying to find some fault in him, but I kept coming up short. Maybe he was just as lost as I was. When I asked Rhonda about his dating history, she informed me that he had none. Her cousin had told her that even before his wife, he had only been with one other girl in his life. That was a little too much information, but helped me understand that he didn't take relationships or sexual encounters lightly. I wouldn't be a fling. And, maybe he just wanted a friend.

I tried to avoid Rhonda's persistent questioning, but she never relented. It was exhausting.

As I was walking into the office, Rhonda ran to catch up with me. As much as she talked and exhausted me to the point where I would literally just have to walk away from her, I truly started to love her. She was my shadow, the closest friend I had in a very long time, besides Rhett.

"Soooo...." She drug out. I knew what she wanted. Details. But, there was nothing to tell. "You eat with Mr. Trimble again last night?"

I smiled. "Call him Rhett. Jeez."

"Okay. I'll ask you what I really want to ask you then. Did Rhett eat you yet?"

I gasped and hit her in the shoulder with the file I was carrying. "Shut the hell up! That was so loud." I shook my head, truly pissed. She constantly embarrassed the crap out of me. I tripped walking in the door and stumbled, plowing into an elderly lady with a cane. I smiled at her and offered my apologies. Rhonda did this every morning. She riled me up about the prior evening, always asking the most inappropriate questions. She was the biggest pervert I knew.

When I recovered, I answered her question. "No. He didn't and he's not going to."

"What?" she screeched loudly. "He would, you know? He's got a thing for you. I'm convinced."

"Will you stop, please? He doesn't. We're just friends."

"Whatever you say." She changed the subject once we stepped into my makeshift office. "So, the man that you talked to on the phone yesterday that said he had some information on Bradley Cravens? The one that was supposed to show up this morning and give a statement?"

"Yes." Of course I remembered. I had been working on this case with several others for weeks. We came up with nothing over and over again. Every day we started at square one. Today would be no different. "What about him?" I insisted at her silence.

She threw a picture down on my desk. "Found dead this morning in his apartment."

I fell back in my chair and looked at the ceiling. "You've got to be kidding me. Our only lead so far winds up dead!"

Treble Jones was a well-known pimp in St. Louis. He dealt in girls and drugs, but the cops went easy on him because he was a bottomless pit of information. When I had spoken with him the day before, he informed me that he "had some pretty bad shit on Cravens." He didn't know anything about his murder, specifically, but information that he thought would be relevant to the case. He didn't want to give it up over the phone, so a staged arrest was planned for the following morning. He could never just walk into the police station. He had a reputation to uphold. So, cops picked him up in fake arrests, just to get him to the station for statements, tips, and intel.

But now, Treble Jones was dead, and all of that knowledge died with him. I rubbed my eyes. "Shit."

To date, the only evidence we had, still, was the broken dog tag which no one could place. Bradley's family and friends had no idea who it belonged to.

I had interviewed dozens of people, reviewed hundreds of hours of different surveillance tapes, and studied the ballistics of dozens of guns confiscated by police, taken from Bradley's family and friends.

Nothing.

It was Friday, and I was looking forward to a weekend of resting. I needed it, especially after this blow. I left the office that morning and headed over to Treble's apartment. I asked neighbors and a few of his contacts if they knew anything about his information on Bradley.

Nothing.

I was back at the office by late that afternoon. I was making a chart that was quickly becoming a web of confusing information, resources, and contacts. From the street thug and homeless to high society and politicians, they all dealt with Cravens. But, none of them were talking.

I finally figured something out, but kept it to myself for the time being. They were...protecting him. Guarding his legacy. All of it made everyone look even more suspicious, especially after the only man who came forward with damning information about the victim was discovered dead. What would be the point of protecting a dead man? What had he promised them? What had he threatened them with? What were they afraid of?

All questions. No answers. And, nobody was breathing a word.

I finally buried my face in my hands and took a deep breath. My phone chirped loudly and I jumped, hitting my knee on the side of my desk. "Crap!" I screamed.

As I rubbed my knee, I reached over and grabbed my phone. I thought it would be the same text I got every night announcing what we are eating for dinner or asking what I planned to cook. But, this time it was different.

Rhett: Have dinner with me.

I always have dinner with you.

Rhett: Yeah, but tonight, let me do the driving and let's let someone else do the cooking.

A date. He wanted to go out on a date. My heart started thudding wildly and my mouth instantly went dry. My breathing accelerated and my hands trembled. Before I could reply, another message popped up.

Rhett: Stop freaking out. Yes, it's a date. Yes, it's going to be fun and amazing. How could it not be? I'll be there.

I couldn't help but chuckle. He acted so cocky and arrogant, but it was all for show. He was sincere and considerate and pretty...perfect. Before I could think too much about it, I answered him.

I'd love to.

His next message consisted of an entire screen of smiley-face emoticons. I wasn't sure where he intended on taking me, but I needed to know what to wear.

How should I dress?

Rhett: You remember what you wore the night you brought me lasagna?

Yes.

Rhett: Wear that.

Casual. This was good. Casual was good. Fancy would have frightened me, but this was more our speed. It would be like a regular night—the two of us, but in public. On a date.

Rhonda walked into my office, already speaking. "Here is that file you asked—"

I cut her off. "He asked me out on a date." I know I looked like a deer in the headlights. Her smile was so big, I think I heard her face crack.

"Really?" I nodded. "Yes!" she squealed and pumped her fist in the air. "I knew it! I called this one! I get to use a coupon tonight! Thank you, Evie!"

I was so confused. "Coupon?"

"Jake and I have these sexual favor coupons that I bought. We have running bets. We have two going right now, and you were one of them. Whoever wins the bet gets to use a coupon."

"You bet on my going on a date with Rhett for a sexual favor?"

"Yes."

"You are so weird."

***

I was nervous and on the verge of being petrified. I had not been on a first date in years. Rhett had sent me a message that told me to be ready at seven. It was a quarter 'til and I was not even close to being ready, physically or emotionally. But, I owed this to him. I owed him more than this, if I were honest with myself.

In little ways and monumental ways, he was helping me. For moments at a time, I felt like I was living. The hours I spent with him were hours in which I was not allowed to wallow in sorrow.

My hair, which was constantly dictated by humidity, looked like a rat's nest. My makeup looked terrible. My shirt, the shirt Rhett had requested that I wear, felt too small. My boobs looked huge, and the knee of my capri's had caught on something and ripped along the entire length of my knee. This just was not meant to be.

I was almost in tears when he knocked on the door a few minutes before he said he would be there. He was smiling when I opened the door, but at the sight of my face, his smile fell.

"What's wrong?" he asked, looking like a freaking super model. His long-sleeve black and gray shirt was well fitted and hugged his chest, and stomach; the long sleeves hid the tattoos that covered his arms. His jeans hung low on his hips and fit him perfectly, and his boots just accented the tattered hems. He looked deliciously perfect while I stood there looking like a train wreck.

My breath hitched when I started speaking. "I look terrible and nothing is working out. My hair looks like doodoo, my shirt is too little, and I ripped my pants." I paused. "I can't go. I'm sorry." I turned around and left him standing in the doorway.

He followed after me, closing the door behind him. "The hell you can't go." He spoke with absolute authority, letting me know that he was leaving me with no option. "You're going, Evie."

I stomped to my bathroom and he continued to follow me. I wiped away a tear before it could escape, but it didn't escape his attention. He grabbed me by the shoulders and turned me around, hooking a finger under my chin.

His sky blue eyes bore into mine. His dark hair he had recently gotten cut stood up on the ends, creating the most handsomely disheveled look. His facial hair was neatly trimmed, his beard being just a tad longer than what he normally kept it.

He spoke softly as he stared at me. "You look gorgeous. Your hair is everywhere and sexy. Your pants look fine and that rip looks completely intentional," he paused looking down at my shirt that felt like it was shoving my lady lumps together, "and, God...this shirt makes me so...happy," he finished with a rascally grin.

I threw my hands in the air and walked around him. "I'm changing," I insisted. I grabbed a sundress from my closet before

Rhett rushed over to me, yanking it from my hands.

He smiled. "No. You're not." He looked at the dress he held in his hand. When I looked at it, I noticed I grabbed the wrong one. The one he held was a short, chiffon, three-quarter sleeve vintage summer dress. He held it out and took another look at it.

He grinned. "On second thought," he tossed the dress at me, "wear this." He walked past me to leave the room. "And don't you dare touch your hair." With that he closed the door behind him.

I'm not one to compliment myself or think much of myself, but I had to admit: I looked beautiful. I am not a size two, or four, or six, or eight. My five foot six inch frame is made up by muscular extremities. I wasn't long and willowy, but I didn't need to be in this dress that brushed back and forth at my knees. After putting on a pair of leather sandals, I exited the room.

Rhett was sitting on my couch looking at his phone. "Okay. I'm ready," I announced quietly, brushing past him to look for my purse. I found my purse and keys and was standing at the door when I turned around to see him still sitting on the couch staring at me.

"Holy shit," I heard him whisper. He continued to sit as his eyes roamed up and down my body. I was self-conscious under his scrutiny, so I busied my hands by pulling my long hair over my shoulder and looked away from him. "Evie…"

I wasn't sure why he said my name, but I did not answer him. I didn't even look at him. I was too scared of what I might see, of what I might feel. I tried to get him moving.

"Are you coming?" I was trying to hide my irritation, but I get that way when I'm nervous.

He smiled unabashedly. "I think I just did."

Even though I fought it, I laughed. "You're disgusting."

He stood, laughing, brushing his hands down his pants. He approached me and I watch him walk up to me slowly. When he reached me, he simply looked down at me and smiled, reaching up to tuck my hair behind my ear.

"If I go to jail tonight, at least I can defend myself," he smirked.

I chuckled, "Why would you go to jail?" I asked, genuinely confused.

" 'Cause if anybody looks at you tonight, that's exactly where I'm gonna end up." He leaned forward to kiss me on the forehead, then he reached down and grabbed my hand. "Let's go, baby."

We made our way down the stairs while he held my sweaty hand. I was so embarrassed, but relieved when he finally released my wet fingers.

While we walked to the parking lot, he informed me that he *was* driving. He warned me, "My truck is pretty ridiculous, if I do say so, myself. You'll need a boost."

"Surely I can—" I stopped talking when I saw what he was talking about. His lifted black truck sat in the back of the parking lot, nearly towering over all the other cars. I glared at him. "My dress?" I slapped him on the arm. "You planned this!"

He smiled and held his hands out in mock surrender. "I swear, I didn't even think about that! I tried to get you to wear pants or slacks or capris, or whatever you girls call short pants these days, remember?" He always drove a two-door sports car, so I never would've expected this.

I rolled my eyes as he opened the door. Not allowing him the pleasure, I reached up to grab the handle. I felt his hands reach around my waist. I turned around and glared at him. "Back the hell up!" I squealed, but couldn't keep the smile off of my face. He backed up and I pulled myself up. I sat down and before he shut the door, he winked and grinned.

"Lacy boyshorts?"

My face flushed red with embarrassment. "You're such a jerk."

He laughed and climbed in, shutting the door. As soon as he did, his scent washed over me. He smelled clean and his cologne was light and masculine. I was barely listening to his small talk. I could hear my heartbeat in my ears, so I was struggling to hear what he was saying. I was still nervous and trying my best to convince myself to just relax and have a good time.

Before he turned on the truck, he buckled his seatbelt and checked his mirror. The boyish charm he possessed that caused him to play by the laws of driving, which no American actually practices after the driving instructor exits the test vehicle, made me double over with laughter.

He looked at me, his eyebrows raised in question. "What?"

"You're such a cheeseball!"

"What?"

I pointed at him and laughed. "You gonna drive at ten and two next?"

He grinned. "I will now."

And…he did. All the way to the restaurant, he held his hands on either side of the steering wheel. I asked several times where we were going, but he refused to tell me. When we reached the restaurant, he lifted me in gentlemanly fashion from the seat and gingerly set me on the ground. He didn't linger. He grabbed my hand and led me inside. His hand was large and strong and held my hand tightly.

While we were led to our table, he placed his hand on the small of my back and guided me. Since we had met, he had never touched me this much—this constantly. Sometimes he would pat me on the back or touch my arm or my side to cue to scoot over, but his touches were never caresses or touches of affection like all of these touches had felt.

It frightened me because I liked it. It terrified me because I felt willing to let someone in after closing everyone out for so long. I only needed my mind to tell my heart that I was ready.

Rhett was wonderful, a dream. He did not scare me or use me. And, I knew, in my heart, that he would never leave me on purpose.

We were led outside to a patio, where overhead, strings of lights dipped low and lit the entire scene with a warm glow. It was beautiful and flawless.

When he looked at me and smiled warmly, tears pricked the backs of my eyes. I pulled my top lip down and held it with my teeth to try and fight the tears. I reached across the table and took his hand.

"Rhett, this is beautiful."

He just winked at me, lifted my hand and toyed with my fingers.

"I'm glad I changed," I teased.

He grinned. "Me too." He paused and his smiled faded. "You are absolutely breathtaking. So breathtaking, it hurts." He leaned back and rubbed his chest. "Right here."

I just shook my head and smiled, looking away from his hypnotizing blues. We ate in relative peace, engaging in light and casual conversation. We laughed like crazy and drank a glass of wine. We looked around us and everyone was staring at us, but not in aggravation. They seemed intrigued with watching us enjoy each other. It was...nice. And, it gave me hope.

I deserved these smiles. I had suffered enough. I deserved to live.

As I sat and stared at Rhett, unaware of my gaze, he was looking to his right and started to rise. When I looked in the direction he stared, a pretty and heavily pregnant woman approached him quickly, followed by a nice-looking man whose face was stretched with a wide smile. The woman threw her arms around Rhett's neck, then the man shook Rhett's hand firmly.

He gestured toward me and smiled. "This is Evie, my...uh..." he paused before finishing, "date."

I breathed a sigh of relief. I feared he would introduce me as his neighbor. That would have stung a bit. But, he didn't. He confessed to one of his greatest discomforts, and it made my heart swell with pride and desire for him.

"Evie, this is my sister Macy and her husband, Nick."

I stood and greeted them both. They both expressed their joy in meeting me. Maybe it was just the fact that Rhett was seen with me that had them ecstatic.

Macy turned to Rhett and mouthed, "She's gorgeous!"

He nodded and smirked. "I know."

They were on their way out and we had finished our meal, so Rhett invited them to join us for a few minutes. While Nick and Rhett chatted lively, Macy peppered me with questions.

She looked like a much shorter, more feminine version of Rhett.

She reached over and patted my hand. "So, where did you guys meet?"

My answers were short, as I could barely squeeze a word in edgewise. "I...uh...live next door to Rhett."

"That's good." Her eyes welled up. "Sorry." She waved her hand in front of her face. "Hormones." She shook her head. "I'm glad. I'm glad you guys are out. It's beautiful out here. He did well."

"He did."

She asked me all types of questions, which I answered without restraint. She told me about her husband, her kids, childhood stories about Rhett, which he adamantly denied, then scolded her brother for not seeing their parents over the past holidays.

She was sweet and asked for my phone number, without hesitation, completely ignoring Rhett's plea to leave me alone.

When we departed, I realized that we had talked for over an hour, and Nick and Macy bid me farewell with tight embraces. One thing was certain. Macy loved her brother. There was no denying that.

On our way back home, Rhett reached over and took my hand and stroked my fingers.

When he spoke, I jumped, "My sister likes you."

"Your sister *loves* you."

"I know."

"She's worried about you."

"I know."

That's all we said until he walked me to my door. He stood, facing me, holding on to both of my hands. He stared down at me and spoke, "I had so much fun tonight."

I grinned. "I did too."

"You looked so beautiful tonight," he whispered.

"So did you," I whispered back.

His gaze flashed from my lips to my eyes in rapid secession. There was no smile on his face. His sky blue eyes were mixed with hope, longing, confusion and fear. I can only imagine that my eyes were filled with the same because my heart was pounding to an uncertain rhythm.

He brought his hands up and cupped my cheeks. His breathing accelerated and his fingers trembled slightly. His breath was warm against my face when he spoke.

"Evie..." he panted faintly. "I think I might kiss you."

The cadence of our breathing was intoxicating. "I think I might want you to."

He closed his eyes. "It's probably gonna be bad."

I smiled and shook my head, bringing my hand to the back of his neck and pulling his face to mine. "With those lips, you couldn't make it bad if you tried."

I watched him close his eyes fully as I pulled his mouth to mine as he chuckled softly. His mouth was soft and warm, undemanding. He simply nuzzled my lips with his until I opened my mouth slightly. He moved one hand to my side and the other cupped the back of my head, pulling me more firmly to him.

He teased my lips with his tongue until I opened fully and touched my tongue with his. His tongue tasted like wine and became more demanding as it tangled with mine. I was breathing heavily and I couldn't seem to get enough. I lowered both of my hands to his shirt and tugged him closer. He moved his lips over mine, sipping from my mouth like I was the oxygen he needed to live.

His beard was soft against my face as I moved my hands up to run my fingers through it and hold his face to mine. He pulled away slightly and looked down at me.

He panted, blowing his sweet breath against my face, and his eyes were glassy. He pressed his forehead to mine and we stood there in silence for several moments. His hands roamed up and down my sides and I relished in the sensation.

It had been so long since I'd felt like this. To be honest, I wasn't really sure if I had ever felt like this. The desire. The want. The need. I wanted him more than I'd ever wanted anyone. In my heart I felt like I was slowly replacing Dash, and I struggled with the guilt of it. I didn't say a word and Rhett hadn't seen my face, but he recognized my internal battle without even looking in my eyes.

"Don't think about him, Evie." I looked up at him and he looked wounded and hurt. "Please." He continued to stare at me. "Give this to me. Don't let him take this away from me."

In that moment, I realized something.

I loved Rhett.

I loved this man who would compete with the memory of a dead man just to steal away this moment with me. I loved the man that made me laugh for the first time in forever, who made me smile on a daily basis. I loved the man who watched over me during the night before he ever really knew me, who insisted that I eat with him every night. I loved the man that made fun of my air freshener and practically picked out my clothes for our first date. I loved his arguments and his knowledge. I loved his smart mouth and his words of benevolence. I loved the man who saw fit to strip down emotionally in front of me, baring his soul to me. I loved the man whose body served as a testimony of the love for his family. I loved the man whose wife and daughter were stolen from him.

I loved his wife and his little girl for letting me have him.

I was in love with him.

I said the only words that I could gather, "Never. This belongs to *you*."

CHAPTER SIXTEEN

RHETT

Evie's mouth was my lips' new favorite place. I had not kissed anyone in over five years, and I couldn't have picked a more perfect mouth to start with. She looked incredible, she smelled divine, and I adored the way she gave me shit. I cherished the innocence in her boldness and the sexiness in her insecurity. She had absolutely no idea how beautiful she was or how much I wanted her.

As much as I wanted to press myself against her and hold her close, I was too afraid that I would jab her in the stomach with the part of myself that wanted to have her in every position physically possible.

If I pushed, I could have her. Despite how I felt, I didn't know if I wanted to go that far with her. Sex is a big deal for me. It always has been. I didn't want to give her a piece of myself that I could never get back, and I don't just mean my man-juice.

Without even being with her in that fashion, when she walked away from me, she would carry away several pieces of my broken heart. Pieces that she had so lovingly restored, broken again with her departure. And, eventually, she would leave me. She was not staying here. She would be going home, and even if she wasn't, when she found out what I was, she would hate me.

I had done the unthinkable. I broke my own rules. Not only did I touch her, I had kissed her and I wanted more. Staring into her hazel eyes, I knew.

For the third time in my life, I had fallen in love. My daughter, first. Sadly, the fall came later for my wife, but I fell eventually. They taught me how to love, and Evie was teaching me that I could love again. I didn't deserve her goodness. I didn't even deserve her at her worst on a shitty day.

We kissed for long minutes outside of her door. When her lips touched mine, I felt at home. I felt like she belonged to me. When she brought her mouth back to mine, I kissed her with passion and possessiveness. I kissed her like I owned her, and she kissed me back just the same. She may have not known it, but she owned me already.

I tore my mouth from hers and our breathing was rapid and unsteady. She held onto my face when I wrapped my arms around her. She pushed her hands through my hair much like she did the night I broke down in front of her. She held onto me just as tightly as I clung to her.

Her eyes remained closed as she spoke, "You want to come inside?"

Pressing my forehead to hers, I refused to give in to what my heart was screaming, along with every other part of me. For once, since the night I met Evie, I would do the right thing. "I better not."

She pulled back and smiled, her watery eyes searching mine. "How do you do that?"

"What?"

"Reject me and make me feel so special at the same time."

"Trust me. It's not rejection. And, you are special. You're nothing short of amazing. I just don't want either of us to do something we will regret or make decisions in the heat of the moment. Going in there, feeling the way I feel, you know what will happen. And, that's a big deal for me. I know we've never talked about it, but that is not something I trivialize. It happened once and it turned into the heartache of a lifetime for me. After you leave, where does that leave me? I'll be alone again. If I go in there with you, I won't come out the same."

Tears streamed down her cheeks. "But I want you."

I cupped both of her cheeks and wiped her tears away with my thumbs. "God, Evie, I want you so much, I can't stand it. I've wanted you since the moment I laid eyes on you. I haven't felt this way about anyone. Ever. You are so perfect for me. You were made just for me. If this ended tonight and I never saw you again, there still would be no doubt that you were sent to me, even if for a short time, by a God I almost stopped believing in. You have brought so much into my life. So much I've lost. So much I never had. You've renewed my faith and hope and joy. I smile all the time now." I felt my eyes begin to burn. "You can't imagine how much that means to me. I smile and laugh without contrition. Five years of living in hate and confusion stopped the day you slammed into my front door. Right now, you're everything to me. And, I want you. I'm just…I'm not ready. And, not because I harbor any guilt or because I don't desire you." I took a deep breath. "If we ever go that far, I want it to be *me* you're thinking about. I want it to be *me* you're seeing and feeling inside of you. You will never be in competition with Arianna's memory. But, can you say the same about me and Dash? You loved him, Evie. So much. I'm not certain I can contend with that."

Her bottom lip quivered and it took everything I had not to lean down and pull it in between my lips and still it with my kisses. She spoke so softly that I barely heard her.

"What if I *do* love you?"

Not possible. She could never love me. To love me, she'd have to love all of me, and she didn't even *know* all of me. If she did, she'd never love me. So, I did the only thing I knew to do. I would plant the seed of doubt in her mind and in her heart, as much as it killed me to do so.

"And, what if you don't?"

She let out a hard sob and buried her face in my chest.

"And besides, what kind of slut would I be if I slept with you on our first date?" I asked her.

Amidst her sobs, she started laughing. "You'd be a big slut. A big, nasty, cheap, disgusting slut," she hiccupped around her laughs.

My chest vibrated with laughter and I tugged her close.

"See? I just proved that I am an upstanding, noble, and respectable gentleman."

She giggled and looked up at me. "Will you kiss me goodnight?"

I took her face in my hands. "Yes, my lady. But kisses are all you'll get from me," I teased before pulling her mouth to mine and kissing her like both of our lives depended on it.

***

After sleeping like a baby following my first make-out session with Evie, I woke to banging on my door. I'm certain my hair was everywhere and I slept so well, I frankly didn't give a damn. I answered the door, smiling like a jackass at whoever decided to disturb my slumber. My brother, Luke, smiled at me in return.

"Morning, brother," he said as he stepped in my apartment and gave me a hug. I hadn't seen him in almost a year. He stopped in whenever a trip he was required to take brought him near me. He and I talked on the phone at least once a week and we texted every day. He's two years older than me and has always been my refuge. Other than Evie, he is the only person this side of the pond who has seen me cry—like ugly cry. He is a Navy SEAL and the strongest man I know.

Luke is the only person outside of *The Guardians* who knows what I do. I couldn't carry that burden alone, and I trust him with my life. I told him about being approached by *The Queen* and what she had asked of me. To my surprise, he encouraged me to do it and told me that revenge was 'sweeter than fuck.' I already knew how sweet it could be because I had gotten a little taste of it on my own before *The* Queen found me.

I invited him in and he pulled me into another bear hug.

"I missed you," he said sincerely.

I laughed. "I missed you, too." I gestured for him to have a seat. "What brings you here?"

"Ah. I was close, so I took a small detour to see you." He grinned and I knew what was about to come tumbling out. "Macy called me."

Told ya. "Did she?" I said, scratching my head. I always knew what Luke was going to say before he even said it. We were so much alike, although we were almost physical opposites. We were about the same height and build, but his blonde hair and warm brown eyes always made me a bit jealous. He always looked so kind and his demeanor matched that. His hope for humanity and love for others is what has always driven him. I've always admired him for that.

He grinned. "She said you went out with someone the other night." I nodded. "Nick said she's pretty damn hot."

"That should piss me off, but I can't argue with him. She's gorgeous."

"How long have you known her?"

"A few months."

"You haven't slept with her, I suppose."

I shook my head. "Nope. Don't plan on it, either."

His eyes went wide. "What?"

"Don't look so surprised. You know me. You know I'm not a manwhore, and she is a good girl. I can't sleep with her, and you know why. If we went there, it would destroy her, man. It would probably destroy me too," I finished softly.

He smiled sadly. "You love her, don't you?"

I brushed my fingers through my beard and pinched my chin, letting out a hard breath, willing away the burning in the backs of my eyes. "So much. I love her so damn much."

He leaned over and patted my leg. "You could always leave the group. They would understand. You know they would. They'd be happy for you to move on."

"And leave Arianna and Haven without justice? I could never do that."

"They would still see it through. Your comrades would make

sure they are avenged. They love you. They'd do it for you. You could move on. Live your life with Evie. Isn't that her name?"

I nodded. He almost made sense and for a split second, it sounded so tempting. I knew he was right. My entire group would get even with those who killed my family. The man who was newly in love was tempted by that. But, the father and husband in me would never let it happen.

I told him all about Evie. Why she was here. How she got here. I told him of the tragedy that made her who she was. I told him the reasons I loved her. I told him that I kissed her like a maniac the day before. I talked for what seemed like forever while he listened, smiling, laughing, ooing and awing whenever necessary. Finally, I turned the conversation back to him.

"How are the boys?"

"They're great, growing like weeds. Jace is in the third grade this year. Brady is in first. Ben is in kindergarten. Jace and Brady are doing well and love school. Ben freaking hates it."

"How's Marlow?" This was a touchy subject for Luke. Ex-wives always are. She was not Luke's wife anymore, but she was still the mother of my nephews. When they met, I was so jealous of Luke. Marlow was so in love with him, and he was so in love with her. When I married Arianna with only obligation in my heart, I felt like I had missed out on what they had. But, over the last few years, they had grown apart, and he still loved her although she fell in love with someone else.

He looked away from me. "Still beautiful. Still perfect. Still the love of my life. And, it still kills me to see the kids get out of my car to get in hers, and drive away from me." When he looked back at me, I knew he was fighting tears. "Don't ever let anything or anyone you love slip through your fingers, Rhett. I know you've lived through terrible things, but in my experience there is not a feeling more painful than seeing the person you love with everything inside of you look you in the eye and tell you that they don't love you anymore." He paused. "If you love her and you know she loves you, you better take hold of that and hang onto it for dear life. Don't let go. Don't you dare let go."

I nodded, fighting my own tears. It pissed me off that I couldn't have a regular conversation anymore. It always turned sappy, sentimental, or too deep for my own comfort. But, since meeting Evie, I was coming into myself. I was finding myself again, and it required me to dig deep and allow myself to experience the emotions and feelings that I had been fighting for so long.

"I still struggle with the guilt, you know? Arianna loved my shitty drawers, and I. Did. Not. Love. Her. What kind of worthless piece of shit does that? I had no reason not to love her back. She was incredible. *Incredible*. She was nineteen when we got married. She was a stupid kid to me. I don't know why I even thought that because she was always so mature about everything. She was so grown up." I paused. "I hurt her. Every day. I remember one day, she was about eight months pregnant, and I had a really shitty day. I lost a huge case, one I had worked on for months. I came in; I was in a terrible mood, but she was ever the good wife. Always smiling. She walked up to me and started loosening my tie, just like she did every day. I remember batting her hands away and telling her to 'stop fucking touching me all the time.' And, that I didn't want to come home to her or her 'shitty meals' or her 'touchy-feely fucking fingers.' You know what she said to me?" I asked Luke. He shook his head. "Not a word. Not one fucking word. I hurt her so bad that she couldn't speak. Her beautiful eyes got all teary and her little nose turned red. She didn't speak at all, but you know what she did do?" Once again, he shook his head. "She stopped touching me. Never again did she touch me without me touching her first. And, I missed it. I missed her touching me all the time." I took a deep breath. "I did love her, Luke."

"I know you did, buddy," he whispered.

"I don't deserve to be loved again."

He smiled. "I don't think any of us truly deserve it. Loving is foolish. That's what makes it so wonderful. I'm older and wiser, of course, and I want you to listen to me. I've never told you this, because I didn't know if it mattered or if you'd want to know. After Haven was born, I went in to see Arianna while you were down at the nursery, staring in the window. I walked in and she was lying there, completely exhausted. She was crying, and I just assumed it was from the labor or just being completely worn out. When I asked what was wrong, she just shook her head. When I finally got her to look at me, all she said was, and I'll never forget this, she said, 'I think he fell in love with me today.' And, she smiled. She knew, Rhett. She knew you loved her."

I dropped my head into my palms, and my breath churned out of my chest. Tears fell with every labored breath and my hands shook like crazy. I sucked in sharp breaths, one right after the other.

"I wanted her to know. I wanted to tell her, I just...I made up my mind that I didn't want her, and it was so hard to go back. I fucked up from the very beginning. I never should have touched her. I wish I could go back to that night and leave that bar before I was head over heels in lust with her. That's how much I loved her. I loved and still love her enough to wish I could go back and walk away from her. That's how I feel now. I'm terrified." I paused. "I'm so scared of losing Evie. I would rather my heart be ripped from my chest letting her walk away from me than seeing her taped to the front seat of a fucking car, man. How do I risk that? How do I protect her? I love her too much. When all of this is over, I must let her walk away. I can't keep her." My bottom lip quivered uncontrollably. "And, I want her so much it hurts." I huffed out a humorless laugh and wiped my face with my shirt. "This was not supposed to happen. I was only supposed to get details about my kill and steer her away from the truth, making sure she didn't get close to it. That's it. I was not supposed to fall in love with her. I know when I did, though."

Luke, in all his love for romanticism asked me, "When?"

"The moment I laid eyes on her. No lie. She literally took my breath away."

"I can't wait to meet her."

"You won't. You can't. You know—" I was cut off by a soft knock on my door. And, I stood to look through the peephole.

"Oh shit."

Luke sat up straight, the smile lingering on his face fell abruptly. "What is it?"

"It's her."

His face beamed in the biggest shit-eating grin I've ever seen, and he leaped from his chair and jogged to the door. "Yes!" he shouted. He looked through the peephole. "Holy shit, man." He turned around and grinned at me. "Holy shit, brother. You lucky bastard."

"Quit. Get away from the door." I shoved him out of the way and she knocked again, clearly able to hear our scuffling behind the door. "Look at me. Can you tell I've been crying and shit?"

He shook his head. "No. You look like you just woke up."

"Okay," I said and answered the door.

There she stood with my freaking heart in her hands and her beautiful body in a long, flowing, pale pink dress. She smiled up at me, and I couldn't help but smile back. Before speaking to me, she inched up on her tiptoes and planted a sweet kiss on my lips. She lowered herself back down and my head naturally followed hers. I grabbed her cheeks and planted one more firmly on her mouth. Luke cleared his throat and she pulled away.

"Sorry," she whispered.

For good measure, I kissed her again. "Stop apologizing," I whispered back. "Come on in." She walked past me and waved at Luke. "Evie, this is my ugly brother, Luke. Luke, Evie."

Luke picked up her hand and kissed it. He's such an idiot. "I've heard so much about my brother's girl," he purred. "You are his girl, right?" Bastard. I knew what he was doing, and I shot him a wicked glare. After I just finished pouring my heart out to him, he's going to be a dick and ignore my fears and push her on me, putting me between a rock and a hard place.

Then, Evie in all her coolness, smiled and answered, "I'm your brother's friend, not sure he'd call me his girl."

Luke chuckled. "Peter in accounting is my friend, and I certainly don't let him kiss me like that."

"Well, Peter in accounting must not look like your brother."

He scrunched his face and grinned. "That would be weird. But, I'd certainly kiss him if he looked like you. Damn, we're shallow." They both laughed as I looked on in horror. This guy was going to be the death of me. "Nice to meet you, really. I've heard a lot about you."

"Nice to meet you, too." She turned to me. "I'm making breakfast if you two would like to join me. I have plenty." She smiled—God, she made me feel like I had been punched in the gut. "Pancakes, eggs, and bacon? Sound good?"

I was all for it, but I really didn't want Luke there, so I started to decline. "Sorry, but—" and that dickhead cut me off.

"We'd love to." The bastard had the nerve to wink at me. At that moment, there was another knock at the door. Luke looked at me, "What the hell? How many visitors do you get in one day?"

Without answering him, I turned and opened the door. "Adam," I greeted. That's just what I needed—another moron slobbering over what's mine.

It was in that moment I knew I had to claim her for myself. She was mine. No one else's. It was one of the most selfish decisions I had ever made. My body became heated and I stared at her until she looked at me. When she met my eyes, they flared with the same emotion they did the night before. I felt my breathing grow heavy with desire and I couldn't take my eyes off of her.

I shook my head to clear the fog when Adam started speaking. "Hey! Woohoo! Rhett. Bro. Luke said we're having breakfast next door."

Before I could say anything, Evie answered, "Yes. We are! You're welcome to come eat with us. The more the merrier!" she chimed.

I smiled at her when she looked at me again. She had changed so much. Her eyes lit up in my presence. Her entire being was shifting. In just a couple of months, her existence had shifted—from being lonely and miserable to spending every minute possible with me, seemingly carrying a torch for me. However, she had no idea how I felt about her. My feelings for her were strong, possibly stronger than her own for me.

I was happy to see Adam. I hadn't seen him since the night I spent the night at Evie's. He never stayed mad at me—a trait he shared with his twin sister. Some days, I wished that he would hate me, but more often than not, I was grateful for his friendship.

I pulled him into a hug. "It's good seeing you. I'm sorry about last time."

He pulled away. "I'm sorry, too. I shouldn't have—" he trailed off.

"No. I'm glad you did. Really glad."

Evie led us all to her apartment and cooked a grand feast. After Luke's whining that he had to get on a plane that afternoon and pancakes were too heavy on his belly, and after hearing his fear of making a dookie in public (his words, not mine), she resorted to biscuits and homemade gravy instead.

All three of us ate like we hadn't eaten in years. To be honest, I hadn't eaten a homemade breakfast since the morning Ari died. The domestic aura of it all was enchanting. I sat and watched Evie cook while Luke and Adam shot the shit. I offered to help, but she declined. So, I watched her delicious curves skate across the kitchen like she was born to cook breakfast for three single losers.

She bit down on her tongue while she measured her ingredients, and cracked the eggs against the counter with her delicate fingers, peeling them apart slowly, watching the yolk and egg white drop into the mixing bowl. The egg plopped, just like my stomach did every time she turned around to smile at me. I rubbed my lips, remembering the taste of her mouth on mine, the texture of her tongue touching mine.

Luke and Adam washed dishes voluntarily and acted like they didn't want to leave. They were drawn in by her charm and vivaciousness and mystery. She was not spirited or vibrant when I met her, but now she was. And deep down, I felt like it was all because we had each other—not because she had me eating out of the palm of her hand, but because she had me, hook, line, and sinker.

After lounging on Evie's couch for half an hour, Luke hit Adam in the leg, getting his attention. "What are your plans today?"

"I don't plan on doing anything now since my tummy is full," he said smiling, lifting his shirt to rub his stomach.

"Let's go somewhere. Let's do something. I have a few hours." Luke and Adam had been close since the night before I got married. Luke got shitfaced and Adam nursed him through his hangover. They talked often, and Adam even went and stayed with Luke right after his divorce to help him through things. He was always awesome like that. Forever the brother. Forever the friend.

I stood and walked them to the door with Evie on my heels. With hugs out of the way, I closed the door behind them. When I turned to Evie, her face was flushed and her eyes were dancing wildly across my face. As much as I wanted to make love to her right where she stood, I wouldn't do that. But, my resolve about giving her something we both needed faded away with Luke's words. I loved her. I couldn't let go. Not yet.

I reached for her and tugged her against me and devoured her mouth. She met me with absolutely no resistance as I turned us both around and pressed her against the door. She tasted like orange juice and sunshine. My mouth danced over hers and my tongue twirled with hers, tasting every bit of her sweetness. I ran my hands roughly down her sides, reaching down, lifting the hem of her dress until I touched her thighs. She whimpered and was met with my moaning the instant my hands skimmed her soft skin. My teeth nipped at her lips and she let out a hard, whining breath, begging for more. Her slim fingers reached for my shirt, and I pulled away for a split second allowing her to pull it over my head. Shaking out my tousled hair, I made my way back to her mouth. Her fingers glided across my naked chest, dipping into every crease they met.

When she started to push down my flannel pajama pants, I stilled her hands, wrenching away from her mouth, panting. "Not that. Not yet. Just…" My breath blew hard in her face. "Not yet."

She nodded and pulled my mouth back to hers. I cupped her ass and pulled her against me, letting her feel how much I wanted her. I was hard and aching. I pumped my hips against her and she breathed heavily in my mouth. She wanted me and I wanted her right back. I pressed my forehead to hers and shared her oxygen as I satisfied my body's need to press into something soft and warm. She turned her head and my face fell onto her neck where I bit it lightly then caressed it with my tongue to soothe the sting.

"Evie," I breathed against her neck.

She panted and whimpered to the tempo of my hips rocking against her. "Rhett, please," she begged.

"Evie, I can't."

"Just touch me. Only touch me, please."

I relented. My hand moved on its own and cupped her over her panties. "Fuck. You're sopping wet." I could resist the urge no longer, and scaled the top of her lace panties and my fingers met her wet, hot core. I groaned loudly and my head fell back. Liquid fucking silk.

I rubbed her gently, teasing that magical bundle of nerves before pulling her leg to rest her inner thigh against me, pushing further and pushing inside of her with my middle finger. "Shit, baby. You're a fucking vise." She moaned loudly as I pumped, never taking her eyes off of mine. I carefully pushed in a second finger and it felt like my circulation was cut off with her tightness. I curved my finger and pumped lightly, pressing firmly against that mystical spot that I was certain would send her over the edge.

Before I could set her off, she reached down into my pants, and I jerked slightly when she stroked me. "Fuck," I screeched. Yes. Screeched. It had been so long since someone touched me. She gripped me within her fingers, wet with my precum, and stroked me, meeting me with the same tempo I pumped my hips and my fingers.

I ravaged her mouth as we touched each other, needing the release. She tore her mouth from mine and exclaimed loudly as I felt her quake around my fingers. Her borderline screams pierced my ears, but I didn't care. As she rode out her orgasm with her pumping hips, I let go, coming in her hand with a yell.

I closed my eyes and rested my forehead against hers, both of us breathing loudly.

Before I could stop myself and before I thought about the repercussions, consequences, or heartbreak it would surely bring, I whispered against her lips, "You're my girl. You understand that?"

"Yes," was all she whispered back.

CHAPTER SEVENTEEN

Evie

"Tell me a secret."

Of all of the things in the world Rhett could require of me while he rested his weight against me, pressing me into the door, that's what he demanded.

As I fought the guilt and tears stung my eyes, I whispered the hardest thing I've ever said, "I've never felt like this before."

As he pumped his hips slightly, softening in my hands, he spoke quietly, "Like how?"

I squeezed my eyes closed and pressed my head against the door. "Like I've been waiting for you my whole life. Like you're everything I never knew I wanted. Like everything happened just so I could have you." I covered my face with my free hand and let my tears flow, and my breathing came in rapid pants. "Like I never thought I'd feel this way. Like I never thought I'd ever want anybody else, but I want you more than I ever wanted him. Like I'm not angry anymore. Like I feel there's more than the hurt and the sad tears. Like I want to try again. Like I want to try it with you."

I felt the little bit of tension left in his body give into his exhaustion, pressing me further into the door. He breathed against my neck. His slack body seemed relieved, like he was letting out the breath he was holding.

"Tell me a secret," I begged in return.

Without looking at me, he mumbled, "You'd run for the hills if you heard my secrets."

I expected him to laugh, or at least snicker, but he didn't. He sounded serious and his words sounded painful. He lifted his head and wiped my face with his free hand, while the other still pressed against my core.

"Please," I whimpered.

His brow pulled together and he smiled sadly. "A secret?" he asked and I nodded, answering his quiet question. "How I feel about you...scares the shit out of me."

"How do you feel about me?"

He dropped his face back down against my neck. "I think you know."

I let out a hard breath and wrapped both of my arms around him. For the first time in over two years, I felt the waters of the boisterous sea of my life calm instantly. The rain and the roaring stopped. The winds died and the clouds parted. He embraced me in return and held on to me tightly. The pure love in his encirclement crashed into my heart like waves beating against the rocks. He lifted his face and kissed me softly.

When he lifted his mouth from mine, his eyes were glistening with unshed tears. He stared at me for what seemed like forever, before saying the last thing I expected, but the only thing I wanted to hear.

"I love you, Evie." Twin tears came plummeting down his cheeks. "I can't make you any promises. Not yet. And please, please don't say it back." He shook his head. "Don't say it back."

"But I want to."

He let out a choked sob. "Don't. Please don't. I can't take it. One day, you'll know everything..." he whispered, "and you'll walk away from me regretting you ever said it back."

I didn't know what he meant. Maybe I should have asked. But I loved him so much, and in my heart, I don't think I wanted to know. I didn't want things to change between us, only deepen. Ignorance is bliss, and I was in paradise in my very own oblivion.

My ringing cell phone pulled us from our stupor. As I took the call, he leaned against my kitchen counter with his arms crossed across his chest, staring down at the floor.

When I answered, Rhonda was on the other end. "Morning glory!"

"Hey."

"Are you panting?"

I tried to cover. "No. Well, sort of. I ran to the phone." I looked back at Rhett who was still staring at the floor.

"Well, I hate to bust up your beautiful Saturday, but we have a lead. We need you to come check it out."

"*Finally.* Okay. I'll get ready and be there in an hour. Thanks."

"You're welcome!" she exclaimed, rather sarcastically and hung up the phone.

I turned to Rhett. "I have to go to work." I smiled. "We've got a lead on the Cravens case."

His face sobered, all residual sadness disappearing quickly. "What kind of lead?"

"Not sure yet, but I have to get around."

He nodded. "Okay. I'll get out of your hair." He turned and headed for the door.

"Hey," I called out to him and he faced me. "Come here." He walked toward me, never taking his eyes off of the ground. I slowly put my arms around his neck and searched for his eyes, finding them closed. "Look at me." He refused. "Look at me, please."

He let out a long, hard breath and did as I asked. His face was torn with every emotion a woman never wants to see after love for her is proclaimed. He looked sad, confused, scared. But worst of all, he looked remorseful. I reached up and took his face in my hands. His beard was soft against my fingers, and I gingerly reached up to brush his dark hair away from his eyes.

Against his request, I softly told him what I felt in the very depths of my soul. "I love you."

He squeezed his eyes closed and shook his head. "Evie, don't."

"I love you," I whispered again.

Suddenly, he reached out and embraced me, pulling me against him. He just held me while he buried his face in my hair.

"I love you so much, Evie. You think you love me, but you won't." His breathing became heavy and his arms tightened. "You won't."

"Why? Tell me why, please."

He pulled away from me. "You'll find out soon enough. I need a few days alone. Okay?"

"Rhett, please don't do this. Don't run away from me." My begging was cut off by the sound of the door closing behind him. I did not understand any of it. Why was he pulling away from me? What did I do wrong? Did I push too hard?

I was suddenly embarrassed of how shameless I had acted in his arms. I had never been that overcome with desire and want in my life. I felt my face heat and my hands start to shake. I looked down at my dress that was wrinkled, with part of the hem still tucked into my panties. I looked rumpled and I felt disgusted by my uncharacteristic brazenness. I wanted him so much, and I wanted him to make love to me against my front door.

Despite my imminent breakdown I could feel coming, I had work to do. I pushed away all of my hopes, fears, and emotions, so I could do just that. But, in my mind and in my heart, I knew that I would never be the same.

***

"So, what's the lead?" I asked Rhonda upon entering my office.

She handed me a small stack of papers that I flipped through as she spoke. "We tracked down the manufacturer of the dog tag. He gave us that, which is a blown up copy of what it looked like. He said that he remembers it well. He keeps a record of all of the tags that he makes, which is a short serial number located on the back of the tag. Fortunately, we ended up with the part with the number on it."

The picture was a little blurry and I could not read it well.

"What does it say?"

"The top line reads *The Shepherd*. The bottom line is a date. *October 28, 2009.*"

"The Shepherd? What does that mean?"

"No idea," she answered.

"Nickname?"

"Maybe?"

"Well, we find out who ordered it and that's one step closer."

She laughed. "You think I didn't check on that? Problem. The buyer paid a higher price for anonymity. That buyer didn't want anyone finding out who he or she was."

"Security tapes? Maybe we can review them and see if we can get a view of who brought the order in."

She pointed to a stack of boxes in the corner. "Those boxes over there are full of tapes taken from the security room recorded the year the tag was made."

"The year? He can't narrow it down to a date?"

She shook her head. "He doesn't keep records that specific. Just by years. He says this tag was purchased about five years ago. We must review all of the tapes, however, he said that he can't be positive as to how he got the order, be it over the phone, through the mail, or brought by a pigeon. He doesn't know. Or so he says."

This could not be happening. I get one step closer and get pushed back ten. That's how I felt. As much as I did not want to leave Rhett, I wanted to go home. I wanted to see my family. I wanted to solve this case or request to be reassigned, but even though I wanted all of that, I wanted to be with Rhett more.

As I sat, not paying attention to the tapes that I should have been studying, I started thinking about a future without Rhett. I didn't like it. He had changed my life for the better. I wanted him in it forever. I needed to talk to someone. I needed some advice.

Without thinking, I looked at Rhonda and blurted, "I'm in love with him."

She jerked, then turned to look at me. "Who? The dog tag

guy?"

"No. Rhett," I said softly.

"You shitting me?" she said loudly as a grin spread across her face. "You're not shitting!"

I shook my head. "I don't really know what that means. I've never really understood that statement. I'm serious. I love him, Rhonda."

She reached over and pulled me into a tight hug. "Oh, baby. I'm so happy for you. Did you tell him?"

"Yes. After he told me not to."

She rolled her eyes. "Ugh. Don't be one of those girls."

"What girls?"

"Please don't go pining after him and feel all sorry and shit because he doesn't feel the same way."

I felt a little offended. "But, he does. He said it first."

She was visibly, and dramatically, relieved. "Oh. Good. Well, that's good, right? You love each other. Ride off into the sunset together and leave us losers in the dust. The end."

"He told me not to say it."

"Say what?"

I shook my hands in front of me, frustrated, wondering if she was deliberately being obtuse. However, her history proved her to be clueless most of the time. "That I loved him! He told me not to say it, and I did anyway. Now, he wants a break or something." I shrugged. "I've not been with anyone in a long time. I haven't dated in years. I definitely haven't been kissed like he kisses me, and I've never jacked anyone off who had me pressed against my front door with his hand in my panties," I said in a rush. "Oh shit." I covered my mouth. "I didn't mean to say that."

"What. The. Hell? You've been holding out on me!"

I shook my head frantically. "I haven't! We kissed last night and the last part happened this morning…right before you called."

"I knew you were panting, you liar!" she said, laughing. "So, wait, wait, wait. Did *I love you* come before or after the uh…mutual orgasms?" she finished, sounding like a psychiatrist.

"After."

"And he still wanted a break?" I nodded. "You were that bad, huh?" I never resorted to violence, but I reached over and punched her in the arm. She laughed. "You hit like a girl with noodle arms. Wait. Is that the hand you used to uh...pleasure Mr. Trimble, because that would explain the weakness?"

I stood up to walk away from her. I really needed a friend, not someone who would ridicule me. But, she grabbed my arm.

"I'm kidding, sweetheart. Come here." My bipolar friend turned serious. "He's probably just scared."

"Of what? I love him. What's there to be afraid of?"

She pulled me down to sit in her lap and pushed my hair off of my shoulder so that it rested against my back. "Think about it. And, I'll just say this. I think he loved you from the very beginning. The day after you showed up when I was at your apartment? I've known him for years, and he's never looked at anyone the way he looked at you." She paused. "Of all people, you should understand the most. He wants you so much, but he's afraid of losing you. His last wife was murdered, for Pete's sake. I'm sure all he's thinking is what if something like that happened to you. He'd die of a broken heart. It would kill him, Evie."

"But I'm willing to take the risk."

She smiled sadly at me. I felt all of the pity radiating from her fingertips as she played with my hair. I would lose love again. Once again, someone may choose to leave me. I wasn't sure what to do or how to feel.

"Then don't back down. Don't let him push you away," she said softly. "You get up in his business and don't leave." I nodded. "So, out of curiosity," she began. I knew where this was going and I wanted to answer her, as juvenile as that sounds. It had been years since I had talked physical relationships with a friend, and I missed that opportunity to share them. I just missed having friends, period. "Is he uh...good with his hands?"

I giggled. "So good."

"And his uh…" she trailed off. I bit my lip, smiling and looked at her. "He's big, isn't he?" I nodded in response. She threw her entire body back against her chair and her entire body went slack. "You lucky bitch," she sighed.

***

The day wasn't entirely a bust. At least we found out what was on the dog tag, and I was able to squeeze in a therapy session. When I pulled back up to my apartment after having dinner with Rhonda, I sat in my car for a few minutes. I wasn't sure what I wanted to do. I wanted to knock on his door and demand he let me in, but I didn't want to scare him away.

As I sat there staring into the streetlamp lit night, my phone chimed with a message.

Rhett: I won't be home for a few days.

Okay? I was typing out a simple and acknowledging reply when it went off again.

Rhett: I'm sorry about earlier. I'm not sure what to do or how to handle this, so I just need to get away. I'm sorry.

Okay. I understand. I apologize if I did something wrong.

Rhett: You did nothing wrong, baby.

Okay then. I love you.

Rhett: Please don't give up on me.

I tossed my phone into my purse and pressed my forehead against the steering wheel. I was flooded with a rush of emotions. I could still taste his lips when I licked mine and I closed my eyes to recall the feeling of his soft lips moving over mine, with his beard tickling my face.

He appeared so raw and rough around the edges with the tattoos and the attitude that fed his reputation. He was not that person around me at all. When he approached me, he seemed to remove the mask and let me see the real man.

My mind drifted and I pictured him with his wife, so young and beautiful. I did not doubt his love for her, and I knew that if she were still alive, they would still be together. He wouldn't be the man that he became. He would not be angry or bitter. He would be happy.

There was a picture on his fridge of the three of them. All of them were looking at the camera, grinning. He had his arm around Arianna and had her pulled up against him, while he held Haven in the other. He looked so different. He was a little more slender, clean-shaven, and totally in love—in love with his entire family.

He didn't love me like that. It was almost like he loved me and he hated himself for it—angry that he allowed himself to love again.

Love made him vulnerable, and that was a feeling he had not permitted himself to feel in years. He had his world ripped away from him, and he was afraid that it may happen again. I understood that. I knew now why he was scared, but so was I.

I broke down in tears when I remembered that Dash nor Noah had crossed my mind at all that day. Without fail, I thought about them every hour of the day. I hadn't stopped to think about them and I was overcome with guilt. Maybe Rhett was right. Maybe we needed to take a step back. I was slowly letting them go. I was trying with everything inside of me to grab hold of Rhett, but he kept slipping through my fingers. He didn't want to be held on to.

I was clearing my face of mascara rivers when my phone chimed again. I slowly picked it up and opened the message.

Rhett: I love you too, baby. I really, really do. I can't even explain the jubilation (yes, I did use that word) I felt in my heart when you told me this morning. These past few months with you have been absolutely incredible. The moment I saw you, I felt like you had cracked open my chest, reached in, and started pumping my cold, dead heart with your spindly and delicate fingers. I was a man lost and driven by hate and vengeance. But, when I look at you and see your beautiful smile, or hear your sweet voice interrupting my favorite movies, or see you fit into my life like you were supposed to be there all along, I can't even remember the hatred. I forget about the retribution. I don't know myself if I don't hate. I don't know this man who loves again. There are so many things that you don't know, some things I'll never tell you...I think. To truly love me, you must know every gory detail about me, and if you hear them, I fear you'll no longer find your heart capable of loving me. But, I'll leave that up to you to decide. I'm not pushing you away and I'm not running away. I just need to step back and see if I still recognize me. If I move on, I don't want it to be downhill, and I don't want to drag you with me if that's what's happening. I love you more than you'll ever know. I never wanted to fall in love again, just so you know. But, no one ever asked me what I wanted. But now that I have you, I can't stand the thought of losing you. You're everything to me. And, I'm sorry if this is the longest text you've ever received in any year of our Lord, A.B. (After Bag phones). I love you.

My hands trembled as I finished reading, and despite my recovery from my waterworks, they started again. I could not imagine anything about Rhett that would frighten me away. I knew that he had served overseas and I have heard stories and witnessed the heartbreak and loss that comes with a loved one suffering with doing what was required of them. I wasn't ignorant. I was aware that he had probably done some things in his past that frightened him or were just to be kept secret.

But, I loved him. Unconditionally.

When I gathered the energy to climb the stairs, I found Luke sitting on the floor, propped up against my door.

"Hey."

He looked up at me surprised and smiled. "Hi." He was handsome, boy next door type. He had kind eyes and a comforting air about him.

"Rhett's not here," I said.

"I know. I was waiting for you."

I pointed at my chest. "Me?"

He chuckled. "Yes ma'am. Can we go inside and talk?" I agreed. He didn't frighten me in the least bit. I trusted him, but I dreaded and feared the reasons that he was here. It was certainly about Rhett, and I had an overwhelming feeling that it wasn't good.

"Want something to drink?"

"Sure. Just anything will be fine."

After retrieving him something to quench his thirst, I sat down across from him. I had stripped off my blazer and tried to get as comfortable as possible. "I see you missed your flight. So, what brings you here?"

He didn't waste any time. "Are you in love with my brother?"

I felt my eyes well up and I bit my bottom lip, nodding. "Yes."

He smiled and sighed. "I thought so."

"Have you talked to him? He's okay?"

"He's fine. I talked to him about an hour ago. He said he was getting out of here for a few days. I asked him if it had anything to do with you. He said yes. But, that's all he said. You two were kind of made for each other, don't you think?"

I nodded. "We've both been through the worst that anyone could ever endure as parents...and spouses. I don't know if we were made for each other, or if we were just made to find each other. He's made me so happy, Luke. I never thought I'd feel alive again."

He laughed. "You two sounded pretty alive after we left this morning." I gasped and covered my face in horror, feeling the red creep over my entire body. "Don't be embarrassed! Adam and I were standing outside the door fist pumping. Hearing you was pretty hot, but when we heard him, it got weird and we shot down the stairs pretty quick." We laughed together and allowed the laughter to die before he continued, "Rhett...I've never seen anyone change more times in their life until him. Everyone seems to hold on to at least a little piece of that personality they had as a kid. But, Rhett...he just didn't. Growing up he was fun, then when he went into the military, he got all serious and shit. Then, when he decided to marry Arianna, he was just pissed at the world. I felt sorry for her. She was so sweet and he was just an asshole. He was so mad at everything and everyone. I called him out on being an asshole just before the baby was born, and he didn't talk to me for a while. When I surprised him with a visit after Haven was born, he was so...happy. Finally. He loved being a dad. He was still a shit husband most of the time, but he didn't seem like such an asshole. Then, after they died, he became…cold." He paused and looked away from me, hiding his misty eyes. "This morning, when I saw him, he was grinning—for what seemed like no reason at all. Then, *the reason* knocked on his door. He loves you and he needs you tonight."

"But I don't know where—"

"He's at a loft he owns downtown." He handed me a slip of paper. "Here's the address." I took it without thinking twice.

"What if he kicks me out?"

He smiled. "Trust me. He won't."

"He doesn't know I'm coming?"

He made his way to the door with me on his heels. "Not a clue." He turned and embraced me tightly. "Please love him no matter what—without condition."

"I will."

"No matter what," he repeated.

"I will love him no matter what."

***

When I found the old warehouse shortly before midnight, I was terrified. My hands were trembling and my whole being was uneasy. The building looked rundown and nearly condemned, and there was not a soul around, and hadn't been for blocks. I almost thought I was in the wrong place until I spotted his truck parked inside of the building that looked to be an old garage. There were lights beaming through the window above me. I sat and stared into it. It was like a beacon that was pulling me toward safety, guiding me from the choppy waters of sickness of the heart.

I made my way inside, trying to be as stealthy as possible. I was shocked by my success because I was normally like a bull in a china cabinet. I looked around the dark and dingy space that looked completely abandoned. I almost called out to him when I spotted the spiral staircase leading up to a catwalk. Naturally, that was the way up, so I started to climb slowly, more so to allow me time to think than just being dramatic and horror-movie-slow.

I wasn't sure what I was going to do or what I was going to say. Beg for him to keep me? Stare at him like an idiot until he told me to piss off? I felt like I was making a huge mistake and I turned around twice before turning back.

When I reached the door, I counted to thirty before I knocked. I jerked when he opened the door, wearing a black pair of boxer briefs, aiming his gun at my face.

The look in his eyes scared me, not to mention the gun and the horrendous noise the door made that already had me on edge.

I was panting like a maniac. All I said was, "I'm sorry. I shouldn't have come here." And I turned around to run away as fast as I could. But, I didn't get two steps before he grabbed my wrist and yanked my body against his and slammed his mouth into mine.

When he began moving his mouth against mine, I felt at home. I knew that in his arms was exactly where I belonged.

CHAPTER EIGHTEEN

RHETT

The last thing that I expected was the only thing in the world I wanted. Evie—standing at my front door in a cute sundress with her kiss-me lips and uncertain hazel eyes. I made up my mind the instant I saw her face. Whether she wanted me that night or not, she was going to get me. More than once.

As my mouth covered hers and I sipped on her lips like an everlasting fountain, I grew hard. Extremely, painfully hard. I pulled her in and closed the door behind her, setting my gun on the table by the door. I didn't stop moving and wouldn't until I peeled her out of her flowing dress.

She whimpered and moaned into my mouth while I wrapped both arms around her and pulled her against me. I slowly moved backward until the backs of my knees hit the bed in the wide open space of my renovated loft.

We did not speak for the longest as we drank from each other, like our kisses contained the sweet nectar that brought us to life. I wrapped my hands in her long, red hair and tugged, pulling her hair until she arched against me and her face was looking straight up at me.

Her hair hung down her back and I slowly ran my hand through her loose and bouncing curls. Her hazel eyes begged for my touch, pleaded for me to turn our words of love into a manifest of carnal engaging. It would only take my submission to create the firestorm that began with just the spark in her touch and the embers in her eyes.

Without speaking, I took one step away from her and tugged her dress off of her shoulders. Her heavy breasts that I had yet to touch, rose and fell in rhythm with my own panting. I looked her in the eyes as I tugged at the straps of her bra and her breasts were unveiled to me. Absolute and utter perfection. Large and heavy and flawless. I tugged her close and kneaded one of them with my free hand, running my thumb over her nipple. I kissed her mouth and she responded with fervor—a passion like I had never experienced. My kisses moved from her mouth to her jaw, down her neck, and further downward until I reached her nipple and sucked it into my mouth. Her eager hands gripped my head and her delicate fingers tugged at my hair. I could feel my beard moving over her bare skin and it was driving me wild.

I pulled at her dress and when I realized it would not slide past her delicious and curvy hips, I unsnapped her bra, sliding it off, and tugged the dress over her head. I stepped back and there she stood. Utter fucking perfection. Her arms hung to her side; her face was ruddy and her lips were wet, swollen, and sexy as hell.

I jerked her nearly naked body to mine and heaved her up, allowing her to wrap her legs around me as I turned and lowered her onto my bed. The single lamp beside the bed provided the only light I needed to devour the amazing woman that lie in front of me—the woman with whom I was completely head-over-heels in love. Speaking of heels, although I had dreamed it and hoped it, I never thought that Evangeline Harrington would be lying on my bed wearing only lace panties and a pair of red stilettos.

I sat on my knees in the juncture of her thighs and stared for as long as I could without touching. Then, when I worked up the nerve, I brought my trembling hands to her collar bone and skimmed all the way down, over both breasts and downward until I reached the top of her panties. When she lifted her lovely hips, I took that as my cue to tug them off gingerly, pulling off her heels in the process. I lowered my body nearly on top of her to cover her in my open mouthed kisses.

As my lips traveled down her belly, she sucked in a breath and winced when I reached the marks left by her pregnancy. Her flat belly of the past had been replaced by the soft, stretched skin that she obviously hated—skin that would never be the same again.

When I opened my mouth and kissed her belly, licking her in the process, she reached down to push my face away to protect herself from my lips. Her eyes met mine, and when I grabbed her quivering hands to still them, I studied her closely.

Finally, she spoke. With teary eyes, she whispered, "Don't."

My brow furrowed. "Why not?"

"I hate them," she answered, as a tear tumbled down the side of her face.

"Why do you hate them?" I asked softly.

She whimpered. "They remind me."

"Of what? That you're a mother?" I whispered, while playing with her fingers, stroking them softly.

Her bottom lip quivered as she spoke, "I *was* a mother."

My eyes went wide and I felt my brows crawl up my forehead. "You *are* a mother, Evie." I paused and allowed it to sink in. "You know, I've always heard that a child without parents is an orphan. A wife without a husband is a widow. But, there is no word for a mother or father who have lost a child. Do you wanna know why?" I whispered.

She nodded.

The corner of my mouth pulled up, smiling at her tenderly and quietly obliging, "There's no need. You never stop being a mother. You're *still* a mother, Evie. I'm *still* a father. We loved them with everything inside of us. We wanted them, but God needed them to come home."

And with that, she wept. I climbed up her body quickly and pressed my forehead against hers. "Say it," I commanded. "Open your eyes. Look and me and say it, Evie."

"I'm a mother," she whimpered, her eyes boring into mine.

While she wrapped her arms around me, I took the opening to push down my boxer briefs, freeing my erection. I leaned forward, pressing a kiss on her cheek and softly saying in her ear, "Yes."

I knew it was not necessary to make sure she was ready for me. I knew she was. Her core glistened when I removed her panties, and I desperately wanted to taste her. But, I needed to be inside of her more. I pulled her thigh against my hip and slowly guided my erection inside of her. I eased in and she was so tight, I wasn't sure I could go any further without hurting her. She gasped and her mouth fell open while her eyes widened with pleasure and pain. She closed her eyes as she released me and her hands fumbled for purchase in the sheets.

I slowly took her hand and pressed it against my heart. It pounded into her hand as she stared up at me with glimmering eyes.

"You're shaking," she said softly.

My eyes burned so badly that I had to close them for a few seconds. She was right. I was shaking like a virgin on prom night. All I could do was breathe deeply and focus on being inside of her.

"I'm so scared," I confessed.

"Me too."

"I love you, Evangeline." I didn't even give her a chance to reciprocate the words before I reared my hips back and thrust into her without delicacy.

She cried out and I bit out a curse, fighting every urge inside of me to scream like a Banshee. With deliberateness, I pulled out slowly and pushed in forcefully over and over until her hips harmonized with mine. She wrapped her arms around me and I devoured her mouth. I reared up, pulling up her entire body, locking her legs behind me, and I sat back on my heels. I knelt on the bed with Evie's body wrapped around me. I pulled my hips back, thrusting into her as she whined and moaned and begged for more. When I pushed my hips forward, her delicious weight brought her down, seemingly impaling her with my body. I knew I wouldn't last very long. It had been so long since I had a woman, and being inside of Evie was unrivaled.

I thrust harder and her breathing accelerated and I could feel her begin to tighten. Suddenly, she tore her mouth from mine, and cried out loudly as her walls tightened around me, coaxing out my orgasm. I couldn't hold back, not after that.

I sped up and slammed into her. "Oh, fuck!" I yelled as I came inside of her, coming harder than I ever had before. She whimpered and whined, riding out her climax as I slowed my pace, drawing out my own pleasure, feeling myself slide in and out easily with the mixture of our carnal desire.

I trembled as I held our position, Evie clinging to me for dear life.

She broke the near silence in the room, occasionally pierced by our sharp intakes of breath. "I love you, Rhett." I felt her tears wet my shoulders. "I love you. No matter what. I promise. No matter what."

The asshole inside of me was going to remind her of that someday.

***

I didn't like the feeling of Evie walking away from me. But a completely naked Evie making her way to the ensuite to clean up after making love a second time, could easily become my favorite thing of all time in the history of ever. As long as she found her way back to me, I didn't care where she went.

I, on the other hand, was wiped out. It's not that I didn't want to move; I just couldn't. My entire body felt like a limp noodle. I hadn't used certain muscles in almost six years, so understandably, I couldn't find the energy to lift my head off of the pillow.

It was after two in the morning when she came strolling back to me with a shy smile on her face and her tangled hair draped over her shoulder, completely covered one of her breasts. I thought I had nothing left in me to give. I was tired, sore, but not completely emptied. Her long minutes tending to herself left me several to tend to mine. I reached under the sheet that covered me and stroked myself until I was hard again, reliving the sensation and consuming release that came with having Evie beneath me.

She pulled back the sheet and saw my condition that could easily be remedied—but not by my own efforts in my fragile state. Without speaking, she straddled me and guided my hardness into her softness. I hissed between my teeth. My tender member was sensitive and she felt even tighter and wetter than before.

She giggled. "How can you still be hard?"

I chuckled and spanned my hands along her hips and thrust up gently. I loved seeing the contrast of my dark tattoos against her milky skin. "How can you still be wet?"

"Well, I kind of rubbed one out in there."

I laughed loudly. "Yeah. I bet you did."

Our laughter died away as I watched Evie ride me like she was made to match my slow cadence. She lifted up and I brought her back down on my rising hips. It was the only part of my body that could move, in all honesty. I massaged her breasts, paying close attention to her nipples that I had worked over and over again while making love the second time. I promised myself that, next time, I would drink from her honey before I made a mess of her. We said nothing as I slowly and tenderly loved her, rocking into her. But now, she was taking what she wanted from me as I watched her slightly sweaty body move rhythmically over mine.

"If I didn't know you were a musician, you'd be giving it away right now." I smiled and mumbled.

She grinned. "And just how would you have figured that out?"

"We're in perfect common time. Four beats a measure. Listen. *One. Two. Three. Four. One. Two. Three. Four,*" I counted as she moved against me. "Four beats a measure. And, I could play this song All. Night. Long."

"You know time?" she panted.

"Of course. I played the quad drums in junior high and high

school."

"I didn't know you were a band geek, too."

I continued to rock my hips against her, speeding up. "Now you do. And no one has ever made love with more harmony than a couple of band geeks. Three four time now, baby. I'm almost there." And for the third time that night, Evie's vessel received everything I had left inside of me. I was acting so recklessly, but I'd be damned if I would ruin this moment with the *you're on the pill, aren't you* question. Frankly, although my mind was racing and second guessing everything that had just happened and was totally freaking out, my heart hoped that her answer would be... *no*. Those were the thoughts of a complete asshole who held no regard for Evie's heart. The very heart that beat against my chest was the same one I held in my hands, possessing all of the power to smash it to smithereens.

I lie there on my back with Evie draped across me. All I could smell was sex and her shampoo. I ran my fingers up and down her back until our breathing returned to normal.

"I'm starving," she groaned in my ear.

"I have some cereal."

"Do you have any with marshmallows?"

"Is there any other kind?"

She chuckled. "Not that I know of." As she climbed off of me, she looked back and smiled. "Will you toss me that afghan?"

I laughed. "That what?"

"That afghan. It's under you a little bit, but I want to wrap it around me."

I rolled over and lifted the crocheted blanket to her—the blanket my grandmother gave me for Christmas one year. It was the weirdest gift ever. Grandma must have thought I looked...cold? Well, a little piece of me looked cold, I guess, because the thing was smaller than shit. It was one of those things, you just grin and say *thanks, grandma*.

I couldn't help my laughter. "This?" I teased.

"Ah. Thanks." She wrapped it around her creamy shoulders. "Man, that's soft. What?"

"Afghan?"

She shrugged, absolutely clueless of her absolute adorableness. "What? It's an afghan."

"Okay. That may very well be, but most people *our* age call it a throw, granny."

She threw her head back, smiling and...growling. "Ugh. Not this again."

I stood up, completely unashamed of my nakedness. A long time ago, I was embarrassed and terrified of what others would think of my damaged leg. It's not completely hideous to me anymore. There is a deep, ugly hole of a scar where part of my inner thigh was missing. But, I got over that. It was Arianna who convinced me that it wasn't bad at all. She always said she loved it because that's why I was sent home—she would've never met me if I wasn't injured. It brought me to her, in a sense. After her death and even up until a few months ago, I hated my injury. If I was never injured, she may still be alive. But, I would've never met Evie. It's hard to love something you've hated for so long, and it's even harder to hate something that has brought you love twice.

I fumbled with my boxers as I continued smiling at her. "What? I'm just saying. You call burgers sandwiches. Skin is hide. Carts are buggies. Druggies don't smoke crack in your world; they smoke dope. The other day, you called that guy at the grocery store a shit-eating codger, for crying out loud. What the hell is a codger? And, now, my little blanket that my real granny gave me is an afghan?" I continued to laugh as she stood there fighting her smiles by biting on her bottom lip. I wrapped my arms around her and squeezed. "I love you. Even though you talk like my afghan-crafting grandma."

"I love you, too," she said softly, her chest, full of laughter, rumbling against mine.

"Just, please, whatever you do, when you tell Rhonda about this, please don't tell her that we did the *horizontal bop* or that I *pounded the punnani pavement*, okay?"

"Well," she drawled out. "I won't make any promises I can't

keep."

I hoped like hell that she was telling the truth. She promised to love me no matter what. I didn't fail to notice the phrase she had used twice after the first time we made love. She said the words *no matter what.*

Luke's words. *No matter what* was his refrain, his exhortation.

He sent her here. Luke and I were the only people besides the tax collector who knew this place existed. Well, the tax collector and *The Queen.* Luke believed in us. He believed in me. He believed that I deserved something good as a reward for all of the horrible shit that I'd overcome. He believed I had earned Evie and was worthy of her love. I knew it was a bullshit claim, but after Luke left that morning, I sort of believed it. That's why I didn't push her away. That's the reason I pulled her in. That's the reason I made love to her three times with no fear that I could possibly be a father again. At least if she were pregnant, she couldn't get rid of me...unless she found out who I was and what I did and sent me to prison.

She may get close, but she'd never find out. I was too good at what I did. I was too untraceable. Or so I thought. I started to believe I could walk away from the duty of *The Guardians* and retire into a quiet life with the woman who was healing me with her sweet smiles, hearty laughter, trembling fingers, and geriatric lingo.

Evie had absolutely stolen my heart—pieces of it and her love was the glue that put it all back together again. I was the broken vase and she was the glassmaker that took what was left of me and turned me into the stained-glass window. She had made me something better than I ever was or dreamed of being. I was the widower, the father of a murdered child, the bona fide killer, the man with only revenge in his heart.

But, now I was a friend, a lover, a nurturer, a man with smiles, hope and happiness written all over my face. Revenge was not what was driving me now. I was driven by a newfound purpose—love. I was smitten with the idea of loving again—loving Evie, specifically.

However, love has this nasty habit of clouding reality, forcing you to forget the minor details…and the major ones.

I would soon learn that reality sometimes hits you right in the face. With a chair.

And, it feels like someone stabbing you in the heart. With a knife.

Scratch that.

With a spike.

CHAPTER NINETEEN

Evie

A month passed. For four incredibly love-filled weeks, we spent the night with each other every night, either in his bed or mine. Our dinner tradition had continued, but this time, we only said goodnight after we made love, usually more than once. Sometimes I would barely make it through the door before he was stripping me out of my 'power suits,' he called them. Then, we woke up and before we started our day, we would make love again. We would get dressed together and part only when we reached the bottom of the stairs in our apartment building.

Every time we were together, he would find his release inside of me. He never asked if I was on birth control, but then again, I wasn't sure he cared. To be honest, I didn't care either. But, I never mentioned to him that I was told after my miscarriage that I may not conceive again—that the doctor was surprised that I had even conceived the two times before. Six months ago, I wasn't concerned But now, I cared. I almost told him, but my desire to reveal that piece of information was drowned out by my gut feeling that things were going to change.

In those weeks, we went to dinner with Macy and Nick. We had game nights with Adam and Luke. I met Luke's children, who were adorable, and we went out with Rhonda and Jake a couple times. We watched movies, arm wrestled, sparred a little in the kitchen (lightly), ate four-course meals some nights and cold sandwiches on others. I didn't care what we did. I just wanted to be with him.

I was still working on the Cravens case vigilantly, but I was getting nowhere. Hundreds of interviews, search warrants, mouth swabs, along with thousands of hours of surveillance tapes from various places were wearing me thin. I was close to giving up, and I had a lurking feeling that I would be sent back to Kansas City any day now. The case had pretty much come to a grinding halt. It had been almost six months, and I knew when that mark came up, I'd be sent packing. I was dreading it. But, for now, I would enjoy what I had. On nights I worked late, Rhett would wait up for me, and he'd answer the door with a smile on his face.

He told me one night that he had never smiled so much in his entire life. He constantly complained that his face hurt. Even people in my office commented that he *must be getting laid* because his mood was stellar. I just laughed it off and tried to hide the blush that came with knowing how true that statement was.

Rhett was an incredible lover. His technique, skill, and style were unsurpassed. Even with Dash, I had never felt the passion that whirled around us every night. I had waited with bated breath for him to be a caveman and flip me over on my hands and knees and drive home. But, he never did. He had me only in ways in which he could look in my eyes. He loved slowly. Lovingly. Tenderly. He whispered that he loved me over and over, and I believed him. I had no reason not to. He would lace our fingers together and press my hands into the mattress over my head and move his hips with the tempo of our beating hearts—the growl of the mattress matched the thundering percussion in our chests, only to be drowned out by the crescendo of our pleasure. I would play him like the cello while he whispered filth into the night with his rolls, diddles, and drags.

It was an all-consuming feeling. His hands were everywhere and so were mine. Our mouths ravaged each other and we could not seem to get enough. Our hearts were on display for the other to see. I was completely bared to him. I could live every night doused in his love…and I planned on it.

***

"We should buy a tree," I said. Rhett was putting groceries away and his arm froze in midair.

His expression was grim. "What?"

"I think we should buy a Christmas tree," I repeated.

"Why?"

"Because Christmas is a few weeks away. I haven't had one since Noah..." I paused. "I never could..." I trailed off.

"I couldn't either," he responded. "In fact, I hate them." He smiled. "But, if you want one baby, we'll get one." His smile held and he shook his head. "And, I won't hate it."

Later that day, we climbed in Rhett's truck and drove to a Christmas tree lot. When I found one I liked, we stood before it for a few minutes saying nothing. Then, Rhett cocked his head to the side and spoke, "I think it's too big."

I couldn't resist. "That's what she said."

I started chuckling and Rhett looked at me without cracking a smile. "Seriously?" I tried to stifle my laughter. "I really don't think you can make jokes like that when it comes to Jesus's birthday." He still wasn't laughing—not even smiling.

"Sorry," I mumbled, blowing out heavy breaths to contain my laughter.

We cut the tree, had it loaded up, and drove to the department store. We bought strings of lights, tons of ornaments, and egg nog—which I spiked.

The warm air in Rhett's apartment was filled with laughter. We turned the radio up and danced to almost every Christmas song that played—even the slow ones..which caused the decorating to take forever.

Once the tree was decorated, beautifully, I might add, we sat down in front of it and just stared at the lights.

"It's beautiful," Rhett said softly. I just nodded. "I can't believe I hate these things. How could I hate something so colorful and happy?"

I put my hand on top of his. "It's not just you. I hate them, too."

He looked at me and smiled. "You know, we didn't even have to write this on a popsicle stick? We did this all on our own." I laughed and he bumped me with his shoulder. "Look at us...growing up and stuff."

I leaned in for a kiss. "I love you...and our tree."

He laughed. "I love you, too...and the tree."

That kiss bloomed into something beautiful. We moved over each other and held each other close. He made love to my mouth and my body like never before.

After we made love so sweetly and so beautifully, we fell asleep on the floor...in front of our Christmas tree.

***

This day all started with a whisper in the dark, a simple request that was so monumental.

The night before, I rested on Rhett's chest and he played with my long hair, which he had said time and time again that he loved. He loved to control the movement of my head as he devoured me by burying his hands in it, refusing to release me.

"I want you to meet my parents."

I sat up and looked at him. "Really?" He nodded in response. "Well, how? When?" I was almost eager. If this man who never dated, who had no other women since his wife, wanted me to meet his parents, I could be nothing but thrilled. This was a big deal to him.

"Macy is having a...uh...what are those damn things called, again? Like a 'baby is almost here party' thing."

"A baby shower?"

He grinned. "Yeah. Why the hell couldn't I remember that? Oh yeah! Because that doesn't even make sense! Baby shower," he grumbled with a smirk on his face. "Why is it called a shower? That's so stupid."

I didn't attempt to even answer his question; I only laughed it off. "So, they're coming up here for that?"

"Yeah. And, I want you to meet them. As my girlfriend." A cheesy grin stretched across my face and I felt my eyes well up. We had never put a label on our relationship since we became closer. We were neighbors, then friends, then lovers. He had called me his girl that one time, but I really didn't know what that meant. He laughed. "Just so you understand this, in your senior citizen jargon, that means, if I had a pin or a letterman's jacket, you'd be wearing it to the baby shower."

Laughter bellowed from my chest then died out when I caught him staring at me with a half-smile on his face. He reached up and wiped his eyes and I reached over and embraced him. "Don't get all misty on me," I whispered.

Still embracing, he rolled me onto my back and made room for himself between my thighs. He lifted up slightly and brushed a kiss across my lips, then reached down and guided himself into me. Upon every thrust, never looking away from my eyes, he whispered, "I love you. Completely. Fully. Unconditionally. With my body. My soul. My heart. My everything. I love your beauty. Your smile. Your laughter. Your tears. Your past. Everything. That makes. You. You." He only stopped speaking when his pace increased, and after he was spent, he buried his face in my neck. His breath hitched as he wrapped his arms around me, burying his hands in my hair. "Promise me I won't lose you. I can't lose you."

"You won't lose me."

"Promise me, Evie."

I reached up and pulled his head from my neck, forcing him to lift and look into my eyes. "I promise you, Rhett Trimble. I love you and you can't lose me. Nothing can make me stop loving you. Nothing can take you away from me."

"I'm gonna hold you to that," was all he said before he rolled off of me and we both fell asleep.

***

"Mom. Dad. This is my girlfriend, Evie."

Rhett looked down at me and grinned. He hadn't let go of my hand since we climbed out of the truck. My hands were trembling slightly as I reached out to shake his father's hand.

He brought his to mine gingerly and spoke, not really smiling, "Cord Trimble. It's a pleasure." His tone was very businesslike and seemed rehearsed.

I smiled at him despite the blatant coolness. "The pleasure is mine." He dropped my hand like it was on fire and stepped back away from me. Rhett's mother, on the other hand, embraced me with open arms. Literally.

She threw her arms around my neck and squeezed. "Oh, sweetie. It's so nice to finally meet you. You are all this boy of mine talks about anymore." Rhett had warned me that his mother loved to talk and that squeezing a word in edgewise would be a difficult feat. He also cautioned me that his father, although the best man in the world in his opinion, had not treated him the same after Arianna and Haven were killed. He asked that I not be bothered by his coldness. However, that was like asking water not to be wet. My nature consisted of people-pleasing. I loved Rhett, and I wanted his family to love me back.

Once the shower was in full swing, and all of the little games were played, I was left alone for a little while. Rhett was with his father and his mother tended to Macy. I watched with unwelcomed jealousy as Macy opened her gifts.

That was me once. An excited mother.

As she held up each little outfit and manicure set, I started to feel a ball of bitterness down in my stomach. I still thought about my son every single day. I was so happy with Rhett, but even with all of his love and promises, I would rather have my son. I fought the tears by biting my nails and bouncing my leg up and down. I sat in the circle of chairs gathered around Macy and watched her smile and laugh while Nick sat at her feet and played with the little toys and stacked up the tiny onesies.

I had all I could stand and left the room discreetly. As I walked down the hall toward the bathroom, I heard quiet arguments coming from the kitchen. Against my better judgment, I held back and waited by the door, not wanting to interrupt. I just stood and tried not to eavesdrop on the obvious private conversation. I only needed a few minutes to regroup.

The voice was raspy, a little louder than a whisper, "What happens when you knock *her* up? Huh? It's just going to be another situation that's no good for anyone involved."

"I'm not a fucking teenager, dad. So, don't talk to me like I am." I recognized Rhett's voice immediately.

"If you're not a *fucking teenager*, then stop acting like one. You need someone who is stable, not a damn train wreck. Your mother told me about her and I looked her up. After all you've been through, you need someone who's not an emotional basket case. She's nothing but damaged goods, and you can't fix her, son. That's always what you've done—tried to fix things. You have tried to fix everything around you. You tried to fix your brothers. You tried to fix your wife. You tried to fix this country and our justice system. We all know you're with her to try and repair something irreparable. You can't even fix yourself. If you're going to finally stick your dick in something, you need to be sure she's not worse off than you are."

I couldn't see his face and he said nothing for several long seconds until he said, "I love her."

"And, you loved Ari, too. And, Haven. Look where your *love* put them," he seethed.

"What the hell is your problem, dad?" he huffed with humorless laughter. "Don't I deserve to be happy?"

"The day you buried your daughter, you no longer deserved happiness. And, the day she buried her son, she didn't either."

"That was not her fault!" Rhett said loudly.

"Both of your kids are dead and you both are doing nothing but living it up! If you have no shame or remorse or hold no responsibility for the lives you've destroyed, you both might as well have pulled the trigger! You both should be ashamed of yourselves."

In that moment, my heart crumbled. If they said anything else to one another, I didn't hear. His father made it sound as if I had *let* my little boy go. In that moment, I truly felt like a killer. All of the guilt and hatred for myself that I had slowly peeled away over the last few months, came crashing down on me.

I pulled my shaky hands to my trembling lips and covered them as tears tumbled from my eyes. I couldn't move. My feet were cemented to the floor. My head fell forward and I squeezed my eyes shut.

I looked up just in time to see Rhett round the corner. When his eyes met mine, his face transformed. His anger fell away and horror took its place. His brows pulled together and his eyes went wide and his mouth fell open, sucking in a breath.

His eyes immediately were red-rimmed with emotion and he sighed, "No."

I wanted to cry out or scream. I wanted to walk into the ocean and let the tide pull me under and hold me. I wanted to run away, never to be seen again. I wanted to die right where I stood.

But, I did none of those things. I simply wiped my face, straightened my shoulders and attempted a small smile, and all I said was, "Will you please take me home?" with a small hitch between the words.

He said nothing as he reached for my hand and led me out. He still said nothing as we drove toward our apartment. I rested my chin on my palm and stared out the window. I watched the world go by—a world my son would never see. Even strangers believed it was my fault he'd never see it. Even strangers believed I didn't deserve to be happy. It seemed that I had fooled myself.

Rhett made no argument when I walked to my own door. I was about to fall apart and I just needed to be alone. With one look back at him, he did not ask questions, recognizing the silent plea in my eyes. His chest rose and fell with loud pants as if he were fighting his own breakdown.

I quickly opened the door and locked it behind me before

slumping against it and sliding to the floor. "Why didn't I call?" I whispered softly before breaking down into sobs. All of my happiness was ripped away by the words of the father of the man that I loved. A man who thought I was too damaged to love. A woman beyond repair. A woman beyond forgiveness.

I walked slowly to the closet and did what I hadn't done in months, but this time I pulled Rhett's shirt off of the hanger and slipped it on my naked body. I stood and stared at myself in the bathroom mirror, disgusted by filth that I saw. I was rumpled and sad.

I walked to the shower and turned on the water, hot enough to sting my skin through the long sleeves. I braced my hands against the wall and hung my head between them and cried, occasionally wiping my face on the wet, purple shirt that I had not even bothered to button.

I stood for several minutes before I felt a rush of cold air brush against my legs and heard the door close. He had come for me. I turned and he stood in front of me, gloriously naked. I caught a glimpse of his bright blue eyes before my face crumpled and I turned it away from him.

"Evie, look at me." He still hadn't touched me or even reached for me. When I shook my head in response, he said it again. "Evie, look at me. Please." When I finally gave in, his eyes bored into mine as he spoke so softly, I could barely hear him over the water pounding into my back. He rushed to me, pulling me against him and pushing me against the wall, under the spray and covered my mouth with his. His kiss was passionate and hungry and attacked mine with a certain vehemence. He pressed his naked body against me, never taking his mouth from mine. He made love to my mouth as he opened the front of the shirt I wore and caressed my breasts with vivaciousness and tenderness. He ran his hands up and down my sides until he reached down and heaved me up, wrapping my legs around his body. His tongue tasted mine and he sucked my lips into his mouth, then kissed me again, smothering our moans and whimpers. He entered me with a bold thrust, and I cried out with pleasure. He pumped with long, slow, deep thrusts until he worked me to the breaking point. But, as much as I wanted him and loved him, I couldn't risk destroying his relationship with his father.

So, I tore my mouth away from his and whined, "Pull out, Rhett. You need to pull out," I managed to say through panted breaths.

"No," he answered and continued to pound into me.

"Please," I begged.

"No," he answered again. His pumping slowed to a lazy pace as he whispered, "Please, Evie. I love you. I want this. With you. Only you."

"But your family-"

He cut me off. "You're my family," he breathed between the working of his hips against mine. "You are. And whatever comes of this," he said in a rush as his pounding sent me over the edge and he came inside of me with fervor. He held me, pinned against the wall with his hips and pressed his forehead into mine. "I want a family again. And, I want you to want that too. With me."

"But, what if I can't…" I couldn't even speak the words. I didn't want it to be impossible for me to bear children, and I didn't want to disappoint the man that taught me to love again.

"You will, baby. You will."

***

"I didn't want you to hear that," Rhett whispered into my hair as he drummed his fingers against my back.

"Why would he say such things? Why does he hate me?"

"He doesn't. He's just," he sighed, "angry. I told you he was a lawyer, but he practiced simply. Small cases, mainly domestic. Nothing big. Nothing dangerous. Ironically, he doesn't like confrontation. He didn't want me to take the prosecuting job, especially after what happened to Arianna." He paused for what seemed like an eternity. "Haven was his little sweetheart. He was absolutely crazy about her."

"Really?"

"First girl? Are you kidding me?" he said, and I could hear the smile in his voice, then his tone turned solemn. "He was devastated when she died. He blamed me. I was assisting on a case in law school. Huge case. Gangs and high profile criminals all tied into one case. He told me that it was dangerous, but I told him that it was my job. He argued that my job was to protect my family and I was being an 'arrogant fuckhead.' I didn't give a damn about what he thought or said. I had that case in the bag. The defendants knew it too." He blew out a breath. "I was the only one with a family, besides the lead attorney, and he had his family taken out of state for the case. I couldn't afford that. Less than a week after the guilty verdict was read, I was burying my wife and daughter. Today was the first day my dad has talked to me in almost six years. He doesn't hate you. He doesn't even hate me. He hates the fact that I've seemed to finally move on and he still can't get over it. I've not gotten over it. I won't ever get over it, but I can't let it destroy me." He lifted my chin and cupped my cheek. "What he said was just his hurt talking. He wants me to leave you alone because he thinks I'll destroy you, too. Hell, he's probably right," he huffed. "But, what he said...about Noah...is not true. It's not your fault and you *do* deserve to be happy." Then he pressed a sweet kiss to my lips.

"I love you," I mumbled against his lips.

"I love you, too."

I decided to bite the bullet and tell him. If he rejected me, then I would be all right. Heartbroken, but all aright. I squeezed my eyes shut because I couldn't bear to look at him. "I haven't been completely up front with you," I admitted. I felt his body become tense under my own. "I was told after my um...," I cleared my throat, "miscarriage that I may not be able to uh..."

The hardest words for a woman to speak. That's what they were. For a woman to say aloud that pregnancy may be unlikely or impossible is one of the most painful feelings in the world. It hurts to lose a child, but feeling the loss of something you'll never have again is an entirely different animal.

He cupped my cheek once more, forcing me to look at him. He smiled softly and shook his head. "It's okay," he whispered. "And, until we know for sure, let's not dwell on that, okay?"

"You do love me."

"Yes."

I knew I was being slightly foolish. I had only known Rhett for six months, and like an ignorant teenager, I was not mindful of protection or risk of conception. I was just overwhelmed by the carnal feeling, totally sustained by love. Not only that, the guilt of being a world-class fornicator had not even surfaced. I was sweating bullets in church over the heavy petting that Dash and I were involved in before we married. But, I was so consumed with affection for this strong man who was doing everything within his power to help me heal and teach me to live again. And, I was helping him too.

***

A week later, two days before Christmas, I received the news. I was being sent home. I had been in St. Louis for six months and every lead had been a dead end. Hours and hours of interviews and screening surveillance tapes and such had gotten me nowhere. My request to stay longer was immediately denied.

A long distance relationship was not something that I wanted to do, but I wanted Rhett. I'd cross oceans or cut through the sky and fly to the moon if he asked it of me. I loved him that much.

Before receiving the news, I had shown up at his work with lunch. Everyone watched with gaping mouths as I walked into his office. The instant he saw me, any worry lingering on his face faded away. He looked so handsome in his suit and his freshly trimmed beard enhanced his gorgeous jawline. The second I closed the door behind me, he reached for me and covered my mouth with his. We ending up having dessert before our main course.

When I whispered, "Please," he set me on his desk after pushing my skirt up to my hips, and released himself from his trousers and pulled my panties to the side. With one swift move, he entered me and worked his hips in tight little waves against me. The absence of our vocal freedom, along with the heavy breathing made our coupling even hotter. My open mouth panted into his chest as I came and he bit down on my shoulder when he found his own release.

When we finally caught our breaths, he smiled down at me, pushing my hair away from my damp face.

"That was a hell of a lunch…and I haven't even eaten yet," he murmured.

We did eat and I left his office with a blush, feeling the evidence of our love every time I moved for the rest of the day. The sensation sent me over the edge with tears later that afternoon when I learned that we would be torn apart by reality.

I let myself into his apartment to prepare our last meal together in this life that we had created. I was dreading having to tell him. I was a blubbering mess by the time I was getting around to preparing the salad.

My search for a lettuce knife had me venturing into drawers I had never opened. When I opened the drawer obviously set aside for junk, my heart completely stopped.

My breath came in rapid pants and I started to shake. Through my tears, I shook my head back and forth, denying what I was seeing.

"No," I said to myself as my trembling fingers picked up the chain holding, what would be, two identical tags, had one not been broken in half. I squeezed the tags in my hand and squeezed my eyes shut as the tears raced down at a rapid pace. I had seen the other half of the broken tag before. I had seen pictures of these tags together.

I should have run for my life. But, instead, I sank to my knees and sobbed.

The life that I finally loved again had been a lie.

The man whom I loved had been a liar—the man whom I had recklessly given my body to.

Everything was a lie.

Then, it hit me…like a freight train. I was not here by

happenstance. I was put here. Somehow. By somebody. My vulnerability, his story, his charm had all been used to blind my heart and cloud my judgment.

The Shepherd. Rhett was *The Shepherd.* What it all meant, I didn't know. But, I didn't care anymore.

The vengeance.

The prominent day job.

The military training.

It all made sense. He had committed the crime that I was trying to solve. And, he knew it all along.

When I heard the door knob rattle behind me, I didn't have the heart or the energy to even turn around and look at him. I sat and squeezed the tags so hard that blood seeped from my palm.

"Baby?" he asked, approaching me quickly. His voice was laced with a fabricated concern. He knelt down and laid a hand on my shoulder. "Evie? Sweetie? You all right?"

I struggled to find my voice. "You killed him, didn't you?"

"Who?" he asked softly.

My slumped shoulders could no longer support my pounding head and I lowered my chin to my chest. "You know who," I seethed.

"Baby," he said in a warning tone.

Then, I snapped. I jerked away from him and stood quickly, looking down at him, holding the tags out. "Don't you fucking touch me! You murdered him! You murdered him in cold blood! An innocent man! Had me brought here for some sick fucking reason where you could play games with me! You made me fall in love with you! I gave myself to you." All the wind had been taken out of my sails. "I fell in love with you," I whispered.

Rhett did not look shocked. He did not deny the things I had said. He didn't look surprised or stunned. He looked...heartbroken.

As tears began to trail down his face, his head fell forward in sad surrender. I had to get out of there. I had to get away from him.

As I walked past him, on a sobbing exhale, he softly said, "He wasn't innocent."

His words stopped me. My heartache instantly fled and anger took its place. "What?" I snapped.

He looked up and his eyes bore into mine. "I don't kill innocent people."

"You say that like you kill people all the time." I spat. He dropped his head once again and I gasped. My heart instantly filled with renewed hurt and my eyes once again filled with tears. I covered my lips. "Oh my God. There are more, aren't there?" He nodded. I leveled out my voice as best I could. "How many?"

"Hundreds," he whispered. "And I don't regret killing any of them." He looked up at me, his gorgeous, tear-stained face, staring right at the barrel of my gun.

"You've killed hundreds of innocent people, Rhett."

He smiled, but it was so sinister, it frightened me. "Innocent?" he questioned. "Innocent?!" he screamed. He lept to his feet and in my attempt to back away, I tripped over the coffee table, dropping my gun and falling to the floor. He stalked over to me like he was on the prowl. I had never seen him so angry or upset. He knelt down beside me and leaned in, just inches away from my face, his hot breath blowing my hair. He spoke with his teeth clenched. "No one that I kill is fucking innocent, Agent Harrington. I shot that piece of shit through the side of his fucking head. His brains splattered on my *fucking* face. I killed that bastard. And, if I could...I'd kill him again."

He stood up and strode to the couch, using one hand to flip it over. Loudly, it busted into the wall. I tried to move, but terror held me there.

Under the couch was a large safe, something I had never suspected. He took off his suit jacket and rolled up his sleeves, then punched in a few numbers on it and opened the door. I could tell from where I sat that the entire safe was full of large envelopes.

He looked over at me, that same sinister smile stretched across his face. "You wanna see the sins of your Golden Boy, Agent

Harrington?" He pulled one out and threw it at me, hitting me square in the chest. "Take a look. You'll be glad he's dead. You'll know I did this world a favor."

I pushed it away from me. "I don't want to look at it. I don't believe you." I tried to back away, but I slipped on my bloody hand and I flew back further, hitting the floor with my back.

Rhett grabbed five or six envelopes and sat down in front of me, with his legs crossed in front of him. He took the first envelope and dumped it out. Pictures and paperwork spread out before me in a heap.

He glanced at a picture and tossed it at me. It landed on my outstretched legs. He spoke with a voice completely and emotionally disconnected. "Roger Hedron. Age 58. First *man* I killed this side of the pond. He kidnapped this girl," he tossed another picture at me, one of a beautiful young girl, "Stella O'Hare, who was fourteen years old, on her way home from a friend's house. He kept her locked in a cell," he tossed another picture at me of her holding quarters, "every day for four years. She was starved and beaten and raped almost daily, according to her testimony. She got pregnant six times, and each time, he beat her until she miscarried. Except the last time, he failed. She gave birth. To this child." he tossed another picture at me. My heart stopped at the sight of the baby in a box "Upon delivery, he killed him. A baby boy. And this is what she looked like when she escaped." The last picture he tossed at me broke my heart. Young Stella was skin and bones, having almost no hair and missing most of her teeth. She had clearly been beaten, neglected.

Rhett dumped out another envelope and pressed forward, tossing the first picture at me. "Chopper Rydell, a.k.a. Siren, Age 32. Serial killer. He traveled mainly along the east coast taking girls from parking lots of department stores. He had raped dozens of women; he had killed nineteen of them. I shot him from four hundred yards away seconds before he claimed his twentieth victim. And, these," he took the other pictures and fanned them out like a deck of cards, "are his victims." He named them off, one by one. He knew their first names. Their last names. Where they were from. Their ages. From Kelly Slayton, age 23 from Charlotte, North Carolina down to Presley Abbot, age 6 from Nashville, Tennessee, he knew them all.

He took the third envelope and dumped it on top of the contents from the first two. He tossed a picture at me. "Rich Wheatley. Age 27. Lured two boys from his neighborhood into the woods behind their house. There he did the unspeakable before dismembering them and burying them in a shallow grave." He tossed three pictures at me—the first two, school pictures of the boys. The third—their dead bodies. "Temporary insanity. Got six months for killing eight-year-old Tommy Prescott and his six-year-old brother Jamie. Got a job at a design firm eight months later making ninety grand a year. Temporary insanity, my ass."

His voice began to waiver as he dumped the fourth envelope. This one was tattered and torn and...blue. Not yellow like the rest. He tossed the picture at me. A young, vibrant girl with a huge smile and long brown hair stared back at me. "Taryn Howser. Age 18. Daycare worker." His voice was breaking so badly, he had to stop and take a breath. "First hit. Self-assigned. Made two hundred dollars to point out the target in a heinous crime and turn her head while that victim was kidnapped." He tossed another picture at me and I looked down and I let out a hard sob.

Little Haven grinned up at me. I looked up at him staring at me, his face tortured with emotion and wet from his tears. "I shot her in the head at point-blank range. She knew who I was. I followed her down a dark alley and when she saw me, she fell to her knees, and begged for her life." His next words, although a statement, seemed like a plea. He wanted an answer. He wanted to know why. "My daughter's life was only worth two hundred dollars." His face crumpled and he buried his head in his hands. "Two hundred dollars," he whispered. "Two hundred dollars," he repeated.

I sat there crying my own tears. I was too scared to touch the beautiful man that I had fallen for. The arrogant lawyer. The ex-Marine. The assassin. The prodigal son. The broken father.

"Shepherd?" I said softly.

"Yes?" he answered immediately, looking up at me. I don't know why I said it. I guess I just needed to know that it was really him. I dropped my eyes down to the floor. "I know you have to go. Hell, I even know you have to arrest me. I wasn't supposed to get this close to you. I wasn't supposed to…" he trailed off.

"You weren't supposed to what?"

"Fall in love with you." I looked up at him and he was staring at me. "I did though." He shook his head. "I know you think it's all a lie, but not that." Once again, his face drew up in emotion. "God, Evie. I love you so much. And, I hate myself. I didn't mean to break your heart."

I sat and watched him as I sobbed. "You did though. What was left of it," I whispered.

He nodded. "I know. That's why I told you not to say it back. I told you that you'd hate me."

I shook my head and stared at his tear-soaked face. "What have you done? You can't do this. You. Are. Not. God. You don't get to say who deserves to die. That's not your decision."

His mood shifted and his eyes narrowed. With an edge in his voice, he spoke quietly, "All you have done is wallow in your self-pity while there are people out there who need you. Wake the hell up, Evie. Criminals didn't stop being criminals because you don't feel like finding them. The world did not stop turning because your husband allowed you to escape his thoughts—allowed your child to flee from the forefront of his mind. Because he didn't really love you. Not enough to see you through this."

I gasped at his words, his hurtful and hate-filled words. With a crippling heartache, I met his eyes. "You don't get to say he didn't love me, either."

I said nothing else. I reached for the envelope he had thrown at me in the beginning. I stood up quietly, straightening my dress like a lady should.

Without arresting him and without my heart intact, I walked

away from Rhett.

With every intention of it being forever.

CHAPTER TWENTY

RHETT

As I knelt there in my living room floor, surrounded by evidence that the people I killed had gotten what they deserved, I was utterly numb. The one thing in my life that I couldn't bear the thought of losing had walked away from me.

She lied to me. She didn't love me no matter what. She didn't love me without condition.

Who could love someone like me? Someone who could kill a man or a woman without blinking, without thinking twice? She was right. I wasn't God. But, I did what I felt I needed to do.

I stood up quickly, picking up anything and everything, throwing it up against walls and doors. I yelled and cried, punching holes in walls and destroyed everything I could touch. I even picked the Christmas tree up, the one we had decorated together, and threw is across the room.

The only thing left unbroken was the picture of my family. I carefully picked it up off of the floor and carried it to my bedroom. I knelt beside my bed, placing the picture on it, atop the thin nightgown that Evie had worn to bed the night before. I teased her body while she wore it before I slowly peeled away the satiny, green gown and filled her body with my own. I rocked into her slowly, declaring my love with every breath.

But, now, she was gone.

Another woman lost. All because of my pride and stupidity.

My chest ached so badly that I could not contain my sobs. At that point, I didn't even care that I was going to prison. I didn't care about living without freedom. I only cared about living without Evie. She was everything to me. She had become the reason I woke up in the morning, my desperate reason to come home; she had become the receiver of my every carnal need. She was my companion, my counselor, my sunshine on a shitty day. I wanted her forever and I wanted to give her everything. I wanted to make her a mother again, despite her fears and worries. I wanted to be the husband that I knew I could be. I wanted to be the father to the child she deserved to have again. I wanted to give her back everything she had lost...and then some.

I picked up the picture and ran my fingers across the smiling faces of Arianna and Haven. "Why did she have to leave me?" I asked them. They answered me with silence. "Why does everyone always leave me? I just wanted to make you proud." My teeth clenched. "Kill back whoever killed you." I sucked in a breath. "Once again, I've done nothing but disappoint you. I've let everyone down. Why didn't I just walk away from that case? I just wanted to win. I wanted to make a name for myself." I blew out a hard breath. "My name killed you both." I stared at Ari's beautiful face and warm brown eyes. "Why did you love me? This wretch of a man. I'll never understand how someone so pure could love someone so damaged. But you did. You fucking did." I smiled as tears rolled down my face.

Then, I turned my attention to little Haven. "Your daddy is a terrible person who never deserved you. Hell, even God knew it." I sighed heavily. "I dream about you all the time. The other night I dreamt that you were all grown up. It was your wedding day, and I stared down at you, with your blonde hair all twisted up. Your dress was beautiful but it paled in comparison to your gorgeous face. You looked just like this, only older." My face drew up in emotion and I closed my eyes. My sweet baby girl. I would never hear her speak a complete sentence. I would never let go of the back of her bicycle without her realizing it. No man would ever have the chance to fall in love with her. All of the wonderful things in life, she'd never experience—worlds of beauty, she would never see. "I still hear you sometimes, in the early mornings, before the sun comes up. I watch videos of you every day. Bet you didn't know that. I sit down at my computer and watch one every morning when I get to work. Evie didn't even know that." My favorite was one of Haven and me—one that Ari had captured when I didn't even know she was filming. Too prideful to tell my own wife, I sat with my one-year-old daughter in my lap, whispering how much I loved them and I couldn't imagine my life without them. I wish I would have imagined it. Maybe it would have prepared me for this hurt—this hurt that I was living all over again.

I looked over to my nightstand and there sat the picture of Evie and me, so careless and so free. She had become my favorite subject for photos. I had snapped hundreds of them—some of us together, then some I asked her to pose for. However, my most cherished ones were the ones I snapped when she wasn't watching.

I picked up both pictures and did something I swore I'd never do. I put them in the nightstand out of my sight. I laid them all to rest in my very own graveyard of women—of every woman who had ever owned a piece of my heart.

I didn't want it to end like this. I simply wanted to disappear out of her life, or maybe even keep her. I never expected her to find out who I really was. Her discovery proved only what I had known from the very beginning: it would be impossible for her to love all of me.

I stood up to close up shop for the night. As I checked the door a second time, something caught my eye. The broken dog tags gifted to me by The Queen almost six years ago lay on the kitchen floor. Somehow, someway, those metal pieces indicated to her who I was and that I had killed Bradley Cravens. She knew before I even confessed it.

The proof needed to identify the murderer of Bradley Cravens lay there, ungathered by the seasoned detective. She was in such a rush to be out of my presence that she forgot to pick up the one thing that would put me away. A mistake on her part could guarantee my freedom, but only if I jumped ship. In my own idiotic mind, I found that to be a cowardly way of going down. For some reason, I wanted to be honorable, even if it meant that, at the end of the day, I was still a murderer.

I could not sleep in this bed anymore—not when I had made love to Evie between these sheets less than twenty-four hours ago. And, I could not stay at my loft—the first place I had her, the place she gave herself to me.

So, I gathered my things and left. I spent the night at a hotel on the other side of the city—away from everyone and everything that reminded me of her.

Before I fell asleep, something that only happened because of exhaustion, I made up my mind to see her one last time.

In the morning, I planned to walk into her office, kneel in front of her, and turn myself in—for the murder of Bradley Cravens.

***

I called into work first thing that morning. I had my hearings continued and told my boss that I would call him later that afternoon. I didn't tell him that I would be calling from jail.

I dressed simply, in a pair of decent jeans and a plain white t-shirt and an old worn out pair of boots. After I tied them, I sat on the edge of the bed with my head in my hands. I never dreamed it would come to this. I never pictured myself in this place. I hadn't even called *The Queen* to tell her that I had been found out. She would have me out of this city within minutes, but in doing that, I would definitely never see Evie again. I would rather be locked away for a thousand years and get to see her face one last time rather than walk away with my freedom and never look into her eyes again.

Normally, I would climb into my truck and turn on one of my favorite songs. I should have since it might have been the last time I ever heard them. But, I rode in silence, glancing over to the passenger seat a dozen times which my sweet love had regularly occupied. Three nights ago, after dinner and a movie, we couldn't wait to get inside. I slipped over to the middle at the same time she climbed on top of me. With minimal effort, thanks to Evie's flowing dress, she slipped me inside of her. I watched her ride me, never taking my eyes off of hers. It was slow and lovely. She barely made a sound. I heard nothing other than our heavy breathing and her quiet, "I love you," when we both found our release.

But now, Evie was not with me. When I pulled up to the FBI office, I sat in my truck for several minutes, breathing in and out very slowly, trying to calm my jittery hands and pounding heart.

I was preparing myself to lose everything all over again, and this time, I would not have my freedom or any hope of ever truly living again. However, I found myself thankful for that time that I had with Evie. A time where I loved again.

I walked into the familiar office and headed straight for Rhonda's desk, avoiding eye contact with everyone that passed. Someone called out to me and I simply nodded their direction. I was silently counting down the minutes until everyone hated me.

As I approached her desk, Rhonda's face lit up, but fell slightly. I found her smile promising. Her smile told me that she didn't know the truth about me. The fall of her expression was something I hadn't figured out, but learned as she spoke.

"Hey."

I smiled, tightly. "Hey. Evie here?"

Her brows drew together and her head tilted slightly. "Evie? She didn't tell you?"

My heart started pounding in my chest. "Tell me what?"

"She's gone."

My heart plummeted to the floor. "Gone? Gone where?"

She shook her head and asked, "Why didn't she tell you? Surely she would've told you."

My panic set in and I raised my voice slightly. "Where did she go, Rhonda?"

"Yesterday was her last day here. She was sent back to Kansas City." I stood like an idiot and just stared at her. "She didn't mention it?"

I only shook my head.

I couldn't do this. I couldn't turn myself in without telling her goodbye, without explaining myself—telling her things that I hadn't told her yet.

She had just left. She left without saying a word about me to anyone. I didn't understand. She was so angry, so hurt by me. She was so convinced that I was this horrible human being—a murderer. Yet, she had said nothing.

I felt like this was a sign that I wasn't supposed to do this. I couldn't confess to my so-called crimes.

I nodded. "Uh. Thanks." Then, I turned on my heel and walked back to my truck. By the time I climbed inside, I was panting like a madman. "Why wouldn't she tell anyone?" I said only to myself. The only reason that I could come up with was that she really loved me, but I knew that couldn't be true.

When I arrived home, I knew I would have to move quickly to clear out. I headed to my room, but upon entering, I stopped in my tracks. On the foot of my bed lay the folded purple shirt—the shirt I had given Evie to replace the blue one she so often found comfort in. And on top of it lie all pieces of my gifted dog tags. And…a note.

I tore it open as quickly as I could as I slid to the floor. I held her handwritten letter in my shaky hands as I read.

Rhett,

By now, you probably know that I am gone. But, I couldn't leave without telling you goodbye in my own way. I cannot see you. You probably think you know why. It's not the reason you think. You think I hate you. That's one thing I could never do. My reason for not hating you and not seeing you one last time has everything to do with love. I cannot tell you goodbye while you're looking at me. I can't feel you watch me walk away from you for good.

I looked at the pictures. I understand. I want you to know that. I understand why you did what you did. Why you do what you do. All those beautiful lives snuffed out by the perversions of one man. Even if they don't regain their lives as they once had them, you have done your part in avenging them. Several of the girls are ones I have seen before—in my own work.

Missing girls. You've found them. You've killed for them. Without apology.

Mothers pray for their daughters to fall for men like you. Fathers can look men like you in the eye. They can go to bed at night and know their daughters are safe. I know Arianna and Haven are never far from your thoughts, and what I just said may find no bearing in your heart, but the man they loved is not the man I love.

I love a different you. Even before I knew the truth, I felt safe with you. Safer than I have ever felt. Even when I learned the truth, a truth that should have terrified me, I did not run. I literally fell at your feet. My heart begged you for mercy.

I thought I wanted my heart back. But the truth is simple. My heart is safer with you.

I cannot keep these things, especially the evidence of your "crimes" that are truly good deeds. Do with them what you will.

Do not come for me. Forget me quickly.

Love,
Evangeline

I dropped the letter to the floor and it landed between my legs. I stared ahead and silently cried. She didn't hate me, but she ordered me not to come after her. She admitted that she loved me.

Which made everything so much worse.

It would have been easier to pick up and leave—walk out of her life knowing that she hated me. But, knowing that she loved me rent my heart in two. Although she loved me, I'd never hold her again. I'd never taste her sweet lips. I'd never wake up to her sweet, sweet face ever again.

The purple shirt that she had taken from my closet—the shirt that had become her new comforter—was neatly folded on my bed, along with two tickets to St. Lucia, my dream destination, with the words "Merry Christmas" written on the tag that was taped to them.

I took the necklace I had bought her for Christmas from my nightstand. I ran my fingers over the inscription a hundred times before I put it away. After sitting for nearly an hour, I finally stood up and left my apartment. I walked to her door, unlocked it, and eased the door open.

Nothing was left to indicate that she had ever been there. The couch that we had made love on several times was still there, but the bright throw pillows we tossed off to make room for our couplings were gone now.

Her curtains were gone—the ones I had talked her into buying to brighten up her apartment, to brighten up her life.

All of her things were gone. But, I could still smell the scent of her. I could smell her shampoo and her lotion both lingering in the air, haunting me with its pleasantness.

I walked to her room and pushed open the door. Her room was completely bare. The bed and the nightstand were there, but gone were the pictures of her and her lost family and the picture of her and myself. And although the softest sheets I had ever slept between were missing from the bed, I took off my shoes and lay down on the bare mattress. I tucked my hands under my cheek and pulled my legs to my chest like a child.

As my tears began to fall again, I whispered the truest words I had ever known into the dark, "I love you, Evie."

Then, I drifted off to sleep, desperate to find rest in the great unknown.

***

I woke up early the following morning. I knew that I had to inform *The Queen* of the events that had unfolded the day before. I was walking out of Evie's apartment when I spotted *The Queen* at my door, wearing an alarmed look on her face. Without speaking, I approached her and let her into my apartment.

As soon as the door closed, she began. "I heard Evie was—"

"Gone?" I finished for her. "Yeah." *The Queen* stood and stared at me. "She knows."

The Queen's eyes went wide. "Knows what exactly?"

"Everything," I whispered.

"You told her?"

I shook my head. "No. She figured it out—about Cravens anyway. But, I did tell her…about the others."

She reached up and grasped her head in her hands. "What have you done? What have you done to us, Shepherd?"

I felt my throat closing up, but I managed to get out, "I needed her to know I'm not a monster."

"You tried to convince her of that by telling her you've killed hundreds of people? Don't you think you went about that the wrong way?" she shot back at me, laced with sarcasm.

"Look. The only fucking thing tying me to Cravens is lying in there on my bed. She stole it from Evidence to save my ass."

"Why? When she had everything she needed to lock you up? When she knows you're guilty?" she asked.

I dropped my head and stared at the ground and said softly, "Because she loves me." I paused. "I gave her everything on Cravens. She understands, or is trying to understand, why I did it." My eyes welled up. "But, she says she can't be with me."

She nodded her head, and her eyes showed absolute understanding. She stood and just stared at me for several long moments before speaking. "I know you don't want to hear this, but you need to get away from here. I requested a leave of absence for you by letter. I hope you don't mind, but I think it's safer for you to leave the area until all of this blows over or in case Evie changes her mind."

Although I didn't want to leave the place that bore my most favorite new memories, I knew she was right. I couldn't stay here. I couldn't stay in this city—maybe not even this state.

"I've arranged for you to stay in a beach house in North

Carolina. I think you need it." I didn't argue. It would be pointless. "Your plane leaves in three hours. So start packing."

After she left and my bags were ready, I loaded everything into my truck and climbed inside. I wasn't sure I wanted to be alone. I picked up my phone to call Luke. He answered on the second ring.

"Hey, brother," he said in greeting. "I heard you're going on a trip," he said, jovially.

"Yeah. For a while. I was calling to see if you want to go with me." He sat in silence for a moment, seemingly distracted. "Luke?" I prompted.

"Yeah. Hang on," he whispered. After waiting impatiently for almost a minute, he continued. "Sorry. What were you saying?"

"Where the hell are you?"

"Around," he answered, avoiding a straight answer.

"I hate it when you do that."

"What?" he asked with a smile in his voice.

"Act all evasive and shit."

He chuckled, "Well, what I'm doing is Official Business, so butt the hell out. And no. I'm not going on your 'man-cation,' okay? You need some time alone. And, I know you're gonna be all depressed and shit. I need to keep the happiness in my life. Your shit'll bring me down with your man-problems."

"Fine," I retorted. "I didn't want you to go anyways."

"And, now you sound like a ten-year-old."

I sighed. "Shut up. I'm getting off of here. Let me know if you change your mind, loser."

"I'm not gonna change my mind. Love you, brother. I gotta go."

"Alright. Love you, too. See ya."

When I got to the airport, I pulled my one-way ticket from my bag, along with the reservations for a six-month stay at the beach house.

Six months could never rid me of the love I carried for Evie. This time away may only protect me from others who would want me killed for killing Cravens.

But, this house could never save me from myself—could never heal my broken heart—could never protect me from my greatest fear becoming reality.

CHAPTER TWENTY-ONE

Evie

Walking away from Rhett nearly destroyed me. I loved him. Nothing would ever change that. The night I walked out on him, leaving him an absolute mess on his living room floor, I ran to the office to retrieve something on the Cravens case, and then I went to my own apartment.

And cried.

I cried like I have never before. I had loss upon loss upon loss. I wasn't sure how I'd ever recover.

Once I finally dried up the blubbering mess, I sat at my kitchen table and stared at the envelope Rhett had tossed at me. It was packed full, nearly bulging at the seams. I was terrified of the stories it would tell me. I slowly peeled back the seal and poured its contents in front of me.

Hundreds of pictures lay before me. All face up. Hundreds of young girls stared back at me. The pictures were not those used for missing persons' flyers. These pictures were of terrified young girls and young women. I covered my mouth with one hand while I spread the pictures out with the other. They covered the table and spilled over to the floor.

Every picture showed the dehumanization of these girls. Some were obviously screaming and crying. Some were being whipped. Some were being tortured, sodomized. Most of the pictures showed naked girls being raped in some fashion. Some of them looked like zombies—drugged, controlled. Girls that looked like they ranged from about sixteen to thirty-five lie wasted in front of me. These were the images of sex-trafficked women.

Some of the girls looked familiar, maybe similar to the ones I've seen in cold cases or missing persons' cases. Something struck me about some of them.

I looked at about a dozen pictures before I recognized a familiar face.

Bradley Cravens—the face and name behind the largest sex trafficking ring I had ever seen in my career.

He smiled, posed, for the picture. He was standing behind a girl, no more than seventeen, who was hanging with her arms above her head. Her naked body hung in front of him while he gripped her chin, forcing her to look at the camera. His other hand was reached to the front of her, cupping her womanhood.

The girl was crying, terrified.

And Bradley Cravens was grinning, delighting in her torment.

I threw the picture down and found another. And another. And another. And another. Dozens upon dozens of pictures of Cravens and these girls. Some looked as if he were posing them for advertisement. Others were photos of Cravens and other men raping and beating girls of all ages.

Under all of the pictures was a disc marked, "Auction." Horrified of what I would see, but needing to know the fate of these girls, I popped it in and sat. And watched. All five agonizing hours of girls being bought. Sold. Raped on the platform on which they were forced to prance. Some screamed and fought in the beginning. The screaming and fighting stopped when the other girls learned what would happen to them if they screamed and fought. I heard only soft cries and whispers from the lips of young girls with closed eyes.

I sat and watched all of these girls who were victims of a "victim." I counted the number of girls that were sold. Two hundred seventy-three. Two hundred seventy-three tortured and broken women. Sold to the highest bidder.

I slid off of my chair into the floor and wept. I could not believe that I had defended Bradley Cravens. This man who had tormented thousands of women—I had taken up for him. I had desperately searched for his killer.

Something slid off of the table and hit me in the shoulder. A spiral-bound book lay beside me. As I reached for it, my fingers trembled. I was afraid of what was inside. The year 2012 was written on the front, and it appeared to be some sort of ledger. The note in the corner let me know that this was the second ledger out of nine. Eight more of these ledgers existed just for said year. As I flipped through it, I realized I held part of the record of girls and women sold in this one year.

The records held their pictures, stated their names, ages, places of residence, physical characteristics, the state of their virginity, their emotional state, to whom they were sold, and the price for which they were purchased.

Tears rolled down my cheeks as I flipped through the pages. Beside each record, Bradley Cravens had signed off on each transaction. His disgusting signature was beside each and every name.

When I reached the end of the ledger, the number at the end was 2,057. If each book held roughly the same amount of records, a transaction for each girl, then that would have meant that in this year there were more than eighteen thousand girls taken, broken, and sold.

Eighteen thousand lives.

Eighteen thousand smiles.

Eighteen thousand futures.

All stolen. All taken by Bradley Cravens. All taken in *one year*.

My stomach wretched and I barely made it to the bathroom before I lost what was left of my lunch. I vomited until I couldn't catch my breath.

After lying on the bathroom floor for over an hour, I lost the battle with not wanting to know more. I had to know. Inside the envelope was evidence that Cravens had been doing this for eleven years. Several hundred thousand girls—someone's daughter, someone's mother, someone's wife—all stolen for profit.

Bradley Cravens had made billions of dollars selling human beings. The records showed that for a girl who was broken, but not a virgin, who had little physical damage, her purchase price ranged from ten to twenty grand.

A non-virgin who was feisty, slightly unbroken, easily brought in thirty grand.

A virgin who was broken and whose body served as the masterpiece behind her brokenness—scars, fresh wounds—raked in one to two hundred grand.

And, a virgin whose skin was flawless, and who was unwilling to be broken, beaten, whose spirit was still present sold for the highest price. Seven hundred thousand dollars.

However, the single biggest transaction was on the very last page of the book I held in my hands.

A girl whom I recognized, but couldn't place. A beautiful girl, even in her brokenness.

Her selling price?

Two million dollars.

I jumped up from the floor and retrieved my laptop to login to the FBI database, and quickly typed in the girl's name. Bianca Turley. When her case popped up, I recognized it immediately.

Bianca Turley was the eighteen-year-old daughter of Charles and Tiffany Turley. Charles was elected as a state representative for two terms. In the middle of his second term, he resigned after the disappearance of his beautiful daughter. She was tall, slender, with creamy skin and long, black hair. Her green eyes were the biggest and most beautiful I had ever seen. She was last seen telling both of her parents goodnight the night of her disappearance. There was absolutely no trace of where she had gone or what had happened to her. She had been missing for over two years, and I held the information to find her.

Trying to find a link between Bradley Cravens and Bianca, I searched the headlines. I didn't have to look far before I discovered that Senator Cravens and Representative Turley had butted heads over several issues. There was even a police report of the two causing a disturbance at a local restaurant.

Bad blood gives a motive. She was targeted. I was certain of it.

I went back to the book to find out who had purchased her. My heart stopped when I read who had paid the high price for her.

Bill Cravens. The Senator, himself.

My emotions were soaring high. I could've dropped to my knees and wailed for these who were somewhere out there—victims of a world driven by greed and sex and slavery. But, I grabbed my phone and called my boss. He answered on the third ring.

"Evie? What is it? It's three in the morning."

"I think I know where Bianca Turley is. Or who has her at least. Who knows her whereabouts," I said in a rush.

"Bianca? Bianca who?"

"Charles Turley's daughter. Remember?"

He sucked in a breath. "Yes. I remember. Where is she? How do you know?"

"Listen, I have solid evidence that Senator Cravens has something to do with her disappearance, and may still have her."

"Where?"

"You need to see all of this."

"Where did you get the information?"

I paused. I couldn't tell him the truth. I was torn when it came Rhett's guilt. Yes, he was guilty of murder. But, he was also guilty of saving thousands of lives in the future—maybe even now if I could track these girls down.

"It was sent by someone anonymously. I received it earlier in the afternoon. It was sent directly to me, not the department. Can you meet me in Columbia by seven? I need to pack up here and I'll meet you there."

"Sounds good. I can do that."

We ended the call and I began packing my things. Quickly. I didn't have much, which was good because I didn't have much time. I put everything back into the envelope and began loading my car.

I pulled Rhett's purple shirt from my closet and set it out on the bed, along with the piece of the dog tag that I had stolen from the evidence room. The objective of the trip I had made after I left Rhett was one that had changed en route. I was certain I would turn him in when I arrived. But, something inside of me warned me not to do it. So, I snuck into the evidence room and discreetly slipped the piece of broken dog tag into my pocket. I had staged the area to make it look like the tag had spilled out and had been lost.

I was officially a criminal. I had tampered with evidence. I realized as I sat there rubbing the tag in between my fingers, that Rhett and I were essentially the same. We became criminals to save someone. However, he was the better savior.

He had saved thousands of people—people who were hurt and saved countless women from the hands of people who would destroy them. He rescued them before they were ever harmed.

I finally understood. I understood why he did it. As a man, he had to protect. As a hurting husband and father, he had a raging taste for blood. As a man in love, he had to betray me.

I had broken his heart, but I could not separate his two lives. He loved beyond anything I had ever imagined, but he was still a killer, even if his killings were justified.

No human could be that detached from the emotions of an assassin and still live a normal life—love like a normal person. I didn't really know who he was. I couldn't understand how he could love me so much, but still reserve so much hurt and hate in his heart.

I left his shirt, but took everything else that reminded me of him. I took our paintings, our pictures, and the unwashed sheets that still smelled like his cologne.

I loved him…in more ways than I ever loved Dash. Dash had stolen my heart. But, Rhett had restored it after Dash has smashed it to pieces. Rhett had repaired me and taught me how to love stronger and purer and all night long.

I knew by the look on his face that he never counted on my finding out the truth. That fact flattered me and terrified me at the same time. I'm not sure who arranged this farce or how, but he crossed lines. Lines he shouldn't have crossed.

He fell for me. He fell for *me* and not because of pity. He seemed captivated by the mess I was, but he fell in love with who I had become. He made me feel beautiful in my own skin. He made me smile and laugh. He made me promise things, not only to him, but to myself.

In the adventure that came with falling in love with him, he made me fall in love with being me.

For that, I could never hate him. For that, I would love him forever.

***

I cried the entire way to Columbia. I couldn't stop myself. I cried over Rhett. Over the lost girls. Over everything.

When I pulled up to the hotel where I had rented a room just for the meeting, Frankie was already waiting for me. Once in the room, without pleasantries, I poured the contents of the envelope all over the queen size bed.

"Oh my…" Frankie paused. "What in the hell?" He fell to his knees by the bed and started spreading the pictures

I showed him all of the pictures, parts of the video-taped auction, and the ledger.

"Can you verify any of this?" he asked me.

"We can only look into it," I answered. "But, if you want my professional opinion, we need to look into the Senator's part in this immediately. No one would just make this up. These pictures aren't staged, not in the traditional sense. We need to have the Senator followed, maybe even get a search warrant. Sir, I don't have a good feeling about this."

Frankie scratched his head. "Twenty-three years of this job and I've never seen anything like this." He pulled out his cellphone.

"Yeah. Betts, here. We need to get a trail on Senator Cravens immediately. Agent Harrington is in receipt of some information that is pretty damning. I need to know his whereabouts at all times. Thanks." He dialed another number. "Judge Howard, please. Frankie Betts." After a short pause, he began again. "Judge, we have reason to believe that Senator Cravens is involved in some illegal activity, and we need a search warrant issued. I plan to contact the prosecutor after I talk to you, but please know that the entire lid is about to be blown off of something huge. Just, be prepared. Alright. Thanks, Judge."

He looked at me. "He's leery about this. Politicians can be...persuasive and evasive. Particularly ones like Cravens who bask in the public's light. This is not going to be good, Evie. For anybody. It might be best if you... "

I cut him off. "I'll be fine, Frankie. What do you need me to do?"

He blew out a hard breath. "Go home. Get some rest. Come in first thing in the morning and we'll brief everyone on this. We'll put a team together; see if we can't find these girls and the men who purchased them." He was walking to the door when he turned around to look back at me. "Looks like whoever killed that son of a bitch was doing this world a courtesy. I want to find out who it was just so I can shake his hand."

I nodded as he closed the door behind him.

I was at a loss. I dropped to the bed that was free of pictures and stared ahead. There was no way we could find all of those girls. A fraction of a fraction is what we may find. My fear was that most of them were probably already dead or out of the country, beyond our reach.

After gathering up the envelope, repacking its contents, I headed home. When I pulled into the driveway, I sat for several minutes just staring at my house.

I didn't want to go inside—back to all of those old memories. Back to the old me.

As I eased the door open and stepped inside, it felt strange—not like home anymore. The silence was deafening. As I set my suitcase down, I slowly made my way to baby Noah's room. Everything was as I had left it. Everything blue. Everything untouched.

Looking around at his things, I knew what I had to do. It was time to pack up everything that remained of his little life. I brought down a box from the closet and set it on top of the dresser. Through quiet sobs and with the gentlest touch, I placed his combs, the onesies, the little overalls, his colorful socks and tiny shoes in the box.

After that box was filled, I filled another. And another. I packed away everything, down to the last diaper and tube of diaper rash cream.

It was past dinnertime when I finally got the crib taken down and set by the back door. I walked outside, into the night, and stared up at the starry sky. I closed my eyes and let the moonlight shine down on my face. I stood and listened to the crickets chirp in rhythm with my beating heart.

I carefully walked out to the barn—a place I had not been since I found Dash's lifeless body. I could never enter that place. I couldn't until Rhett helped me face my fears.

I was no longer angry with Dash. I still missed him, but I was slowly letting him go. He gave me the best thing that had ever happened to me, but all of my best things had vanished into the night.

When I finished loading everything inside, I walked over to the place he drew his last breath and sat down. And...I talked...as if he were sitting right beside me. Through my tears and deep breaths, I spoke to him.

"I, uh...packed away Noah's things today." I closed my eyes. "It was so hard...putting everything left of our baby boy into boxes. I used to see his face every time I closed my eyes." Through hitched sobs, I admitted, "He's...fading...away...from...me. I don't see him all the time anymore. I feel...guilty. But, I finally feel alive, you know?" I smiled. "I remember the first time I saw you. You were so adorable. That blonde hair of yours was everywhere. I wanted to jump across that counter and jump your bones. Remember our wedding night? Our first time?" I chuckled. "You were shaking so bad, I thought you were having a seizure. I threatened to get a spoon to hold your tongue down. You were just nervous, I know. I was nervous, too." I paused and sucked in a deep breath. "I can still see your face when you saw those two lines. That's something I'll never forget. I didn't feel like a failure anymore. If nothing else, I wanted to be a mother just so you could be a father. You were too good to never be a father. Then when he was born..." I sucked my lips between my teeth and bit down and held them for several long moments. "I don't hate you anymore." I brought my knees up to my chest and set my chin on top of them. "I met someone." I dropped my head and closed my eyes while I confessed. "I fell in love with him. I *am* in love with him. I already lost him, but I had him for a little while. He taught me that I could be happy again." I inhaled slowly. "Dash...I found happiness outside of you and my memories of you. I can't be happy and hang on to you." I nodded. "I'm bringing your things out here too. I need to move on. And, the only way I can do that is to let go of you," I said on a whisper. "I love you...so much. But, I love me too. And I can't move when I'm anchored to you, baby. I just can't. I love you and I'll never forget you...as long as I live."

Slowly I stood and brushed myself off. I made my way into my bedroom and did just what I said I was going to. I reverently packed up all of Dash's things and placed them in the barn alongside Noah's.

I couldn't rid my home of them completely, so I did something that I had learned from Rhett—something he helped me discover the strength to do.

Before bed, I took out all of the framed pictures that I had packed away long ago—and I hung them up—where I could see their faces smiling back at me.

After I climbed between the sheets, I reached over to turn off my lamp. On my nightstand sat the men whom I loved—Dash, grinning at me from my most favorite selfie of him, Noah, with baby food smeared on his face, smiling at me, and Rhett…holding my face against his and beaming at me from the picture frame.

That night, I fell asleep, knowing that I was healing…that I was conquering my fears and facing my demons. That night, I fell asleep beside the men that I loved.

***

I woke up early the following morning and headed to the paint store. My entire life needed a fresh coat, and I was going to start by painting over the baby blue. It was going to be hard, but I knew it was something I had to do.

I picked out a soft brown, almost the color of my coffee after I've added my milk and sugar. When I arrived home, a woman sat on my steps—a woman I had met before. Her white hair was just as pristine as her pant suit. I looked frumpy compared to her in my shirt with holes in it and baggy overalls.

As I approached her, I smiled and she smiled in return. I shook her hand. "Nora, right?"

"Not…exactly." Her answer clearly caught me off guard. "May we speak inside? I have a lot to tell you."

I knew this woman was tied to Rhett, and everything inside me was screaming to send her away. But, my love for him had to know all truths, not just the ones that I had uncovered on my own. So, I invited her inside, asked her to make herself at home, and gave her the floor. And, she talked.

"Your meeting Shepherd was no accident." I wasn't surprised to hear that. "I arranged it. I orchestrated everything—down to putting you next door to him. I know all about you, Evie. I am about to tell you things that Shepherd doesn't even know."

"Shepherd. Rhett?"

"One and the same. Yes. My name is Katarina Nottingham. I have worked for the CIA for thirty-nine years. My husband worked for the FBI for many years before me. After seeing the decline of the world's values and morality, we started a mission. Since we had access to everything there was to know about a person, we began to realize that we had enough information about criminals to destroy them—to clean up the streets that were so quickly turning to shit. So, he can up with a plan." She paused and drew in a deep breath. "These criminals were slipping through the cracks of our justice system. Killers were getting off with slaps on the wrists and just kept killing. The first time he decided to assassinate a criminal was in the spring of 1978. A man by the name of Billy Kingston was acquitted of some heinous crimes. He got off by reason of insanity. He had kidnapped, raped, tortured and killed three teenage girls from the Ohio River Valley area. He was found to be sane by several examiners, several who ended up not being able to testify. One was murdered, one was arrested for illegal activity for which he claimed he was never involved in, and one disappeared without a trace. The only examiner that found him clinically insane was a doctor whom I found out after the trial had been paid fifteen million dollars for his testimony. I knew there was nothing wrong with him. My husband, Duke, did too. You see," she paused, "one of those girls was our daughter, Nadia. She was fifteen when she disappeared walking home from a friend's house. She was missing for seven months before her body was found in a wooded area less than five miles away from our house. She had been dead for less than twelve hours when her body was found." Her eyes bore into mine. "Duke tracked Billy Kingston down…and avenged our beautiful daughter's lost life." Her face dropped to the ground. "After that, we started to dig and find criminals who committed terrible crimes and had not paid the price. Duke died nine years ago, but I still carry on our mission."

I sat in stunned silence for several moments. This sweet, old woman was part of something huge—some type of organization whose sole purpose was justified murder; however, it was only justified in the moral sense. She was heading up and carrying out tasks that everyone truly wants to be a part of. She was using her resources to kill people back.

"So, you still do this? And Rhett...or Shepherd...is a part of this?"

She smiled like a proud mother. "He is my most favorite part." She took a deep breath and reached over to touch my hand. "I'm not sure what all he has told you about his life—maybe everything, except the role that I play in it. When I heard about his wife and child's murder, it devastated me. Here was this handsome, upstanding man, just trying to do good and had just received life's cruelest punishment for it. I was contacted by a friend in the FBI about the case, and in my down time, I worked to locate the person or people responsible for it. I learned about the daycare worker just a day before I met Rhett. Acting alone, I had tracked her down and I planned to assassinate her, myself. She was in my line of sight when Rhett seemed to have come out of nowhere.

"I had followed him some and knew enough to recognize him. And I did. Immediately. He beat me to the punch. Through the scope of my rifle, I watched a heartbroken father exact his revenge. He didn't stick around, but I followed him. I assumed he would go home and shut himself in for days, but he didn't." She blew out a hard breath and said quietly, "I followed him to a cemetery. In the night, he went to the place where Arianna and Haven were buried. He dropped to his knees before them and wept. After about an hour, he fell asleep lying prostrate before their headstones, right in the middle of where they rested. I walked up to him and sat beside him all night while he slept. When he woke up, I introduced myself, told him what I knew about him. I made a proposal. He could work for me and carry out these assignments and I would throw myself into finding his family's killers." She looked at me, her eyes boring into mine. "He's worked for me ever since. He has never yielded. Never argued. Well," she chuckled, "until you came along."

"Me?"

"Yes. He has not had a mark since he met you, because you were his assignment. He was supposed to steer you away from any truth you may find. He was supposed to find out information from you. He wasn't supposed to fall in love with you." She smiled. "But he did." I looked down at my fidgeting hands and I felt my bottom lip start to quiver. "I know, as an investigator, it's difficult for you to see that what he does is somehow justified. But, try and look at it as a woman. As a wife. As a mother. What would you do? What would you want to do to someone who hurt your mother, your sister, or your child? If given the opportunity? If you're honest with yourself, you know what you would want to do."

I met her eyes solemnly and whispered, "I'd kill them."

She smiled just slightly. "Exactly." Her eyes fell to the floor. "He didn't want to get involved with you, but I made a promise to find them. But, I have hit a brick wall. I don't think I'll ever find them—you know, actually pinpoint *who* it was. I don't know what else to do. He's come through for me so many times, and I may have to break my promise to him. He may never get his revenge."

I sat and thought about everything that she had said. Of course, not all of it sank in right away.

I closed my eyes and could picture Rhett falling asleep, alone in a graveyard, and this sweet woman keeping watch over him. She loved him. I loved him. She loved him differently. She loved the strong man, the man with the purpose. I loved him in everything—his happiness, his weariness, his brokenheartedness. I loved the broken father, the shattered widower. I loved the wounded man. But, I loved the man who was healing slowly as I was healing.

I spoke the words before I realized it. "I want to help. I want to find them. It might help…having a fresh pair of eyes… I think Rhett deserves that."

She looked at me and smiled. "I think that's a wonderful idea."

After another hour of speaking with the woman who loved Rhett dearly and most likely saved his life, we bid farewell. She promised to have the boxes of evidence she had accumulated sent to my house the following morning.

Before she walked down my steps to her car, she turned around and looked at me. She asked, "Why didn't you turn him in? You had everything you needed to bury him, and you didn't. Why not?"

I already knew the answer to that and it wouldn't benefit me to keep it to myself. "Because I love him."

"So, why is he there and you're here?"

I whispered, "Because I'm not strong enough."

Without another word, she turned and walked away from me.

***

I took an eight week leave of absence from work the following day, and dove into the case of Rhett Trimble's murdered family. There was so much documentation, pictures, and pieces of evidence that I felt like I was drowning in it.

On the second day of the third week, I woke up sick. What felt like a dizzying head cold turned into a stomach bug. It wiped me out completely for an entire day. I felt like I was working too hard. I had done some traveling, even to St. Louis, to do some questioning. I had studied the records Katarina had given me for hours upon hours. I stayed up until dawn some mornings. I chalked my illness up to being overworked, but when I woke up sick every day for the rest of the week, I started to entertain the notion that something more serious was going on.

I sat on the tub and waited the full three minutes. I was terrified to peer over and take a peek at the answer that sat atop my bathroom counter. I sat there for five minutes after time was up without looking at it. It was useless, because I already knew the answer.

I squeezed my eyes shut and picked up the test. I opened up my eyes slowly and through my tears, I saw two little blue lines.

To my own astonishment, I smiled. Then, I laughed. Then, I wept.

I smiled because, in my heart, it's what I wanted.

I laughed because I was overjoyed.

And I wept because Rhett would never know.

***

After five months of searching diligently for the men responsible for the deaths of Rhett's wife and daughter, my work was complete. I placed the sealed envelope inside of a box along with a letter to its recipient. I taped the box shut—sealed it ever so tightly and wrote its destination on the top with a black marker and no return address.

I drove to the shipping office with shaking hands. I watched warily as the box was measured, weighed, and posted.

I observed as the box that held my finest work, the details of the deaths of the girls that belonged to the man that owned my heart, my most cherished task, made its way away from me.

Straight into the hands of *The Queen.*

CHAPTER TWENTY-TWO

Luke

Evie easily ranked as one of the most beautiful women I had ever laid eyes on. Not only was she lovely to watch, but I liked protecting her—even if she was unaware of my presence. I protected her because she loved my brother, my best friend.

The Queen had tracked me down after she discovered Evie had gone home. She had finally found my brother. He was devastated. He had lost everything. Again.

The Queen had learned the Senator, whose son's fate had fallen into the hands of her *Guardians*, was onto Evie. He had been snooping around the headquarters when his son's perverse actions had gone public. He had learned that Evie was the one who had busted the case wide open. Although her identity was kept out of the media, he had his avenues he often used to gain that knowledge.

Katarina knew that Evie was in danger. But, she also knew that Evie would never agree to any type of protection. She was stubborn and had become independent again—a quality that she gave my brother the credit for restoring.

So, Katarina called in a personal favor from me. I took an indefinite leave to watch out for Evie. I sat outside her house at night. I followed her to work. I trailed her to her doctor's appointments. I slept underneath the stars when she went to visit her parents.

She had been home for nearly four months when I noticed the swelling in her lower belly. After the third doctor's visit, I thought she may be pregnant. My suspicions were right. I could've easily found out for sure sooner, but I still wanted her to have some privacy.

I sat in my SUV in front of a small shopping center and watched her walk to her car, walking into the wind; it blew her flowery knee-length dress taut against her front, revealing the small mound protruding below her navel. She reached down and placed her hand on her belly and smiled.

She wanted it—my brother's baby. Keeping that baby a secret was one of the biggest lies I ever told to my most favorite person in the world. It was almost impossible not to call him up and tell him that he was going to be a father again. But, as much as it killed me, I didn't need to be convinced of why she made that decision.

She hadn't turned him in. And, that spoke of her love for him. She hadn't told him about the baby. And, that spoke of her fear of him. Maybe not the kind of fear where she would fear for her life in his presence—that would never happen—but, maybe the fear of not knowing who he really was.

But if I know my brother, he showed her who he was. I had never seen him so infatuated before. I definitely had never seen him so incredibly in love.

A few months had passed and there seemed to be no retaliation coming from the Senator or his henchmen. I was starting to believe that Evie was in the clear. But, I didn't want to give up watching her. It was easy to see why Rhett fell in love with her. Her movements (most of the time) were graceful, she smiled at everyone, she was patient and kind. She helped anyone she could.

One day, I watched her sit down and have lunch with a homeless man near her work—a lunch she bought for him. She sat down right beside him on the sidewalk. Right when she sat down, he said, "It's been a long time." She just smiled at him. Then, for the remaining hour, they made small talk about things that were not important. He told her she looked happy. She told him she was, and even I was convinced. He mentioned her pregnancy that was becoming obvious and he asked her if she knew what it was going to be. She just spread her fingers over the bump and told him she wasn't certain, but she had a feeling.

"You have a name picked out?" he asked her with a smile stretched across his dirty face.

She nodded. "I do."

After a long day at work and a long day of my voyeurism, she called it a night. I was sitting down the road, watching Evie's house about eight o'clock when my phone buzzed.

"Hey," I said right when I picked up.

Sniffling is what I heard for the first twenty seconds. Then, a sobbing Rhett said, "I don't know if I can do this, man."

"What can't you do, buddy?" I asked him softly and tenderly, like I'd talk to a wild horse I was trying to break.

"Live. I don't *want* to live anymore."

I sat up straight in my seat and leaned forward. I had not shed tears in a long time, a very long time. But, my eyes burned with the sensation that it was going to happen any second.

"Don't talk like that. Don't you dare talk like that."

"I should've died. Why did it have to be them? Why didn't they just kill me?"

"You have a lot to live for, brother."

"Like what?" he snapped. "You fucking tell me what I'm living for and I won't pull this fucking trigger!" he screamed.

I panicked. I knew Rhett. He was hurting more than he ever had. He was completely destroyed. I knew he would do it. My voice broke, "Don't you fucking dare! That's a coward's way out and you know it! If you seriously have a gun, put the damn thing down!" I couldn't stop my sobs. "Please, Rhett. Please." I squeezed my eyes shut. "I'm coming to you. Give me until the morning. I'm coming to you."

"If you're not here in the morning…."

"I'm fucking coming!" I screamed. "Just go to bed. I'll be there by dawn."

"Okay," he whispered.

"Rhett?"

"Yeah?"

"I love you. I'm coming. Just…wait for me, okay?"

"Okay," he said softly. "I love you, too, Luke."

I called Katarina and let her know that I had to pull myself from Evie's detail. I assured her that I thought she would be safe, at least for a couple of days. Nothing had happened since I'd shown up. I was certain I could slip away and pop back up completely unnoticed.

I didn't tell her all of my plans, especially the ones that involved knocking on Evie's door.

When she opened her door, she stared at me in shock. Her yoga pants and tight blue t-shirt hid nothing from me. It was pretty obvious from my red eyes and flushed face that I was upset. Her smile faded when she saw me, but the tortured look on her face after taking me all in nearly brought me to my knees.

Her hand covered her mouth and she took in a sharp breath. "Luke? Is Rhett alright?"

I just shook my head. "I hope so."

She was clearly shaken. "What happened?"

"Nothing yet. But, he's not dealing well with everything."

She touched my arm. "Please. Come in."

"I can't. I have to go. I just…" I paused. "I just needed to tell you that you might be in danger. There's nothing concrete, no proof or real threats, just please be vigilant. Be careful." She dropped her eyes to the floor, and I saw the look on her face when she realized that her baby bump was not concealed in the least. She looked up at me and I smirked. "I've known for a while."

She just nodded. I didn't explain further. Maybe it's because she knew. She knew someone would watch out for her. She knew that none of us could let her walk away so easily.

"I have to go to him. So, I need you to keep an eye out. If you notice anything out of the ordinary, call me." I took my phone out and called her phone. "There's my number. Don't call the police. If something happens while I'm gone these next few days, call this number." I handed her a business card. "He's a friend of mine that lives about two minutes from here. We served together. His name is Trevor Jamison. Call him. No one else. Got me?"

She nodded jerkily and I turned to walk away from her. Then, she called out to me, "Luke?" I turned around. The moonlight cast upon her and I saw her silhouette move toward me. When she reached me, she stood on her tiptoes and wrapped her arms around my neck. "Give him this for me." She sniffed. "I love him so much, Luke. I just..." she trailed off.

"He loves you, Evie. He needs you. He doesn't want to live without you. That's why I have to go him. He says he *won't* live without you." Her body stiffened against mine. "I might tell him...about the baby."

Her breath hitched and she squeezed me tightly. "You can't, Luke. He can't know."

"He *needs* to know. It might be the only thing that saves his life."

"Luke..." she pleaded.

"Evie." My bottom lip quivered, and I bit down on it. "He's my brother. I can't lose him. Maybe you could go. Instead of me." She shook her head. "You love him. I know you do." She nodded. "So, why don't you go to him?"

"I can't."

"Evie, if you'll just try to understand..."

"I understand, Luke. More than I should. That's one reason I'm having such a hard time with it. Those people he killed...they weren't innocent. Hell, I even think they deserved what they got. But, what kind of person does that make me? It makes me someone that I don't recognize. I don't want to live my life with my heart filled with hate. I feel like he can't love me when he is consumed by that hatred."

"He's not consumed by hatred, Evie. He's consumed by you. But, you want to know what I think? I think you *have* to hate in order to know what love really feels like. He's lived without Arianna for over five years. But, I've never seen him like this. He was devastated then. Distraught, yes. But, he's lived without you for three months, and he's ready to stop living at all. He's killed for them, but he'd die for you." I shrugged as she backed away from me. "Please remember that."

With that, I walked away, leaving her in the dark. I climbed in my SUV and drove away. I boarded the redeye flight with only a carry-on. The woman beside me was on her way to see her mother who was dying of cancer. When I asked her about her destination, she told me, "I'm going to tell my mother goodbye. Where are you headed?"

I smiled at her. "I'm going to tell my brother that he's gonna be a daddy."

CHAPTER TWENTY-THREE

RHETT

That was what rock bottom felt like. It felt like every possession of mine, especially my favorite ones, were all ceramic. Then, one day, I took a hammer and smashed all of them until there was nothing left but the dust. After that, I tore my chest open and ripped my own heart out. I threw it down on the ground and beat *that* with a hammer.

What's worse than a regular heartache? A heartache that comes to a heart that was nearly mended.

I was almost over it. I was almost ready to walk away from everything that I had known that I hated. I even considered a new career. I just wanted to take Evie away from all of this.

These months away were supposed to be a retreat. I was to enjoy myself, go out and meet people. My second day here, I met my neighbor—an eighty-seven year old widow named Emma Bradshaw. I saw her lounging on the beach and decided to introduce myself. It was completely out of character for me, but it was something that Evie would've done.

Ms. Emma had met her husband weeks before he went to war. She instantly fell in love with the smart-mouthed Texan. Two days before he left, they were married. The love in her eyes raged, especially when she told me that they didn't sleep at all from the time they left their reception until he boarded the plane that would take him away from her.

She got pregnant within those two days and she waited for him to come home to her. And waited. And waited.

For six years, she waited. All the while, she raised her son alone. She had heard nothing of his whereabouts, or whether he was alive or dead. She loved him, so she waited.

She was outside picking tomatoes from her small garden when she saw a figure in the distance. The man emerging from the horizon was tall but lanky. The limp in his gate was obvious even from far away.

After what seemed like forever, he finally walked up to her—the man she had patiently waited for. She said his face was bowed to the ground. He was ashamed that he was not the same man that walked away from her. No longer was he the strong, flawless, handsome man that she remembered. His cheeks looked hollowed, nearly starved. His face was scarred, his nose was crooked, his leg was damaged, and his arm was missing.

"What did you say to him?" I asked, curious to know what her wisdom would reveal.

She smiled. "I reached up and touched his face so that he'd look at me. All I said was, 'You're beautiful.'"

I smiled back at her. Those words were familiar to me from a time in my life when I found myself in a less dramatic, but similar situation. They were the same as Arianna's words to me.

"He wasn't ever the same."

"I don't imagine," I responded.

"He was better," she said, grinning at me. "He never told me everything that happened. But, whatever happened made him a better man. Our kids idolized him."

"You had more children?"

"Oh, yes," she laughed. "We had six more," she said chuckling. "He and our first boy, Wynne, were inseparable. The day Wynne died, I thought Harlan was going to die, himself. I'd never seen a man so devastated. He blamed himself."

"What happened to him? To Wynne?"

Her eyes shone bright with tears. "Harlan sent Wynne to run trotlines one night. Harlan was so sick; he couldn't get out of bed. Wynne was sixteen and was accustomed to doing most of the work anyway, but that was the first night he went alone. He fell out of the boat, got tangled up in the lines and drowned." She paused and looked out across the water, letting the setting sun dance on her face. "That would've killed some men. But not Harlan. That tragedy renewed all his love for us. Before the accident, there were some days that Harlan got wrapped up in his self-pity and self-deprecation. Some days he would ignore us. He was still a good man, a great husband, wonderful father, but he was still human. He would get that way sometimes. But, not after that. Never again did he feel sorry for himself. Wynne's death changed him…for the better."

Almost every day for four months, we would meet out on the beach or the back porch and share stories. Most nights I would just sit there and listen. So many things she said took me back to the lives I had lived. My childhood. My life as a Marine. My life with Arianna and Haven. My life with Evie.

Everything that she said resonated with me. I just liked listening to her. She was witty and funny and wise.

I told that woman everything. Literally everything. She told me to hold nothing back, that she'd "take it to the grave." She said that she was only allowing me to unload on her because she was on a fast track to eternity. So, I did.

After some small talk, which included her confessing that her children, because of their own monetary success in life, asked her to leave her house to a charity organization, and my admission that I absolutely loved the house and it was big enough to raise a family in, she laughed and said, "Well, I'll leave it to you. How about that?" I just laughed. That led into a therapy session that I wasn't sure Ms. Emma had the heart for.

We stayed up until three in the morning while I told her the edited version of my life in a nutshell. By the time I finished, we were laying on our backs in the sand, staring up at the moon.

We sat in silence for several minutes before she said, "That was a beautiful story." She paused. "How does it end?"

I chuckled. "With me. Here. Talking to you."

She let out an outraged huff. "That's no ending! Lying in the dark night, looking at the stars with a nearly ninety-year-old woman!" She slapped me on the arm.

I laughed. "Well, maybe I'll tell you the ending tomorrow."

"Today is tomorrow. It's past midnight!"

I chuckled. "Yeah, you're right. Tomorrow's tomorrow."

"Okay," she responded.

Ms. Emma's tomorrow's tomorrow never came. When I stood on her porch at a quarter after nine and she wasn't waiting for me, I knew something was wrong.

I quickly picked the lock and found Ms. Emma lying in her bed with her eyes closed, as if she were asleep, clutching a picture of Mr. Harlan and all seven of their children to her chest.

Ms. Emma had left me.

Just like the rest.

I tried desperately to resuscitate her, but my efforts were in vain. She would not come back to me.

She loved me. She had told me many times. She told me she prayed for me every day, and that she hoped that I found my happiness with the woman that I loved. She gave me peace in a tormenting time in my life, and I loved her for that.

I sat on the beach as her children came and packed up her things. Her son, Charlie, who was old enough to be my dad and whom I had met on several occasions, walked up to me holding a brown paper bag and handed it to me.

"Here you go, Rhett. This has your name on it."

"Thanks," I said, taking it from his hands.

"Well, everything is cleaned out. We'll probably have the house on the market soon—or as soon as we find out what mom's intentions were with the place." I nodded. He stood and I sat while we both occupied an awkward silence—until he filled it. "She adored you. Thank you for looking out for her."

I shook his hand. "It was truly my pleasure. She was a special woman."

He nodded. "My dad would say to us, 'If I had a nickel for every woman like your mother, I'd have…one nickel. But, it'd be *my* nickel.' I always loved it when he said that." With that, he walked away.

The next month was absolutely brutal. Once again, I was alone. All I could do was dwell on my life and the things I had done to royally screw up every good thing I had.

I had not been drunk in years, but it was becoming a regular occurrence. And, with no outlet, no way to really express what I was feeling, no one to talk to, I started to go crazy.

The night I called Luke, I don't know what I was thinking. I was being pathetic and irrational. I upset him. I know I wasn't serious. I just knew that saying those things and acting out like that would make him run to me. I needed someone. I needed someone badly— someone who knew why I hurt so much. My other brother and my sister had no clue. They thought that I had taken a job on the coast. I didn't tell them differently. But, Luke knew. I needed Luke.

I went to bed that night not able to remember at what point I fell asleep. I woke before dawn to banging on my front door. My hangover was so bad; I didn't even grab my gun as usual. I didn't even check to see who it was. I simply opened the door.

The Queen stood before me. Her face held almost no expression. I motioned for her to enter and she did, reluctantly. I sat down in my recliner. I hadn't said a word. I should have been mortified, but I was too far gone to even be ashamed. She said nothing either.

From the bag she carried on her shoulder, she extracted a large envelope whose contents were stretching the limits of the seams. She handed it to me face down.

I reached for it and flipped it over. My heart stopped.

Scrolled across the front was written, "Rhett Trimble," in the most beautiful cursive I had ever seen.

My hands started to shake and I could only sit and stare at it. I was panting, trying to catch my breath. This was so surreal. What I had waited almost six years for was finally in my hands.

"You found them," I said on a heavy sigh. I looked up at her guarded face.

She shook her head. "Not me."

"Who then?" I asked curiously. She said nothing for several moments. I grew impatient. "Who, Queen?"

She held my eyes. "Evie. Evie found them. She wanted me to give that to you."

I started to cry. Hard. *The Queen* just stood there and held a silent vigil for my mourning. And for my soon-to-be victory.

After ten minutes of wailing, I finally stopped and she spoke. "There is a lot of information and documentation in there. You could look through it all. Study it. Contemplate something terrible and truly vengeful. You could do that. But, if you want to carry this out quickly, so you can get to her faster, you can use this." She pulled a piece of notebook paper from her bag and unfolded it and handed it to me. I took it quickly and saw Evie's handwriting staring back at me. Another letter. Addressed to my *Queen* on the outside, but meant for me. The letter read:

Dear Rhett:

Your wait is over. I have found them. Every last one of them. Doing this for you is the least that I could do to pay you back for what you did for me. I am no longer the person that I was when I met you. I'm not even the person that I was before my heart needed to know you. And, I'm not the person that I was when I thought I had everything.

I can wake up in the morning and not hate the daylight that begged me to wake up. I can lie in my bed at night and finally hear complete silence—total calmness in my mind and in my heart. I can find peace in the things that almost killed me. I can smile and not hate it. I can visit my friends again. I even held my friend's baby a few days ago…and I loved it. I fell in love, even with a broken heart. I became someone who could live again.

I did all of those things…all because of you. I think about you every single second of the day. I fell in love with you. I fell in love with your family. I fell in love with the ladies in your life. They deserve justice. You dedicated six months of your life to me—baring yourself almost completely. So, I decided to dedicate some of my life to you.

This letter provides the shortcut to your chase. Everything in the envelope proves their guilt—beyond a shadow of a doubt. It's all there for you. But, I want you to use this as your map to complete this final task.

You'll need the help of your entire team. Katarina is already aware of this. Your team knows as well. They're sitting on 'go' waiting for your instruction. So, below are the identities of your final marks along with a rundown of the most pertinent information. My suggestion is that you have a member assigned to each person and carry out this assignment simultaneously as to avoid quick retaliation.

Names and addresses to residences are given below. They are all members of the drug cartel which you already suspected—the cartel whose member you prosecuted. Of the hundreds of members, the following seven are the ones who are responsible for your greatest loss.

Raul Ortiz—2569 Pine Valley Cove, St. Louis. Took Haven from daycare.

Tommy Dunn—62 Peach Tree, Carthage. Called Ari on the morning of murder to report your faked car accident.

Vito Lopez—85 Cheyenne Loop, Ashland. Attacked Ari in parking lot, kidnapped both mother and child.

Quinton Tupelo—9 Dakota, Bates City. Actively assisted Lopez.

Bobby Price—725 Third St., St. Louis. Also actively assisted Lopez.

Robbie Fortner—24 Third St., St. Louis. Physically abused Ari. Wounded her, by firearm, in both legs.

Carl Helton—65 Valhalla, St. Charles. Mastermind. Taped mother and child to driver and passenger seats. Pushed into river. Left note with clue as to location of the vehicle on patrol car.

Never ask me how I got this information. After you carry out the assignment, never speak of it again.

I love you with everything that is left of me.

I sat and looked at the names and address of my family's murderers. Despite everything I did to Evie, she still loved me. She loved me enough to do what *The Queen* had been unable to do.

I looked up at her. "When did you get this?"

"The moment I received it, I caught a plane to bring it to you."

I looked back at the letter. "Who's Katarina?"

"Me."

I finally knew her name—after all of these years. It seemed odd. She suddenly seemed more human to me. She must have seen Evie. She must have spoken with her. "Did you ask her to do this?"

"No. It was her idea. She wanted to do it."

"I can't believe this. It says here that I need the entire team. There are only five of us. There are seven marks here. How do we...?"

She smiled and cut me off. "Who do you think did this before you? You think I'm too old to carry out an assignment?"

I smiled at her. My face felt like it was cracking because it had been so long since I smiled. "No ma'am. I don't think that at all. So, you and who else?"

She smiled. "An old friend of mine. Get dressed. And hurry. We're going to St. Louis. We have something to do tonight."

"But, it's not Friday," genuinely stating.

She smirked. "I don't give a damn what a day it is. We are doing this. Tonight."

"Yes ma'am."

In a daze, I jumped up and gathered my things.

I was going to get my revenge.

I would finally be at peace.

And whether she wanted me to or not, I was going to get Evie.

While packing up my things, I retrieved the bag containing my inheritance from Ms. Emma. I was not her son, but she loved me just the same.

I turned the bag upside down and its contents fell out. I picked up her late husband's dog tags and put them around my neck. Then, I reached down for the little box and popped the top open. Inside rested a vintage three carat diamond wedding set that was polished and shined to perfection. Tucked inside the box was a note that I had read a thousand times. It read: "This ring better be the beginning to your happy ending."

I smiled because I knew this was the end of this life for me, and I would do absolutely anything to win her back.

***

I did not follow Evie's orders exactly. Although her plan was a good one and would get the job done, I would not feel the satisfaction of carrying out my revenge completely.

I had to be the one that did them in. Every. Last. One. Of. Them.

It had to be me.

In the late night hours and the wee ones in the morning, we drew them out. All seven of them.

In their own strategic ways, the team members baited their marks, gagged them, and brought them all here to our warehouse.

There they sat. All seven of them in a line before me. Their arms were tied behind their backs and they remained gagged. Lights shone down on them while I leaned against the wall in the darkness. I studied them. Two of them were crying. The other four sat stoically and almost looked reflective—almost appeared accepting of what would surely be their fate.

And, Helton sat in the center with a smug look on his face. Where I found some contrition in the faces of the rest, there was none in his. It took six years for them to be gathered here for this reason. They would not linger in suspense. Truthfully, I was ready to get it over with.

While the members of my team, including *The Queen* remained against the wall in the blackness, I pushed off and made my way into the light. I didn't bother concealing my face. There would be no point because my face was going to be the last thing they would see.

I stood in front of them and waited until seven pairs of eyes landed on me. Recognition blazed in their expressions. They knew exactly who I was. They knew exactly why they were here.

Bobby Price sat at the end on my right. His face was wet with his own tears, and the moment he saw me, his face crumpled and his head dropped to his chest. I walked over to him, pulled off his gag, and dropped to my haunches in front of him.

"Look at me," I ordered. Slowly, he lifted his head and did as I had told him. "Do you know who I am?" He nodded. "Speak. Do you know who I am?"

"Yes," he said softly. "You're the lawyer."

"What did you do to my family?" I asked with a steady voice. His face drew up with emotion and he shook his head. "Answer me. Now."

"We killed them," he whispered.

"Specifics. I want specifics. What did *you* do? Did you touch my wife? Did you touch my daughter? Tell me what you did," I said almost tenderly, under the pretense of calm and comfort.

His eyes fell to the ground. "I pulled...I pulled your wife from her car and threw her down to the ground once we had her cornered. Lopez was yelling at me to kick her, so I did. I did. Hard. I kicked her everywhere I could." He paused and I said nothing. I closed my eyes. This was my torture. This was the price I had to pay for letting them die—knowing of every detail of their deaths. "She cried out for you." I felt my breathing grow heavy as I fought my tears. She called for me, and I didn't come. "I can still hear her. In my nightmares. Saying your name. The rasping. The gurgling. I hear it all."

I took a deep breath. "And my daughter?"

"I uh...stepped away from your wife when I heard your daughter crying in the back seat. Lopez told me to shut her up. I knew what he wanted, but I couldn't kill her. It wasn't in me. So, I walked around and opened the door and took her out of her car seat.

I bounced her and shushed her until she stopped crying." Tears poured down his face and his entire jaw quivered. "She smiled at me. I hate that she smiled at me." Then, he broke down.

This man had hurt my wife and soothed my daughter all in one terrifying day. As worthless as he was, I almost respected the gesture. Almost.

As I looked up at him, fighting my own tears, I asked him, "You know I'm going to kill you, right?"

He nodded. Then wept.

After I replaced his gag, I stepped over to the next one. Once again, I removed the gag and squatted in front of him. Quinton Tupelo stared back at me. He was not crying, but he was scared. His breathing was unsteady; his pulse was pounding; and he was shaking.

"What did you do to my wife? And my daughter?" I asked him, my voice coming off strong, renewed.

"I did what Bobby did. Not as much because the damage was done. She was hurt bad. And, I just couldn't bring myself to do more than watch."

"Was she assaulted? Sexually?" The reports said that she hadn't been, but I needed to know if it had been attempted.

He shook his head rapidly. "No, sir. Lopez tried, but she fought. She fought like crazy."

I nodded. "And my daughter?"

His eyes welled up. "I didn't touch her. I swear."

I nodded once more, and then I looked up into his gray eyes. "You know I'm going to kill you, right?"

"I deserve it," he whispered. I replaced his gag and pressed forward.

Every one of the men surrounding Helton confessed their crimes to me. Lopez was the only one of them, besides Helton, that appeared smug and sure of himself. When I asked him if he knew his life would end by my hands, he said nothing. He just stared at me. Maybe he thought I was bluffing. Maybe he thought I wouldn't get away with it. Maybe he thought his gang members would bust him out in a grand escape.

He was wrong.

Tommy Dunn and Raul Ortiz actually apologized, tearfully. Raul pleaded for his life. They both admitted that they too were actually apart of Ari's physical abuse. Dunn also admitted that he was the one that buckled Haven back into her car seat. He even mentioned her Halloween costume and through sobs told me that she looked at him with huge, blue eyes…just like mine. It took everything inside of me not to take his head in my hands and wrench it quickly beyond its limits.

My tears fell when he told me that. "She was beautiful, wasn't she?" I asked him.

He nodded. "Yes, sir. I'm so sorry." He also wept, but remorse would not save him from my wrath.

"You killed my baby," I whispered to him. He nodded. "You know I'm going to kill you back?" Once again, he nodded.

Raul Ortiz was inconsolable. He was beside himself with grief and fear, begging to be spared, after he tearfully admitted that he had kidnapped Haven from her daycare. I asked him, point blank, "Did my wife beg for her life?" I was certain she did. I was only pointing out that his begging was like hers—absolutely futile.

But, his answer stopped me dead in my tracks. "No," he answered. "She begged for her daughter's life…and yours."

Anger came over me like a tidal wave. For the first time since her death, I was angry with Ari. I hated her selflessness. She didn't even ask to be spared for her own sake. She only wanted her daughter safe. And her husband—the man who had put her there in the first place. Unfortunately for Ortiz, that anger was unleashed on him. I laid into him with strong and forceful punches until I knocked him out. His nose was broken, clearly. And his jaw. And I didn't care.

Robbie Fortner had the greenest eyes I had ever seen. They were haunting. He, too, told me of his role in the death of my family. He explained he owed a debt to the gang and couldn't pay it monetarily. So, he agreed to "rough someone up," that's what he was told he was going to do. With a shaky breath, he admitted to shooting Arianna and helping place her in the car. He also said that he put Haven in the front seat beside her mother. "I know you're going to kill me," he said softly. His green eyes bore into mine. "I have a daughter," he said as his bottom lip trembled. "I wasn't a father then. I am now. And, if any man hurt my daughter the way we hurt yours, I'd do exactly as you're doing now. There's one major difference between you and me, though."

"What's that?"

"What you're doing...this is merciful compared to what I would've done. You're a good father." With that, I replaced his gag and turned to Helton—the man behind my greatest heartache.

When I took his gag off, his demeanor and expression was unlike all the rest. He smiled at me. I hadn't taken the time to look at him when I lured him outside. I simply put him in a hold and he quietly passed out in less than a minute. But, now, in the light, I recognized him.

He was in the courtroom every day during the trial of Trenton Black, a member of a drug cartel on trial for murdering a doctor and his wife in cold blood—the case I had won. The case that cost me my family. But, he was there. Thinking back, I remember him sitting behind *me*, not Black, the defendant. He even asked me how I was doing every day.

I felt my blood run cold.

I had told him about him about my wife. I had told him stories about my daughter. I had shown him pictures of them. He baited me with kindness and interest, claimed he was part of the advising team for my law school. Naturally, I trusted him.

And, I had sold my family out to him. After the trial, I never even thought about him again. He grinned at me.

"You remember," he stated.

"You motherfucker," I seethed. I vaguely heard footsteps behind me and saw *The Queen* step partially into the light. Her presence was almost forgotten, but she stepped forward as reinforcement, a reminder for me to carry this out rationally.

He shrugged and grinned. "It was cute, you know? You always called her *my Ari*. She belonged to you, but in the end, I owned her life. Didn't I?" I breathed heavily, my nostrils flaring. "You think I'm going to be like these other pussies and apologize? Beg for your forgiveness? Please." He huffed. "I still like the sound of duct tape being pulled away from the roll, wound around and around and around..." he trailed off. "I love that sound." He held my gaze as he spoke. "My brother went to prison because of you. He was killed the same day he went in. Did you know that?" I did know, but I didn't give a shit. "Your family. For my family." He paused. "That little wife of yours was something else, a little fighter. Hot little bitch, too. Tight little body. Nice little tits. Firm little tits." The fucker chuckled. "And that little cow costume was the most precious..." He was cut off by his own screams when I reached for my pistol and shot him in the top of his left leg.

"You fucker!" he screamed. "I'll have you killed for this!" he screamed. And again, cut off by his own screams when I shot him in his right leg. He was moaning and panting.

I leaned down to look in his eyes. "Did that hurt?"

He spit on me. I've always hated that. Even in movies. "If you had a family now, I'd kill them too."

I looked behind me and all of *The Guardians* stepped forward into the light. The corner of my lip was tugged up by my grin. I looked back at Helton, bleeding out of both legs, completely vulnerable. Completely touchable. Completely damned.

"That's my family. Think you can kill them? Because you can't do a fucking thing bound to that chair." I lifted my pistol and aimed.

His eyes met mine and he spoke, "Killing your wife and your daughter was the sweetest thing I ever did. I relished in what I had done. I loved that they suffered. I love that I..."

I fired six times, unable to hear any more. The first shot certainly killed him, and the last five were *just because*.

For the remaining six, because of their remorse, I showed mercy. I did not let them go. However, I made their deaths quick and painless.

After I fired my last shot, I dropped to my knees. And wailed. Finally.

They were avenged. My sweet wife and precious daughter could finally rest in peace.

And so could I.

***

After *The Queen* sent me away from the warehouse, promising to take care of the rest, I drove to my loft to sleep. I was incredibly tired and I needed rest. I needed to be completely rested up for when I went after Evie. I didn't turn on my phone. I didn't check the time. I just laid down in bed and passed out.

For the first time in almost six years, I actually slept soundly. I slept peacefully knowing that my family's murderers were dead. Some may think that my taking of their lives was just as bad as what they had done. But, I saw it as justice. I still see it as justice. It was the upright thing to do.

When I woke up the following morning or midday rather, I watched one of my hundreds of videos of Haven. I didn't cry to my surprise. I smiled for the most part, listening to her and to Arianna.

I was recording when I walked into the room where Ari was breastfeeding Haven. She was about two months old. I remembered this day because Ari had turned twenty the day before. I had taken her out to celebrate. We ate cheeseburgers and cheese fries. We went to the driving range and we laughed like crazy. She hit three people with wild balls and we were eventually asked to leave. I carried her to the car, then I carried her into the house, and I loved on her like crazy…a few times. Her neck was still red from my five o'clock shadow.

"Hey, baby. Whatcha doin'?"

She smiled at me. First thing in the morning, she was gorgeous. "Feeding your daughter." She cocked her head to the side. "Are you

247

really recording?"

"Yeah," I chuckled.

"Oh my goodness! Really?" She leaned forward in the chair to reach for a blanket.

"Don't cover up. It's just me."

"My boob is hanging out."

"I love your boob. Oh, and it's the left one. My favorite."

"What? Your favorite?" she laughed.

"Yeah. It's just a tad bigger than the right one." She smiled. I knelt down in front of her. "She's pretty perfect, huh?" She nodded. "She looks so much different, even in the last few weeks. Who do you think she looks like?"

"You."

"Really?" It secretly thrilled me. I thought Ari was beautiful, but there's a special primitive feeling of ownership that comes when a daughter looks like her daddy.

"Yeah. Look at those lips. Those are your lips. And those eyes, definitely all you. She's even got that slight dent in her chin just like you. She *is* perfect." She looked up at me, shirt open, no bra, our daughter receiving nourishment from her mother's body—absolutely beautiful. "I love you," she said.

Nonchalantly, I said, "I know."

With that, I saw something that I had never really taken the time to notice. The little quiver in her jaw. The low hitch in her breath. She nodded and looked back down at Haven.

I didn't notice when it happened. I was wrapped up in keeping myself at a distance that I didn't even notice the little things that hurt her. I knew I hurt her every day. But, even in this special moment we shared, I hurt her heart. I had never watched this particular video before. But, when I saw the expression on Ari's face, I backed it up and watched it over and over again. After I watched it, I let the video play out. I didn't know that I hadn't turned off the camera and it was still rolling. I couldn't see either of them in the picture, but I heard her voice, talking to our daughter.

She sniffed. "You think he'll ever say it back?" Of course, Haven didn't answer, but I could hear her grunting and smacking. "When I saw him, I was swept away. And, when he kissed me…for the first time in my life, I felt wanted. I couldn't believe someone like him wanted someone like me. I was so happy to find out about you. Because…I wanted him forever. I already loved him—the moment I saw him." She sighed heavily. "But you gave him to me. I think he loves me. I'm almost certain he does. I just wish he would say it back. But, as long as he says it to you, that'll make me happy. As long as he loves you."

She, along with her selflessness, put little Haven back in her crib. Captured on the camera was Ari standing there just staring at her. She reached down and touched Haven's belly and smiled. "Just like him. You look just like him." Then there was silence as she left the room, leaving Haven asleep.

I sat there and stared at the blank screen. My phone rang loudly and startled me. It was Luke.

"Hey."

"Where the *hell* are you? I've been trying to reach you since yesterday! You knew I was coming to where you were staying! Where are you?" He sounded panicked.

"I'm at the loft. St. Louis. I came home. I have a lot to tell you…"

He cut me off. "That shit can wait. We have got bigger fucking problems."

My heart dropped to my stomach. "What happened?"

He didn't even hesitate. "Evie's missing."

CHAPTER TWENTY-FOUR

Evie

I was shocked to see Luke at my door that night. However, I was not shocked that someone was watching out for me. I could always feel someone watching me, but it wasn't an eerie feeling or any feeling of uncertainty. I actually felt safe. Over the last few months, I had seen someone who resembled Luke, but his thick facial hair and longer hair concealed his true identity. I just thought I was mistaken on those occasions and went about my business.

As the months passed, the baby inside me grew. The baby was healthy and growing beautifully. I wanted to wait to know what it was. I needed the anticipation in my life. However, I gave in and asked the doctor what I was having.

Telling my parents that I was pregnant was the most terrifying thing ever. I felt like a little girl who had cut all of her bangs to the scalp and was waiting for her mom to get home to find out. Or a teenager who got pregnant on prom night and had to tell her dad that she got knocked up by the quarterback.

I told my parents two weeks after I found out. I wanted to wait to see the doctor before I told them anything. They first asked me about my relationship with Rhett because they knew I was trying to move on with someone. I told them a whitewashed version of the truth, and just said that it wasn't going to work out.

"I have something to tell you both," I said quietly while we sat on the back porch. I couldn't look at them, so I just stared toward the evening sun.

"What is it, sweetie?" my sweet mother asked.

I blew out a heavy breath. "I'm pregnant." My mother gasped and my dad stared at me. I waited with bated breath for their reaction.

My dad was the first to move. He slowly stood from his chair and walked over to me. When he reached me, he leaned down and hugged me. He quietly whispered, "Wonderful news, baby. This is wonderful news." He leaned back and looked at me with teary eyes. "That man is a fool, if you ask me."

"That man is the best man I've ever known," I responded. "He just doesn't believe that." I looked at my mother who was smiling and sobbing. Even with all of her wisdom, she had no words for me. She clung to me and cried...tears of joy.

Over the next few months, they both helped me decorate a guest room in my home for the nursery. My dad made a beautiful crib for the baby. My mother helped me pick out new furniture to match it. I had reconnected with one of my best friends from before the accident. Once again, I told the short story of how I came to be in the condition I was in. She was ecstatic and offered her helpful hand. We had been shopping together. I had visited her on several occasions. I had even babysat their eight-month-old baby while she and her husband went out on a date. Being a mother, doing motherly things, was truly like riding a bike. I never stumbled. I never got caught up in my heartache. I just cared for their munchkin as if he were my own.

I was being more social, catching up with friends and loved ones—actually reaching out to those I had turned away from. Once I made that move, they received me with open arms and wet faces. I was even asked out on a date, pregnant belly and all. I kindly declined because only one man owned my heart, and I didn't think I could ever love anyone else.

Every month, I would visit the doctor and learn of my baby's progress, and afterwards, I would leave with a smile on my face. My situation wasn't perfect. My heart was still sore, but I finally had a reason to live. So, I smiled. I laughed. I cracked jokes. I wasn't exactly coming into my old self. I was becoming someone new—someone better. And, I loved her. I loved who I was becoming.

I was this new person all because of Rhett…all because of the things he had taught me. All because of this gift he had given me.

I hardly slept the night I saw Luke. If not for the exhaustion that growing a baby caused, I probably wouldn't have slept. I was worried about Rhett. From what Luke had told me, Rhett was acting irrationally. I prayed that he wasn't considering what Dash had done. As much as I loved Dash, his weakness and unwillingness to forgive himself had been his downfall. I knew Rhett was stronger than that.

I sat in the new glider in the nursery and stared at the walls. My mom and dad had painted the room a cool, beautiful aqua color. They hung gray curtains with white dandelions on them, and other gray accents throughout the room. Big black and white canvas photos hung on the walls. There were several of Noah, a small picture of Dash and I on our wedding day, and a larger picture of Rhett and me—a selfie that he had snapped as we lounged in bed on a rainy Saturday. I was pregnant when the picture was taken, but I didn't know it.

My father had brought in a large canvas, larger than all of the rest, flipped around so that I couldn't see the photograph. He simply stated that it was a gift from him. When he turned it around, my hands flew over my lips as I sucked in a breath.

It was a picture of Rhett and little Haven. Her face was ruddy and she was smiling. Rhett held her close, and the picture captured them facing one another, his lips planted on her forehead. His eyes closed.

"Where did you get that?" I asked him quietly.

He shrugged. "The picture came in the mail—addressed to me. There was no return address. The postmark says it came from North Carolina." He took the original from his wallet. I took it from him and flipped it over. It said, *from one father to another. R.*

Rhett.

"That's him isn't it? Rhett?" I nodded. He sighed. "Oh, thank God. This would've been awkward if it wasn't. You have that picture, but he looks a little different in this."

I chuckled and stared at the picture in awe. "I can't believe he sent this."

"That's his little girl? That he lost?" I nodded. "She looks like him." I nodded. "You think you'll have a girl?" I shrugged. "What will you name her if you do?"

I smiled. "If the baby is a girl, I think I'm going to name her Ellie."

"I like that, but why Ellie?"

"It means *shining light*. And, that's exactly what she is to me."

I closed my eyes, thinking about Rhett. I wondered where he was. What he was doing. If he had gotten the envelope containing the information on his revenge. If he had already carried it out.

I was worried about him and the reasons why Luke had to rush to him. I knew that I was breaking his heart, and that I could easily make it all go away by running back to him. However, his deeds, that I even saw as justified, were hard for me to accept. Not only that, I had this huge secret that I could tell no one. I knew the suspect in a headlining murder and I had said nothing.

The only upside is that the real life of Bradley Cravens had been exposed to the public. We started working on the case immediately. To my own astonishment, in only three months, we had recovered over four hundred girls. The records we had were impeccable. The information contained within them was astounding. Sadly, we discovered that almost two hundred of the girls were dead.

The FBI had raided the home of Bradley Cravens; they recovered several more books like the one Rhett had given me. Not only that, they had discovered several properties belonging to Cravens which were also raided. More records were found. A total of fifty-seven books were found—all records of human transactions. Many of the girls had been sold to people or companies overseas.

We had people working everywhere trying to find these girls.

We kept looking. And we found girls every day. We made many arrests. It was the largest takedown in criminal history, especially in sex trafficking. Katarina had proposed a rehabilitation program endorsed by the CIA, which she ran, coincidentally. So, she was hard at work trying to get the girls back into society.

Rhett did so many good things, and if I were smart, those would be the things I focused on. But, I was scared. However, I had convinced myself that if he came for me, I could not run away from him. Maybe that's what I was waiting for—him to come after me. But, he never did.

The strong flutters in my protruding stomach reminded me of reality. I would most likely be a single mother, but I would be a mother. Even if it was not ideal, I would finally have, again, what I had always wanted.

I finally laid down in bed and stared at the ceiling in the darkness. Into the night, I whispered, "I love you, Rhett." Then, I fell asleep.

***

When I woke up, I felt strange. There was something eerie about the morning. When I stepped outside, the sky was ominous and it was so quiet. The calm before the storm.

That morning, I had a doctor's appointment. Everything was going well. I had asked for an ultrasound just to make sure everything was still okay. It was, but my paranoia needed some reassurance.

I went to work, as usual, and worked a full day. I was beat and my feet were tired and swollen, and my pants were too tight. I was looking forward to pajamas and a good night's rest—as good as I could get when worrying about Rhett. I desperately wanted to call Luke to check on Rhett, but truthfully, I was terrified of what I might learn.

It was after nine when I left work—much later than I normally left, but something came in from the local police station that required my attention—requested specifically by an officer whom I was vaguely familiar with. According to him, this certain report had to be reviewed and signed by me that night. I hated leaving late and arriving home in the dark, but duty called.

When I stepped out of the office, I looked around me and checked my surroundings as always. Still, I had this sensation that someone was watching me. However, I knew it wasn't Luke which made me uneasy. I made my way to my car quickly and climbed inside. I lived about seventeen miles from work, which included the six mile stretch off of the main highway.

When I turned down the road with thick brush and tall trees lining each side, I became more alert. I always watched for animals anyway, but tonight, I looked for something else. I wasn't sure what.

A car approached me quickly from behind and my heart started pounding. But, when the blue lights flipped on, I let out a sigh of relief. Naturally, I looked down at my speedometer and I was going the speed limit. So, I wasn't sure what the problem was.

I pulled over slowly and watched in my mirror as the officer approached the window. When he leaned down, I recognized him immediately.

"Hey, Chase."

He smiled. "Hey, Evie. How are you?" Chase was the same officer that had requested the paperwork for which I had stayed late to finish. Although boyishly handsome, something was strange about him. Untrustworthy.

"I'm fine. What's this about?"

"You…uh…have a tail light out. Were you aware of that?"

I shook my head. "No, I wasn't. Thanks for telling me. This thing on the dash is supposed to tell me if it's not working, but I guess it's messed up. But, I'll get it fixed tomorrow, for sure."

He just stared at me. "Could you step out of the car, Evie?"

I was taken aback by his request and huffed out a laugh. "Why?"

He leaned down into my window, inches from my face, reached

in from the outside and popped my door open, and gritted out, "Get out of the fucking car, Evie."

Nervously, I released my seat belt. He pulled the door open and grabbed the back of my shirt, pulling me up from my seat, turning me around and slamming me as hard as he could into the car. I grunted at the impact and tried to pull away quickly and turn to protect my baby. He quickly grabbed both of my arms and pressed his huge frame into my back and held my arms, pinned between our bodies. He reached into the back of my pants and retrieved my gun, then threw it into the woods.

He pressed so hard into me, I couldn't catch my breath. I couldn't scream.

"What are you doing?" I managed to ask.

He spoke in my ear, spitting on the side of my face, "Shut the fuck up before I shut you up. You're goin' for a little ride. Someone important needs to talk to you."

He bound my hands with a heavy plastic tie then whirled me around. "Please don't hurt my baby," I pleaded.

He smirked. "I don't give a fuck about your baby. Or you."

His forehead flying toward mine was the last thing I saw before everything went black.

CHAPTER TWENTY-FIVE

Senator Bill Cravens

My life had officially gone to shit after my son was murdered. I wasn't so much upset about losing that bastard as I was when those million dollar checks stopped rolling in. Girls. Girls. Girls. That was the name of our game.

Now our game was over. And, I was pissed. I was determined to find out who fucked me over and fuck them right back. Nobody was going to get one over on me, especially some piece of shit whore who walked around headquarters like she owned the fucking place.

I had been watching her since she came back to Kansas City, and she was nothing too special. She had been recognized for her performances earlier in her career, but she had accomplished nothing too significant for the past few years. I did learn recently that she had come dangerously close to solving a crime committed by my son many years ago while working on cold cases. I needed to snuff this bitch out and fast. But, first, I needed to know who or where she got her information from. I needed to know who was screwing me and take care of them too.

The media knew everything. Although the entire sex trafficking ring was solely pinned on Brad at the current time, I knew that I would inevitably be brought down by it as well. The FBI was watching me, so I only had a short time to get my hands on this bitch and get the information I needed and hopefully draw out the assholes that did me in.

Never did I sell any girls, but I did collect the fees and drew a percentage of the profit, and kept the money in offshore accounts. I was filthy rich. And, I loved it. There was no paper money exchanged, just paperwork, but I got my paws on my adversary's daughter—a girl that I still had.

I offered Chase five grand to bring Evie to me. I also had him leave a little piece of evidence to indicate my whereabouts. Whoever got their hands on the information about our girls had to be a professional. We told her rescuers exactly where we were. No professional investigator was needed. It wouldn't take long for them to find us.

I waited with four of my henchmen a few miles outside of Kansas City, but I didn't wait long. At eleven thirty at night, Chase walked in pushing a stumbling woman through the door.

"Got the bitch," he said. He pushed her down at my feet and lifted his foot, ramming into her back. She screamed loudly.

I laughed. "Now, now. Easy. Can't hurt her too bad. When someone comes for her, I want them to think that she's still intact…before we kill her, of course."

Chase leaned down and yanked her hair back and put his mouth against her ear and said, "Not before I have a piece of her, I hope."

I chuckled. "You've been most helpful. I think that will be a good reward for all of your hard work. Don't you, Agent Harrington?"

She said nothing. I didn't figure she would.

I led them both down to the basement and ordered Chase to tie her hands to a bar above her head in the dark room where we would wait. It was hot, humid, and pitch black, except the dangling light bulb above Evie's head.

She would stand with no food. No water.

I would wait however long I had to…for this bastard to come to me.

CHAPTER TWENTY-SIX

Rhett

I swear my heart stopped in that moment. Luke was obviously shaken and I was angry with myself for being so consumed with myself that, once again, the woman that I loved could be in grave danger.

"What do you mean missing? How do you know?"

"I've been following her for months—watching out for her. You called, and I had to abandon her to make sure you were fine. We were just taking precautionary measures to protect her."

"Who's 'we?'" I asked.

"The Queen and me. She contacted me right after Evie left, so I've been detailing her. But, I leave and in less than twenty-four hours she's missing." He took a deep breath. "Shit!" he yelled. "How could this have fucking happened?"

I was getting my bag ready like I would for an assignment when I heard a knock at the door. "Hang on," I told Luke.

With my pistol drawn, I pulled the door open. Pops stood in front of me. He didn't waste any time. "Get your things. There's a helicopter waiting for us."

"Okay," I replied. I put the phone back to my ear. "Luke, I gotta go. I'll talk to you in a few."

"We've got to find her, Rhett."

I already knew how right he was, but I needed to stay calm and keep my bearings. I could not lose my head. That would be the worst thing for her. Hopefully, she was just out of pocket or on her way to see her parents or broken down somewhere. But, my gut was screaming something entirely different.

I knew she was in trouble.

"I know. I'll see you in a bit."

On the helicopter, I was briefed on where Evie was last seen. I learned from Blue that Evie's car was found off of the main highway near her house. Her belongings were in the car and her door was left open. Her phone was lying on the ground. I was told it was found under some dirt and gravel and the footprints and marks indicated a struggle.

My Evie fought. She did the only thing she could've done. *The Queen* had learned that Evie stayed late after work. The request for her to stay was made by a certain officer that no one could locate.

When we landed just outside of Kansas City, Luke was waiting for me. He was visibly upset. He was standing with the rest of my team along with *The Queen* and another man whom I didn't recognize.

Luke approached me quickly. "I'm so sorry."

"It's not your fault. You need to get it together. We need to save her, and I need you to be at the top of your game, man."

"Okay." He gestured to the man I didn't know. "This is Trevor Jamison. He's a friend of mine. He was Evie's contact while I was gone." I shook his hand.

"What do you know?"

He spoke and his voice was a deep, low rumble. He was intimidating and I could tell right off that he did not tolerate bullshit. "She had been getting home by seven or so every night. When she wasn't home by nine, I started driving around. I drove to her work and her car wasn't there. So, I continued to drive around. I headed home to see if she was there. That's when I found her car. I found this in the front seat." I took the piece of paper from his hands.

"What is this? An address?"

He nodded. "Yeah. To Senator Craven's house."

***

We surrounded the senator's large house. We had a foolproof plan, but it wasn't guaranteed to go off without a hitch.

Strangely, there was no one outside—no resistance at all when we approached the property. That in itself was completely unexpected and made us wary. We stood yards away from each other and glanced at each other. Luke stood not far away from me. When I looked at him, he shrugged his shoulders and shook his head. Covertness was not an issue. The electricity to all outside lights had been shut off. The inside of the house, however, was lit up like a Christmas tree.

While the others cased the house and checked everything on the outside, Wist motioned for me to enter the house. Surprisingly, the front door was unlocked.

I knew in that moment, it was a trap and I backed out slowly. I made my way to the tree line on the property and the others followed. They were confused at first by my actions, but followed me.

Pops questioned me first. "What the hell are you doing? If she's in there...."

"She's in there," I stated with absolute certainty.

"You saw her?" he asked.

"No. But, this is a fucking trap. She's in that damn house. I can feel it."

"You think he knows about us?" Blue asked.

"I don't think so. He knows someone, a professional of some sort, gave her that information." I looked at Luke. "He obviously knew that we had a detail on her. That's why he took her when you left."

"There's no way he knew that," Luke said.

"Somehow. Some way. He found out." I paused for a long moment. "I'm going in there alone."

The Queen argued. "Not going to happen, Shepherd. You will not go alone."

Luke spoke up, "I'll go with him." I started to object. "Don't even argue. I'm going."

I nodded. "Everyone else, just hold your post outside. If you hear shots, come in. Get Evie out. Don't worry about me. Just get her out. Understand?"

Reluctantly, everyone gave the affirmative and Luke and I headed back up to the mansion.

"I'll take this floor. There's probably a basement. You take the top two floors."

"Got it," Luke responded and headed up the stairs. The house was still and quiet.

I slowly made my way through doorways, scanning rooms and checking closets. With my gun drawn, I checked every room on the main level.

I opened the last door on the first floor that led to a dark stairwell. At the bottom of the stairs was another door. The stairwell was dark and there was no overhead light. I eased the door shut behind me and made my way down the stairs, hoping and praying they didn't creak. I stood by the door for several moments and let my eyes adjust to the darkness. As I stood there, I heard a low murmuring.

I had found them. My brain was screaming for me to wait for Luke, but my heart wouldn't listen.

I eased the door open. My eyes landed first on Senator Cravens who sat in a chair behind an old desk. I should have shot him right then.

But, I glanced to the right where a dim light dangled from the ceiling.

And, standing on her tiptoes with her hands tied above her head was my precious Evie.

Her long, red hair was wet and stringy. Her back was to me and I wasn't completely sure if she was alive or dead until she shifted her weight on her legs and let out a small whimper. She was wearing nothing but a dirty shirt and her panties.

My eyes shifted to the senator and I made my way to him. "Motherfucker!" I yelled.

"I wouldn't do that if I were you." he said to me. I looked over and a man stood beside Evie with a gun aimed at her side. "He will kill her," he promised.

I looked at him. "Let her go and I'll let you live."

He laughed. "Oh, Mr. Trimble. You put that gun down and back away and I'll let *you* live." I was shocked to know that he knew who I was. I was in the news often because of my job, but the way he said it, I knew he knew more about me than he would've learned from the news. "What? You're surprised? You look surprised. Give me some credit, will you? Smart man, educated man, military man. Who else would be aiding her in this," he gestured to Evie, "sexy piece of ass, if I do say so myself. She could draw a pretty penny on the market even though she's not unfucked." He smiled at me. "She's passionate, isn't she? I could tell by the fight she put up. That red hair. Mmmmm. If she's passionate in a little scuffle, I can just imagine what she's like when someone's inside of her." He pointed at the man standing beside her. "Chase, over there, will know what it's like before this night is over."

"What do you want?" I yelled.

"What any father wants, Mr. Trimble. I want my son back."

I smirked. "That's too fucking bad."

His eyes narrowed on me. "Do you know who killed him, Mr. Trimble?"

I didn't want to answer him, but I wasn't going to lie to him. "Yes."

"Who was it?" he demanded, slamming his hand down on the desk in front of him. "Who killed him? Why did they kill him?" he screamed.

"I had a city to watch, Senator. I had people to take care of, people to save. And, your son was a disgusting bastard who desecrated everything pure and wonderful in life. I killed him, you son of a bitch. Because of his sins," I seethed. "Just like I am going to kill you. For your sins."

I aimed my gun and was about to pull the trigger when I heard a loud blast from behind me.

"No!" Evie screamed.

The pain and the familiar burn spread through my back as it arched, and stopped me in my tracks.

My eyes landed on Evie who had turned herself around to face me.

I fell to my knees before her as I felt blood pour down my back.

"Evie," I whispered.

I decided right then that was the best way to die.

I knew I tried to save her.

I was able to see her one last time.

And, I would die at the feet of the woman I loved.

I looked up at her gorgeous face that was wet with her tears.

I whispered, "I love you," one last time before I heard another blast that tore through my left shoulder—a shot meant for my heart.

When I tasted the warm copper in my mouth, I knew it was over. I fell forward and my face touched her skin. I turned my head and pressed a sweet kiss on her dirty, bare feet.

I would die here. With my lips pressed against the skin of the woman who saved me.

I closed my eyes, knowing I would wake up in the presence of the family that was waiting for me in a heaven I almost stopped believing in.

CHAPTER TWENTY-SEVEN

Evie

I knew what would happen. They would trap him here. I screamed a one-worded plea for his life, but it fell on deaf ears and evil hearts.

As Rhett fell forward, blood seeping from between his lips, I tried to scream for him, but I couldn't breathe. I couldn't find my voice. I couldn't even tell him that I loved him too.

Everything happened so fast after that. Luke burst through the door, guns blazing. He took out all four of the senator's men and Chase with five efficient shots. He shot the unarmed senator once to wound him.

Luke then ran up to me, stepping over Rhett in the dim room.

"Don't!" I screamed at Luke. "Get him! Get Rhett!" I watched as Luke rolled over Rhett's lifeless body, and revealed a large pool of blood underneath him.

Luke spoke to him as he ripped Rhett's shirt open. "You're okay, buddy. You're okay," he reassured a silent Rhett. He reached up to check Rhett's pulse. "He's still alive. Barely."

I faintly heard sirens in the distance as several people, dressed like Rhett and Luke poured into the room. A tall, broad man approached me quickly. "Hi. I'm Tink," he said softly and reached up to cut the ropes that held me. Before he cut the rope completely, he scooped my body up with his other arm and caught me when the rope separated.

A young, attractive woman ran up and covered me with a blanket. She smiled warmly at me. "I'm Blue. We're gonna take care of your boy, okay?"

I started to weep and tried to wiggle free from Tink's strong hold just as the paramedics came down the stairs.

"I need to see him," I cried. "Let me down."

He held me tightly. "Just let them do their job. It's best if you're out of the way," he said with authority. "I'm going to carry you up. You need to be checked out too."

"I'm fine," I argued.

"You'll need an I.V., I'm sure. They'll need to check on the baby."

I started to weep uncontrollably. In all of the commotion, I had forgotten. I was so concerned with Rhett staying alive that it didn't occur to me that he might have seen that I was pregnant.

If he didn't survive, it would devastate me. Because of me, he would have another child.

But, because of me, he would never meet…her.

***

Nine hours later, I was cleared to go home and Rhett was in the recovery room.

He had been shot in the back and low in the shoulder. He lost so much blood, that he had to receive several pints to replenish it.

I sat beside his bed for two days as he slept.

I cried.

I wept.

I prayed.

I kissed his pale lips.

I stroked his still fingers.

I whispered that I loved him.

I promised to never leave him again.

The only time I left his side was when Luke asked to be alone with him. So, I sat outside the door on the floor and listened as Luke sobbed. Luke insisted everything was his fault, but even my assurances wouldn't change his mind.

As I sat on the floor, I stared blankly ahead. I was so deep in thought that I barely noticed when someone dropped down beside me. I turned my head and was shocked to see who had joined me.

Rhett's father.

I straightened my gaze, taking my eyes off of him. His low voice filled the air between us.

"I'm sorry," he started off. "About what I said. About what you heard. I don't even know why I said those things. I know I hurt you. And, I'm sorry. That may mean nothing-"

"It means something," I cut him off.

His head dropped. "You know, Arianna almost left him." My eyes shot to his face that was still bowed. "A few days before they were killed, she came over and talked to me about it. She told me that he would never love her." He looked up at me. "I told her to stay— to stick with him. And that I thought he did love her, despite what she thought."

My eyes flooded with warm tears. "He did...love her."

He smiled. "I know. But, I hate myself for telling her that." He paused. "I haven't talked to Rhett in years because I felt like it was my fault. If I would have told her that he didn't, she would've left. And, maybe. Just maybe, they would still be alive."

I nodded, completely understanding his heart. But, he had to know. "They still would've died. Whether he was in love or not, he would've still cared for her. She was still his. They would've still found her and did what they did."

"That's what I try to tell myself. Every day." We sat in silence for a long time before he spoke again. He turned, facing me completely, and held out his hand. "May I?"

"Of course," I said quietly. I leaned back a little and put my palms on the hospital floor and closed my eyes while my daughter's grandfather stretched his fingers over my belly.

When I opened my eyes and turned my head toward his, tears rolled down his cheeks. I said nothing. I only smiled.

He smiled warmly back at me. "Thank you," he whispered. "Thank you," he repeated.

He pulled his hand back and placed it over mine. We sat in silence for a long time when Luke appeared. He stood and looked down at me from the open door. He face was ruddy and wet, and his hair was sticking up everywhere.

His warm eyes met mine and the corner of his mouth tilted up. "He's awake. He's asking for you."

My heart started pounding out of my chest and I felt frozen. Rhett's father stood immediately and helped me to my feet. I leaned in and hugged him, and passing him, I hugged Luke too. As he held me in an embrace, Luke spoke quietly. "He doesn't know."

I pulled away and looked up at him. I slowly blew out a breath and my eyes welled up.

I loved him.

I needed him.

And, I wanted him forever.

I opened the door slowly to enter his room with every intention of telling him just that.

CHAPTER TWENTY-EIGHT

RHETT

I wasn't sure if it was my dry mouth or Luke's bawling that pulled me from my drug induced slumber. Whatever it was, I woke up. Luke's body was leaned forward with his elbows on his knees and his hands pressed against his head.

It took everything I had, but my speaking jolted Luke to attention. "This can't be heaven cuz you're here. I don't think they let ugly people in."

His head shot up and he smiled at me. "Not heaven. God evidently didn't want to put up with your attitude today. So, he left you here for me to put up with your miserable B.S."

Suddenly, I remembered why I was here. "Evie?" I asked him in a panic.

He stood quickly. "She's okay, brother. She's all right. She is sore, a little dehydrated, but she's fine."

"Where is she?"

"Just outside. She's been here since you got here."

I smiled. She was waiting for me. I knew she loved me, but I almost thought that she would disappear again. Hell, it was still a possibility. Maybe she was just making sure I was okay before walking away from me again.

I was weak and in great pain, and probably looked like shit, but I wanted to see her. I had to see her.

"Will you get her? Please?"

He leaned down and hugged me. "Well, since you said please…"

Luke stepped away and stood in the doorway and spoke, before easing the door closed.

I waited for her.

My blood was pounding. My hands were shaking. My breath picked up.

I was scared—scared she would reject me one last time.

I didn't know what was in the future for us. Hell, I wasn't even sure we had a future. I wanted a life with her, but I had betrayed her. She was a stranger who filled me with life. She became a friend who made me want to live. She was my lover who drained me of hate and filled me with a love that I thought was dead and gone.

My room was dim, but when the door slowly opened, it gradually filled with light. We looked in each other's eyes and held each other's gazes.

I spoke first. My voice was wobbly and uncertain. "You're so beautiful, they should play music when you enter a room."

She let out a huff of quiet laughter and walked slowly to me. When she reached me, she was crying. My eyes scanned her face and made their way down her body.

That's when I saw it. She stepped even closer and I stared at her distended belly.

My face twisted with emotion and I covered it with my hand. I started to cry.

Something unexplainable happens to a man when he sees the woman he loves carrying his child. We become protective. We are filled with pride. We want to beat our chests. We want to tell the world. We're happy. We're thrilled and excited.

But, mainly—we fear.

We're afraid we won't be enough, do enough, and be fast enough, strong enough. We're afraid our children won't love us back. We're terrified of doing the wrong things, saying the wrong words, being too harsh, crushing their little spirits.

And, as I lay there with tears rolling down my face—my face that I had hidden, I was afraid.

And, I was happy.

And proud.

I felt a gentle tug on my hand, pulling it away from my face. My eyes were still pinched closed and my lips were tucked between my teeth. Evie slowly turned my hand and laid my palm on her belly.

With a hitch in her voice, my sweet love spoke, "She kicks like crazy."

I chuckled with a tear-filled sobbed. "She?" I asked her. She nodded. "The baby?"

She smiled at me. "*Our* daughter. She."

Had I been able to move, I would've held onto her forever. But, I couldn't and had to settle for touching her with my right hand. I rubbed her belly as she stood right beside me. We stared at each other for what seemed like forever.

We were both crying as she steadily ran her fingers through my hair. Hoarsely, I told her the only truth I knew, "I love you, Evie. I love you. I love this baby. I love everything you are. I love everything you did for me. I know I hurt you. I know I lied." I took a deep breath. "You may think you loved a lie, but I was more real with you than with anyone in my life. I don't want to live without you. But I understand if you can't love me that much…can't love me enough to forgive me for everything that I've done. I understand. But, I will never, ever stop loving you. You can't make me."

She smiled at me. "Never once have I thought I could make you do anything." She paused. "I'm not going to lie to you. I never wanted you to know about this. I was going to keep her a secret. I was going to keep her to myself. I…I was trying to protect myself. Protect my heart. But I started thinking, if I did that, it would make me a liar." She held my gaze. "I told you once that I would love you…no matter what. And, the first time something jeopardized our love, I ran away. I had proved to you that I didn't love you no matter what. I forgive you for deceiving me, but I do not forgive you for making me fall in love with you. There's nothing to forgive. You were only trying to fix this broken world and save lives of people you have never met, but loved them just the same." Tears plummeted down her rosy cheeks.

"How could I keep my daughter from a daddy who would try and change the world for her?" She shook her head. "I couldn't do that. I couldn't do that to her. Or to you."

Through my tears, I finally spoke the words I had been waiting years to say, "Thank you...for finding them. For letting me... For understanding... For loving my girls enough to do this for them."

Evie's beautiful lips quivered and tears streamed down her cheeks. "You're welcome," she whispered. "You deserved that. Who you are is what every father should be. It was the least I could do."

"I love you. Evie, with everything I am, I love you. You know you're gonna marry me, right?"

With that, she smiled warmly at me. She leaned into me. Her beautiful face neared mine and her round belly pressed into my body. She kissed me sweetly on the lips. "Yes, and I love you, too. No matter what."

CHAPTER TWENTY-NINE

RHETT

Four weeks later, I stood on the beach, Ms. Emma's beach, with the sun on my back. My family and my team, along with Evie's closest friends and family sat together.

And we waited.

When Evie rounded the corner, wearing a heart-shaped necklace, a pale pink dress and no shoes, she took my breath away. She walked into the wind and it embraced her, wrapping her dress around her beautiful body. Although she wanted to wait until she had the baby and lost her weight to get married, I absolutely refused. She had never been more beautiful to me than she was in this moment.

When she approached me, and after her father gave her to me, I knelt down in front of her and pressed a single kiss on her belly. Evie ran her fingers through my hair just like she did the night she first saw the real me.

There were a million things that I loved about Evie, and traditional vows could never express the promises I would make. When I gave Evie the ring that Mr. Harlan had given Ms. Emma decades before, I told her that I wanted us to write our own vows. She laughed and said that she was not a writer and she would only embarrass herself. But, I convinced her, charming her into submission.

As I stood before her, I took her feminine hands in mine and held them. And, I promised to never let them go. I rehearsed my vows over and over, but decided at the last minute that speaking from my heart was the only justice I could give her. So, that's exactly what I did.

"Evie, I could never, in an entire lifetime, name all of the things that I love about you. There are not enough words to describe the love I have for you. I could fill the oceans with ink and stretch scrolls across the sky, but even with that, I could never write all of the things about you that have changed me.

"I was lost. Broken. Angry. Alone. And, the moment I laid eyes on you," I took a deep breath, "I was none of those things anymore. I was captivated by your beauty. I was found in your arms. I was happy in your presence. I was healed by your love. You deserve so much better than me. But, I know, in my heart, you'll be the last person I will love like this. You accepted who I was. You make me who I am." My lips started to quiver as my confessions continued to pour from my lips. "You love my family from yesterday. You'll never know how much that means to me. They will always be a part of my life and you love that about me. You've never asked me to forget. And, I know you never will.

"So, because of that, I promise to be yours forever. I promise to make you laugh and make you smile and make you breakfast. I promise to be patient and kind to you every single second of the day. I promise to trust you and be someone you can trust. I promise to always have faith in you. I promise to dream about you, comfort you, and be devoted to you. I swear to be the best husband to you. I swear to be the best father to our baby. I vow that not a single day will pass that you can't count on me. I promise to be here. For you. For our children. As long as I live. I love you. I love you more than life itself."

I never took my eyes off of hers. Her gorgeous hazel eyes were red-rimmed and little clear rivers rolled down her cheeks, then off of her chin, onto her chest.

"That was beautiful," she whispered.

She released my hand and turned to Rhonda who stood behind her. And, Rhonda handed her a light blue piece of paper. I smiled at her preparation. She was adorable. And nervous.

She looked up at me and tucked her pouty lips between her teeth and closed her eyes for a moment. She finally opened them and smiled at me. And read. My Evie and her letters…

"Rhett, I feel so many things when I'm with you. When I first met you, I felt safe. But, I knew my heart was in danger—I knew I would lose it, what was left of it. I was a shattered woman, a heartbroken widow, a childless mother. I did everything in my power not to live. But you…you wouldn't allow that. You never forced me to love you, but you did force me to love myself. Because I love myself now, I could never deprive my life of the love that I have found in you. I have felt happiness again. I'm no longer lonely or alone. I feel renewed. I feel forgiven. I feel like I can live.

"I have fallen in love three times." Her face drew up in emotion as she spoke, and I couldn't stop mine from doing the same. "And, each time it's happened, it's only gotten sweeter. You love the family that brought me to you." She looked up at me. "You'll never know how much that means to me. *My* family from yesterday.

"Because of that, I promise to love you forever. I promise to always be your best friend. I promise that my heart will always be yours. I vow to put you before myself. I will honor you by sharing every story of my life with you. I promise to hold your hand during our prayers, to make you dinner every night. I promise to tell you I love you every day that I live. I promise to love you with actions, not just words. I vow to make our life adventurous and make your favorite cake for your birthday. I vow to be a wife you can be proud of. I vow to be good to our children and teach them the love that makes good men. I promise to tell them that their daddy is the best man I've ever known. And, I promise to tell them that he's tried to save the world. Just for them."

She placed my ring on my finger after I placed Ms. Emma's on hers. I pulled her hand to my lips and kissed it.

As we danced under the stars for the first time as husband and wife, I leaned in and kissed her lips. When she pulled away, I mumbled, "You know we'll probably never use those tickets, right?"

She laughed loudly. "Oh? You didn't go without me?"

"Not a chance, baby," I said, smiling.

She would never regret her vows to me. She would never be lonely again.

That night, as the world faded away, I made love to my wife. I whispered that I loved her over and over again. We made love under the stars, on a beach, behind a beach house, given to me by a woman who loved me like a son and who taught me that an ending to a story that was not a happy one was no ending at all.

***

Seven weeks later, Evie gave birth to beautiful baby girl. I wept like a silly woman, especially when I realized that she looked so much like Haven.

I sat in a chair holding my daughter as my wife slept at my side. I had never felt the joy I did when the doctor laid little Ellie on Evie's chest, wailing and screaming her little head off.

I kissed her forehead and played with her fingers while she grunted and yawned. What a gift I was given. What a beautiful life born from the makings of a lie.

I was not a perfect man, but after all of the tragedy I had suffered and after all the heartache I endured, I was finally granted a perfect life.

A life with a wife and a daughter who saved me from myself.

EPILOGUE
Six Years Later

RHETT

"Watch me, daddy!" Ellie yells from the backyard. I smile as I watch my daughter do cartwheels in the sand.

"Whoa!" I exclaim, thoroughly impressed with my little one's tumbling skills.

"Now, watch me, daddy!" yells Ada. She absolutely idolizes her older sister and attempts to do everything Ellie does. Unfortunately, her skills are not as good as Ellie's and it makes me chuckle. She looks at me and sighs after getting to her feet. "Please don't laugh at me, daddy," she coos.

Ellie is a spitfire and holds her own, but little Ada wears her heart on her sleeve.

"I'm not laughing at you sweetie. I'm just smiling because you're absolutely adorable."

Just as I finish speaking, I hear a soft voice behind me. "Daddy? I go pee?" I'm not certain if it's a question really or a statement, but I'll find out soon. We've been potty-training our little Brooklyn for a few weeks now, and she doesn't really have it figured out yet.

That's right. Three girls. Ellie will turn seven in a few months. Ada will start kindergarten in the fall, and Brooklyn is the most independent eighteen-month-old I've ever known.

After Ellie was born, Evie left the bureau; and, she and I moved into the beach house that Ms. Emma left me. I started my own law practice in North Carolina and Evie got her license and started teaching classes at a local university. It was difficult for her to walk away from all of the cases that needed to be solved, but she made the decision to do so and left that work to someone else. Criminal investigation was really her forte, and occasionally she teaches those courses, but for the most part, she teaches American History, her true first love.

After I exacted my revenge on those who robbed me of my first family, I left *The Guardians*. Everyone understood. *The Queen* recruited someone to take my place whose story is much worse than my own. Occasionally, they contact me for little things—help in training or intelligence, which I am happy to provide.

Senator Cravens lived, but was arrested. *The Queen*, through her resources, had notified the FBI of Evie's kidnapping and no charges were brought against Luke for killing the senator's men. *The Queen* has a special way of making things…disappear, if you will. He tried to tell the police that I had admitted to killing his son. Because his credibility was shot to shit, and because of who I was, and because no one really cared about Bradley Cravens anymore, no believed him.

Bianca Turley was found in a secret room in his house. She was malnourished and skinny as a rail, but she was alive and was returned to her family. She is doing well.

Girls are still being found and brought home. Those girls are getting their lives back because of Evie's efforts and the lost life I took with my own hands. The FBI still rescues one or two girls a month. There is no way in a hundred lifetimes that all of those girls will be found, but at least there's some hope for some. *The Queen* still runs her division with the CIA to help rehabilitate them. Every once in a while, Evie will volunteer and do what she can to help the victims of the worst crime she had ever seen.

That's just who she is.

Every single day, I fall more and more in love with Evie. I have never known anyone like her. I say that, but in some ways she reminds me of Arianna—every fiber in her being is held together by love. That only makes me love her more.

She is the most perfect mother to my perfect children. Twice a year, we all travel to St. Louis to visit Arianna's grave. And twice a year, my girls stand in front of Haven's headstone and sing her a song. When Ellie was three, she sang *Twinkle, Twinkle Little Star* on her own accord. They sing hymnals to their big sister now. And, when we go to Kansas City, they sing to their big brother.

Evie speaks of Noah often. He lived and she does and says everything she can to keep his memory alive. Ellie is so curious about them, especially Haven. She asks questions about her constantly.

Last week, I took Ellie to get some ice cream while we waited for Evie and the other two girls at the doctor's office. She ordered her favorite—mint chocolate chip.

She looked up at me with her huge eyes and asked me, "Do you think Haven would have liked mint chocolate chip like me?"

I smiled and rubbed her head. "I think she would've loved mint chocolate chip...just like you."

She smiled. "Do I look like her? Just a little bit?" she asked me, holding up her index finger and her thumb with about an inch of space in between.

I laughed. "Yeah. Just a little bit."

I wasn't certain that I ever wanted to really tell my girls about Haven or about Arianna. I wasn't sure how to even break it to them. As luck would have it, I didn't have to. Evie did it for me.

A couple years ago, I sat outside of the girls' room as Evie tucked them in one summer night. I was about to enter the room when Ellie asked, "Mama, who is in those pictures? The pictures in you and daddy's room? That little girl with daddy? And that little boy with you?"

I stopped in my tracks and slid to the floor outside their door. I stared at the ceiling as tears raced down my face as I listened to their mother tell them about the siblings they'd never meet.

"Well," she said softly, "a long time ago, before I met your daddy, I had a little baby boy. His name was Noah. And, your daddy had a baby girl. Her name was Haven."

"What happened to them?" I heard her ask. I felt my chest began to shake as I heard my Evie answer her in the sweetest way.

"You see," she started, "God did not give your big sister and your big brother to your dad and to me like he gave us you. He just let us borrow them for a while and made us promise to care for them until he needed them back. And, we did that. And, we did such a good job that he knew we were ready for you. We just had to find each other first."

Ellie understands a little, and Ada just follows her lead. We will wait until they're much older to tell them the whole truth, but for now, we want our girls to experience the innocence we did when we were kids. Innocence is disappearing quickly, but I want my girls to be kids, not little grown-ups, so for the most part, we tell them half-truths.

I tell all of my girls that I love them every chance I get. Little Ada groans and says, "Daddy, you say that all the time."

"Because I mean it all the time," I always answer.

Evie and I have mended old relationships with friends and family, and we've even made many new and wonderful friends. I still see members of my team all of the time. I even know their real names now.

Our parents are thrilled with the life that we have built and the girls we have given them. My brothers and sister adore their nieces and they are adored right back.

Luke has finally fallen out of love with his ex-wife, which is the best thing for him. He deserves someone good and who will love his ugly ass back. He has found that, and that girl is lucky to be loved by someone like him.

Adam surprised me when he showed up at Christmas dinner with *Blue* on his arm. It's still a struggle for me to call her by her real name—Haleigh. He cares for her, and I think she wants to love him, she just doesn't know how to love anyone. I did admit to her that I thought she liked women. She laughed and shook her head. "No. I like Adam, though. He's the first person I've liked in a really long time." When she got weepy, she walked away from me.

The rest of *The Guardians* are still doing what they do best.

Rhonda and her husband still make bets in exchange for sexual favors.

And just last week, I welcomed a new attorney to my small firm. He just passed the bar exam and I was the first person he called with the news. I immediately offered him a job. Who is it, you ask?

Fitzgerald Coulter, III, Esquire—remember him?

So, that's where everyone is now—everyone who really matters.

Today is a special day. Today, I turn thirty-seven.

After six years from the start of our happily ever after, we have three beautiful little girls. I've told you a little bit about them, but I've not told you what they look like. Little Ellie is a fiery little redhead—my attitude trapped inside of the spitting image of her mother, but her eyes are the color of the cloudless sky. Ada looks just like me with the eyes and heart of her incredible mother. I pick little Brooklyn up and put her in my lap as I ease down into a chair on our porch. With her blonde hair and green eyes, she looks exactly like my mother—that in itself is a gift to me from the Almighty.

"Girls!" I call out to them. "No more cartwheels. Get up here. Your mama's coming!" They quickly run up the steps of the porch and take their places on the bench that sits beside me.

I watch my wife stride toward us holding a birthday cake in her hands with a huge grin on her face.

"You ready?" she asks.

I smile at her. "For anything," I respond. She grins and walks toward me singing *Happy Birthday* as our little girls chime in. She makes her way to us with the cake held way out, so she doesn't get icing on her rounded belly. She sets the cake in front of me, never taking her eyes off of mine as their song ends in a soft cadence.

"I love you, baby," I tell her.

"I love you, too. No matter what," she sweetly responds.

After three beautiful girls, God finally gave Evie another little boy, my first son. I was happy with my girls, but when I learned we were having a boy, I admit…I cried a little.

Every man wants a little boy to take fishing. To take hunting.

To play ball with. To teach him how to be a man.

To carry on his name.

So, by God's good graces, Evie and I are excited about having a boy.

A baby boy whom she insists we call...Shepherd.

ACKNOWLEDGEMENTS

For starters, I'd like to thank my husband—the man this entire book is dedicated to. The night I realized I was in love with Buddy, a sad reality came upon me—a dark cloud hovered over my newfound love. I knew I would have to tell him *the secret*. It was a truth I dreaded to tell. In all of his sweetness and love, he looked down at my wet face as I quietly and tearfully told him of the heartache of my life. The two little words he mumbled to me in the darkness changed my life forever. I knew in that moment that he would never walk away from me.

I've promised him that if my words ever make us rich, he has my permission to quit fixing tractors and open a bait shop on the lake of his choosing.

I'd like to thank my mom who has always thought that I could do anything. The words that Evie's mother used as comfort within these pages are the exact words my mother has spoken to me. I cry when I read the dialog between those characters because I hear my mother's voice.

Thanks to my little sister, Melanie. You have an imagination and possess creativity from out of this world. So many of these scenes came from the mind of you, my best friend. You always cleared my writer's block, and your honesty is something I love and can always count on. I love you...for real.

I'd like to thank my childhood friend, Stacy, for reading this book and loving it. I've adored you since the sixth grade. Seriously. Thank you for your encouragement and your kind words. On more than one occasion, you have expressed that I have a "gift with words." For a girl who has never thought she has much to offer anyone except a decent joke and a pat on the back, those words mean so much to me…more than you'll ever know or understand. Thank you for being my friend.

I also want to thank Kayla, a girl after my own heart. Thank you for reading this in its entirety. I love you. You know that. You read this in its very early stages and loved it. And, I am thankful for that because it made me want to keep going. You're always excited when I have something for you to read, and I love that about you. You make me feel like I am capable of anything, and I love you for that. And, thank you for reading every word of this aloud to Tyler, because I love telling that story.

Thank you, Tyler, for being the first man to hear this story and love it. For that, you have earned a spot in my next book, in Luke's story. Absolutely adore you.

Finally, a huge thank you to my close friend, Dusty. If it weren't for you, this book would have never been completed. You would literally hang on my every word—as I sent you all that I had written, leaving you with cliffhanger after cliffhanger. The fact that you texted and called me so many times—even in the late hours and early mornings—is truly the reason this book ever came to complete fruition. You had a zeal for this book, moreso than I did some days. What you truly gave me was the best kind of harassment I've ever experienced, and I absolutely love you for that. Thank you for pushing me and awakening the passion for writing in me on days I just wasn't feeling it. You will never know the depth of love I have for you, because that is so special to me.

And thanks to all my friends…who love me just because.

ABOUT THE AUTHOR

D.L. Beaumont lives in the South with her husband where they try to build their tiny life. She has many titles: daughter, sister, wife, friend, author, artist, and musician just to name a few.

Poetry saved her life. In a time where she felt that no one could hear her, she turned to pen and paper.

She is a woman shaped by happiness and heartache.

Luke's story. Coming soon.

THE GIRL I CALLED MONTANA

By D.L. Beaumont

PROLOGUE

Luke

In the darkness, twelve of us scaled the tall wall surrounding the village that the militants had taken over in Yemen. This operation would be my last and I prayed that it went as planned. I was tired of touring. Even though I got the greatest satisfaction of my life from this, I was ready to be at home with my boys. I've been over here most of their short lives, and I was just ready to finally be their father.

After this, I would be going home. But, this was a dangerous operation, and I always had to face the fact that I may not make it out alive. We were to rescue two Marines who were made prisoners of war sixteen months prior. Along with them, six others were to be lifted out as well--two American missionaries and four humanitarian workers. We had no knowledge of their condition, just that within the last six hours we had received word that they were alive.

Wordlessly with rifles ready, we crept in. As the leader of our team, I had located the makeshift prison where our men and the others were being held and orchestrated the retrieval.

As we silently eliminated militant threats one-by-one, we drew closer to our target. When we finally breeched the shanty and entered the room, I made a quick assessment of the prisoners. Through my night vision goggles, I could see that they were all asleep. I quickly spotted one of the Marines whom I had recognized from a picture.

I knelt down in front of him. "Corporal Langston?" I said
quietly. He started to stir, and he winced as if he were in great pain.
"Corporal Langston?" He slowly opened his eyes and when he saw
me, he gasped and attempted to back away from me. I put my hand
out to signal him to stop. "Calm down. We're here to get ya." I
watched as realization crossed his face and he let out a hard sob. He
was dirty. His head was shaved. His body was emaciated. He
covered his face with his hands and started to cry. I spoke softly,
"Straighten up, Corporal. We need to get everyone out of here. Got
it?"

"Yes, sir," he answered, his voice cracking.

"Two missionaries? Four humanitarian workers? American.
You know them?" I asked.

"Yes, sir," he answered, nodding and wiping his face with his
hand. He pointed to a few others in the room and my sight followed
his motions. "The missionaries are Richard and Paula Denton in the
corner." The Dentons were a couple who looked to be in their
forties, but they too were dirty and looked nearly starved. They
could've been younger that that, but it was hard to tell. "The
workers," he continued, pointing out three men in the room, are
"Trace, Caldwell, and Tyler." All three men appeared young but
were skinny, unclean, and bald. Then, he pointed over to the other
Marine which one of the other team members was attempting to
wake. His hands were draped over a woman's head that appeared to
be sleeping in his lap. "And, Ms. Grace," he paused, "Ms. Grace
Parsons is in Lance Corporal Whitaker's lap."

"Okay," I acknowledged. "Can you stand? Can you walk?"

"Yes, sir," he answered and slowly stood. The others he had
pointed out began standing very slowly...all except Lance Corporal
and the woman Langston had called Ms. Grace. I made my way over
to them and squatted.

"Lance Corporal? Can you stand?" I looked at his face and
tears were streaming down his cheeks. He had tucked his lips
between his teeth and attempted to suppress his weeping. "Lance

Corporal, we need to wake her. We need to get you out of here."
He opened his eyes and stared at the ceiling. "Lance Corporal, we
need to..."

"She's dead," he whispered. I looked down and the woman he
was holding had clearly been beaten. Her clothes were torn--what
clothes she wore, and her body was covered in huge welts and dark
bruises. "I did everything I..." he trailed off. "I told her to do what
they said," he whispered. "She's dead," he repeated.

I set my rifle down beside me and leaned in toward the woman
at his feet. I took off my glove and pressed my fingers against the
small cross tattoo on her wrist, a tattoo so similar to one I had
touched in my past. My own blood was pounding, so it was hard to
tell if I was actually feeling what I thought I felt. Her long, red hair
was ratted and covered her face. I pushed my night vision goggles up
slightly and pulled a penlight from my pocket to check her pupils.

When I brushed the hair away from her face, I froze. This
couldn't be happening. This couldn't be real.

I remembered this beautiful face, and I had not seen it in a
decade. I had held this face in my hands while I kissed these lips that
were now pale and cold. The eyes closed in seemingly eternal sleep
were the same color green as my youngest son's. The last time I saw
this face it was wet with tears and rent with heartache before it slowly
turned and walked away from me. No one, not even her own family,
had seen her since.

My fingers searched for the beat within this heart...the same one
I had broken...the day it learned I was in love with someone else.

This lifeless woman that everyone here called Grace Parsons was
not Grace Parsons to me.

The woman that spent what appeared to be her final hours in
the lap of a Marine was not really a woman to me at all.

She was a girl...the girl I called Montana.